Dorothy Berry,
6, Tan y Foel,
Borth y Gest.

Penguin Books
Gentleman and Ladies

Novelist, playwright and literary critic, Susan Hill was
born in Scarborough in 1942 and was educated at King's
College, London. She has also written several radio
plays and broadcasts frequently. Her works, all of
which have received considerable attention, include *I'm
the King of the Castle* (Somerset Maugham Award),
A Change for the Better, *A Bit of Singing and Dancing*,
The Albatross and Other Stories (John Llewelyn Rhys
Memorial Prize), *Strange Meeting*, *Do Me a Favour*, *The
Bird of Night* (Whitbread Award for 1972), *In the
Springtime of the Year*, *The Magic Apple Tree*, *The
Woman in Black*, *Through the Kitchen Window*, *Through
the Garden Gate* and *Shakespeare Country*. She has also
edited Thomas Hardy's *The Distracted Preacher and Other
Tales* for the Penguin Classics.

Susan Hill is married to the Shakespeare scholar Stanley
Wells.

Gentleman and Ladies

Susan Hill

Penguin Books

PENGUIN BOOKS

Published by the Penguin Group
- 27 Wrights Lane, London w8 5TZ, England
Viking Penguin Inc., 40 West 23rd Street, New York, New York 10010, USA
Penguin Books Australia Ltd, Ringwood, Victoria, Australia
Penguin Books Canada Ltd, 2801 John Street, Markham, Ontario, Canada L3R 1B4
Penguin Books (NZ) Ltd, 182–190 Wairau Road, Auckland 10, New Zealand

Penguin Books Ltd, Registered Offices: Harmondsworth, Middlesex, England

First published by Hamish Hamilton Ltd 1968
Published in Penguin Books 1980
Reprinted with an Afterword 1988
10 9 8 7 6 5 4 3 2 1

Set, printed and bound in Great Britain by
Cox & Wyman Ltd, Reading
Set in Linotype Pilgrim

Chapter One

IT was a pretty churchyard. An ugly church, monstrous and vulgar as the cloth merchants who had built it. But a pretty churchyard. Hubert Gaily liked churchyards, they gave him a curious sense of well-being. If the worst of it all, he often thought, ended in a place like this, then nothing was ever so bad as you pretended. Ma agreed with that. Ma had some nice opinions on churchyards.

'Churchyards are the way of nature,' she said, 'not like those Crems. People forget you too quick if you're burned up. They don't find it so comfortable to forget you with a nice headstone.'

The headstones here were all erect and orderly, close-shaven, loyally inscribed. Hands in his clay-coloured raincoat, Gaily, myopic, bent down and read one at random, wonderingly.

SACRED TO THE MEMORY OF
ALOYSIUS ALBERT QUENTIN SAVAGE
SON OF
ALBERT AND JEMIMA SAVAGE
BORN 5 FEBRUARY 1801
DIED 28 DECEMBER 1883
Quidquid agas prudenter agas et respice finem

Gaily straightened up. His bus was about due. Above his head, above the outrageous tower, rooks wheeled and the sky was crimped and furrowed like the underside of tripe.

At his feet were seven early snowdrops, fronded with grass. Gaily picked them – they did not belong to any grave – to take to Ma. She liked flowers, liked even more the thought behind them, but Gaily only remembered when he caught them staring him in the face – or in the feet, as now.

He took a last look at the green churchyard, turned up his

collar and picked his way respectfully round the side of the church. At the head of the path, beside the porch, Gaily stopped snowdrops in hand.

A funeral cortège was making its way towards him.

The Reverend George Jocelyn Bottingley, six feet four and stooped like a crane, awaited them inside the porch. It upset him that all the mourners should be women. Thirty, forty years ago, that would not have been allowed to happen, and fifty years ago, the women would not have been allowed here at all. Male mourners only. For funerals, the Reverend Bottingley felt, were not a woman's occasion, they were too hard on the emotions, and on the feet and knees, and he did not like to see women weep in public.

Not, he observed, raising his eyes a little, reverently, as they approached, not that any of these women were weeping. Their faces were tucked and grey, scooped out or nerveless, but they were tearless faces. Poor Miss Lavender (Miss Faith, the eldest Lavender), he thought. And then thought again. For Miss Lavender would not, perhaps, have cared, Miss Lavender would never have cried at her own funeral.

They had reached him, with Miss Faith Lavender alone in her grained and silk-lined box. They shuffled on the gravel, and a February gust cut cold across the green churchyard.

The Reverend George Jocelyn Bottingley turned and bowed his head.

Hubert Gaily was not in the habit of thieving, still less of being caught thieving. Standing before the coffin, with seven stolen snowdrops in his hands, he flushed with shame. The fact that nobody noticed him, let alone the flowers, did not give him ease of conscience, but that was what he sought. Pointless, quite, to return and replace the plucked stems. In the end, Gaily followed the clergyman, the coffin, and the small bunch of women, black as crows, into the dust-smelling church. It was the least he could do. As he passed through the doorway, he heard his bus go grinding by the church and away up the hill.

*

Twenty-three miles away, at Number 14, Maxstone Villas, Mrs Ada Gaily decided to defrost the refrigerator. She had no idea how to go about it but she disliked waking an hour early from her rest and having nothing to do, and she disliked even more the idea that there was some household task or mechanical appliance which might defeat her. Ada Gaily had known how to do things all her life.

The very reason she had always forbidden him to bring a refrigerator into the house was this fear that, because she was old and no longer so quick of eye and nimble of hand and foot, it might defeat her. The television had not defeated her because nothing had ever gone wrong with it, and it had only to be switched on and off or, scarcely more complicated, over. In any case, the television provided entertainment, information and company and Ada Gaily knew when to keep quiet.

Refrigerators were different. 'I'll not have one in the house,' she had said, 'we've a larder, haven't we?'

'The food goes bad.'

'I'll thank you to remember when you ever ate bad food, in all the years I reared you and there were no refrigerators.'

'Fishmongers had them,' Gaily had said.

'Fishmongers had ice. Slabs of ice.'

'Refrigerators *make* ice.'

'You'll not bring one into this house.'

But he had brought one. Ada Gaily had begun to realize just how much her son did in spite of her. Secretly, under layers and wads of protest, was her admission that he was right, that these things were for the best. Like the refrigerator, which she was determined to defrost before he came home.

Gaily knew very little about the ways of church services, and so he sat halfway towards the back, looking at the coffin and the windows full of pale saints carrying lilies and the dust motes in the groin of the roof. His snowdrops were already wilting like wax candles in the warmth of his hand, and as he copied the mourners ahead of him and stood up, one flower slipped between his fingers on to the rust-coloured floor. Gaily dared not bend to retrieve it. At that moment, they were passing slowly by him on their way out, the tall parson with the crumpled clown's face, the coffin with its bearers, the black-clad women. This time, one by one, they noticed Gaily. He stared down at his hands as each pair of eyes ran over him swiftly, took in his face and his boots, his snowdrops and his clay-coloured raincoat. Each pair of eyes questioned and then looked away, wondering Gaily followed them at a discreet distance and watched as they lowered Miss Faith Lavender into her last resting place.

After they had all begun to move away, twitching up astrakhan collars, eyeing him sharply, Gaily remained beside the new grave. He examined the three wreaths:

'From Kathleen and Isabel, with our dear love and remembrance.'

'Remembering always my dear friend Faith, with deep affection, Alida Thorne.'

'With love from Dorothea.'

And a thin sheaf of forced daffodils, 'From the Reverend and Mrs G. J. Bottingley.'

Then, Hubert Gaily dropped the six remaining snowdrops on to the coffin. They made a faint brushing sound as they fell. It was not a sentimental gesture, and Gaily felt nothing save curiosity, though there was, perhaps, a slight element of touching wood. But he was a man for the proprieties. The stolen flowers had been, in a manner of speaking, restored. It was the least he could do.

Gaily turned away, the last to leave Miss Faith Lavender in the green churchyard.

'An old flame, perhaps,' suggested Dorothea who, often an unthinking woman, felt vaguely that the afternoon might now benefit from a stroke of the unlikely. She should not have done so. The other three turned their eyes on her like a trio of hanging judges. They had no need to speak and they did not do so.

Dorothea flushed from neck to hairline and, bending her head, took a sip from her tea-cup. But there were only soft, cold leaves remaining, and they got sucked in beneath her plate, to rest there clammily until she could get away to the bathroom. Alida shot her a glance of triumph.

'I noticed,' Isabel Lavender said, 'that he wore *boots*.'

Through Dorothea's head flitted the tune, but she had been too facetious already, to her shame. If she was really too old to cure herself of facetious *thoughts*, at least she could bite them back from the tip of her tongue. So she kept the tune trapped in and it marched up and down inside her head. Isabel was going on about the boots.

'Black,' she said, 'well polished and without broken laces. But they were boots.'

'And yet he wore a collar and tie,' put in Kathleen, tipping Madeira cake crumbs deftly from her plate into the little blue tin always brought in for that purpose with the tea trolley. Dorothea had often wondered about the crumbs, whether they stored them up in some kitchen jar and you got them, months later, coating your fish.

The two remaining Misses Lavender continued to discuss the stranger at the funeral. Alida Thorne, who had not finished eating, listened, her thick jaws chomping up and down, her back turned just perceptibly to Dorothea.

Dorothea Shottery herself was bewildered. As far as she could remember, she had never seen the man before, he was no friend of Faith's. And even if he were? All this talk of his clothes, his grubby raincoat, his boots – what did they matter? He was a man at Faith's funeral and they should be grateful to him, shouldn't they? For what a poor showing they had made, the four of them, that afternoon! Of all Faith's friends, of all the correspondents and visitors, who had come? Every one had slipped away into the mists during the past two or three years until only she, Dorothea, was left. Alida was really the sisters' friend. It was not much, for a lifetime, two sisters, and a handful of neighbours. Whoever the man had been, with his blue eyes and thinning hair, Dorothea was grateful to him for his presence.

She said, 'Anyhow, it was kind of him to stay.'

The eyes turned on her again.

'Yes, Dorothea,' said Isabel Lavender, her small mouth pointing the consonants, 'but you could hardly say he *took part*.'

'He hung about,' said Alida Thorne.

Dorothea still protested. 'He was probably a stranger – just a visitor,' she said, 'who might easily have rushed away. So polite . . .'

Isabel Lavender pursed up her mouth. The conversation was at an end. But the women continued to think about Hubert Gaily's presence at the funeral. Dorothea merely remembered it, occasionally, with gratitude. Alida thought about the man once, to decide that he was not worth thinking about, and then thought no more. Isabel and Kathleen Lavender, however, gave considerably more attention and care to the subject in the silence of their own minds. But they would not be ready for some time to admit the fact to one another.

The tea trolley was wheeled out. Behind the net curtain, the sun was setting on cushions of soft mauve, pearl and beige. No further conversation was opened, no invitation to supper was proffered, and so Dorothea could do nothing else but leave for home.

Isabel's quick kiss was like the peck of a very small bird, Kathleen's cheek was downy as a fern-leaf but as cold. Out of view of the front window, in the last light of a late February sun, Dorothea Shottery wept a little, for her own loneliness and for the absence of her friend.

Ada Gaily had remembered to switch off the refrigerator. Indeed, to make quite sure, she had switched off everything, electricity, gas and water, at the main. She put a red plastic bowl on the refrigerator floor and sat down to wait for the ice to melt. She half-expected it to be a beautiful sight, the white-furred blocks crumbling and cracking like Arctic floes under the August sun. From below the Welsh dresser, the cat watched with sulphurous eyes, disturbed by this small change of routine.

Her son would be annoyed. His hand would come up to his head and he would wipe back his hair in a little, unconscious gesture of annoyance. Ada Gaily grinned, squatting on the kitchen chair. Let him be.

When, after perhaps quarter of an hour, the ice was opaque and solid as ever around the sides of the refrigerator, she became impatient and tried to chip at it, first with her fingers and then, finding them painful as well as useless, with the point of a kitchen knife. But she had to bend almost double and she was too large a woman, thickly fleshed, for that. At the last, clumsy thrust of her knife, a sharp sliver of ice chipped off the surface and flew into her eye. It hurt enough to frighten her and she was not a woman easily frightened. At the kitchen door, the cat, neck-fur upstanding like the spines of a hedgehog, wailed to be let out.

Ada Gaily was seventy-four. A recalcitrant refrigerator, an aching back, an eye stinging with pain, a wailing cat, any of these would have sapped a lesser woman's determination. But to her they merely served as spurs and she was used to those. The texture of her life was roughened with the stubble of physical work, lack of money, personal and public sorrow. The world believed that women like Ada Gaily were uncomplaining; the world was wrong. Ada Gaily complained, had always complained, loud and long and bitterly, against the tenor of her life. The descant accompanying it for fifty years had been one of complaint. But complaint was – had to be – an end in itself. It was a small release, like swearing or spitting. Ada believed that nobody could grudge you the right to complain.

Now, she hitched herself upright, ejected the cat, and sat down again to think about the refrigerator. Heat, plainly, was needed but in what form she was unsure. Always a resourceful woman, Ada Gaily knew she would come up with the solution. Meanwhile, she dabbed her handkerchief at her eye, ate a soft-centred peppermint and wondered where her son had gone.

But he was coming back. From the village which was called Haverstock, through twenty miles of Warwickshire countryside and three of brick and brown Midlands, home to 14 Maxstone Villas.

All the way, on the back seat of the long bus, Gaily smoked a Park Drive and thought about death and dying. You had to think of it, now and then. Ma was seventy-four. You had to admit the possibility. Out of the bus window he saw a manor house, with barley-sugar-stick chimneys. He enjoyed his days out.

Of course, she might have another twenty years, which would make *him* seventy-four and what would there be left to speak of then? Gaily looked back over his shoulder at the rosy-bricked manor house, for he was too near to remembering the time he had wished his mother dead. He cringed from that single revelation of himself and of his motive, even while knowing it wasn't really true to his nature, that the instance had come, gone and never would return.

It was just after he had come home in 1945, with his raw imagination still straining to assimilate the only excitements of his life and the strange dust of Italy and Egypt still upon his boots. Returning to his old job, he'd learned of the opportunity. L.M.S. would give selected staff a London training, to be followed, if you were lucky, by a London job – at Euston, or King's Cross, or at least a post in one of the large cities, at Snow Hill, Crewe or even Edinburgh. Gaily had thought he stood a chance. He had eleven years' good service before the start of war. He was not clever but he was interested and thorough. A reliable man.

'Take your chance,' Monks had said, Monks his friend, who was already accepted. 'Take your chance and come with me, you'll do no good stopping here.'

Monks' curry-coloured eyes had filmed over lasciviously at the vision of London, of freedom and promotion and advance. That night, Gaily had told his mother, told her, not asked her, since he was thirty-two now and master of the house. Ma had sat, large, aproned, silent, whilst he talked. On the mantlepiece, above and between them, stood his father's photograph.

When Gaily had finished, he sat back, his heavy legs sprawled anyhow over the hearth, and ran an anxious hand over his already thin hair. Ma Gaily had not spoken.

On either side of the shiny-faced photograph of Harold Herbert Gaily were four more photographs, two pairs. On the right, nearest his father, Hubert, best-suited school-leaver with a downy boy's face and sharp cheek-bones. Next to him, Eric, the long-dead little brother. On the left were his sisters, May, in Australia, and Alice, gone on the first available post-war ship to America and her man. Gaily felt them looming over him.

'Well,' he said tonelessly, shifting.

Ma heaved off her chair. 'So you'll be gone too, then,' she had said, her own voice flat as lead. She went off into the kitchen, Gaily had shaken his head. He knew that he would not.

Only once had he let himself begrudge it, only once, that night, and never since, for he knew it was his duty and his right to stay at home with her. He was too much a man of his tradition to resent it, to take flight. And he knew he had not the justification of genius. He had none of Monks' clever ideas. All the same, that night Gaily had wished her dead. Then he might have gone with Monks.

The bus stopped to pick up a passenger off one of the first terraced streets of the town. She was old, small, shrunken, a woman unlike his mother, to blow away with a single puff. Gaily was again reminded of death. He got up, as the only other occupant of the long bus, to help her to her seat.

'Lovely,' she said, appreciative of his firm grip. A reliable man.

The smell, when he opened the front door, took him back half a century. Electricity was erratic in the old, two-up, two-down house and as often as not the children had gone to bed with candles. It was candles Gaily smelled now, the thick, snuffed-out smell of candle-smoke. Ma peered at him over the top of the evening paper. Her eyes were shifty with guilt. She said nothing. Gaily followed the trail of the smell.

'God help us!' he said, finding it, 'God help us!'

Except that it seemed to him rather funny. Upon the rack immediately below the ice-box was a tin baking sheet and stuck on to the baking sheet were innumerable dirty candlestubs. But the ice was still inches thick, furred as tongues, and the smell hung acrid inside the refrigerator doors.

When he went back into the room, she got her word in first. 'You can say what you like,' she said, 'but show me another way it can be done. You show me. Because it can't. It can't be done.' It sounded defiant but they both knew it was defensive.

'I've tried all ways.' Her eyes never lifted from the newspaper.

'You'd no call,' Gaily said, standing his ground, 'no call to try anything.'

'No machine has ever seen me beaten.'

'*Candles!*' he said, but half-laughing at her enterprise. 'Lighting candles!'

'Common-sense.'

'It's common-sense the ice'd drip and wet them all out.'

'I'm not arguing.'

'The food'll smell. Smell of smoke.'

'There's other places to put the food. Always has been. I never wanted one in the house.'

There were layers of Gaily's patience, built up grain by grain over the years like geological strata. 'You switch the refrigerator knob to zero, you pull out the plug and you put a bowl of boiling water inside,' he explained sweetly. 'And you leave it. An hour, two hours. Changing the water every now and then.'

'There's a man here,' Ma said with an air of wonder, 'been down a pothole for one hundred and thirteen days. Now why would anybody want to do a thing like that? I don't see it, myself.'

'Next time you think a job needs doing,' he said, knowing her to be listening, 'tell me. I know the way of things.'

'Black as pitch,' she said, 'I don't get it. Might just as well bury yourself alive.'

A picture flitted across Gaily's mind. 'I went to a funeral today,' he said. She glanced up. The pupils of her eyes, black as sloes, dilated a little. 'Fancy,' she said.

Gaily turned back into the kitchen. It was a tiny, unjustifiable triumph and he felt mean. She came heavily in.

'Get out of the way,' she said, flapping at him. 'Get out, you want your tea, don't you? Get your great body out of my way.'

He knew better than to offer help, after all these years. Neither of them spoke again until she brought his meal to the table.

'Anyhow,' she said, setting it down. 'You can't expect me to go hefting bowls of boiling water. Not at my age. You've no call to expect that.' She sat down. 'I near blinded my eye as it was. Flies up like coal under the hammer.'

'What?'

'Yes,' she said, and put a dainty forkful of fish – it was one of her distinctions, this dainty way of eating – into her mouth. Gaily sighed.

'I can't carry bowls of boiling water about the place,' she observed again to the bread and butter plate. Gaily fought against any reply.

'Whose funeral was it then?' she asked, her composure about the subject regained now. It hadn't been fair to hurl it at her.

'Miss Faith Lavender,' he said, giving the words more sonority than they deserved.

'Oh,' she waited a second. Gaily allowed himself a smile.

'Friend of yours?'

'You could say that.'

'Speak plain!' She snapped, 'I can't do with that.'

'I wonder what he thought about, down the pothole all that time,' Gaily said.

'You didn't tell me anyone had died.'

'No.'

'So she was a friend of yours, then?'

'Yes,' he lied. Ma frowned. Quits, he thought.

Chapter Two

AMONG the petit-point and apple-green cushions of her bedroom, Alida Thorne stood, waiting for the postman. From behind the ruched net curtains, she could see him plodding his way around the green.

Alida Thorne, soft and nerveless and firmly-bounded as a fruit, expected at least one, possibly two, small parcels. Since her inheritance, ten years ago, all her pleasures and hopes and excitement had come to her in such small parcels. Perhaps more than the end of work, these had continued to spell riches and freedom. Or no, she thought, no – for that last, golden day at the girls' preparatory school, which had coincided with her fifty-first birthday, that had been a joy such as she had never dared to hope for, a once-in-a-lifetime joy.

Aunt Fosters had died at the right time. Wasn't that a hideous thought to have? Yes, probably, but it did not lessen her joy in the past ten years of leisured, ladylike existence and in the arrival of innumerable small parcels.

Hearing a slight sound, a scraping noise through the wall, Alida, though she ignored it, stiffened her corseted thighs. Aunt Fosters, her mother's last surviving sister, might have had the wit and grace to die in time but it was not a family trait.

Alida knew better than to follow up that particular avenue of thought. All the same watching the thin, lemon beam of sun catch across the postman's bicycle bars, she let herself think it unfair that her dear friend, Faith Lavender, should have died so suddenly and so much younger than the husk of a woman left in the next room.

Blattern the postman reached her gate. He propped up his bicycle and opened his bag. He took out two small parcels. Alida

Thorne turned away from the window with a pursed smile of pleasure.

'Seven counties,' she told him wonderingly, 'Imagine that! *Seven* counties.' For that was what she had been brought up to believe, that was how the rhyme went:

> God rolled seven counties
> Down Tantamount Hill.
> They fell at the bottom,
> They lie there still.

'Imagine that!' she had said again, to her escort, who wore white gloves, of course, because it was evening, but whose name she could never remember – it might have been any one of half a dozen – and whose fresh, young face was in shadow. He must have been a stranger to the village, that was why she was telling him. And he seemed to disbelieve her, which was ill-mannered. Eleanor Thorne changed her mind about her partner.

'I would like to go back now,' she announced, and they set off down the grassy path in the scented April darkness, back to The Gantry. Other couples wandered in their wake, or else lingered on the hilltop by the Commemorative stone, happier in their partners. For, of course, you could not see the foot of the hill, let alone seven counties, under the stars.

'Seven counties,' Eleanor repeated as he held open the paddock gate. '*Seven* counties . . .'

Eleanor Thorne jerked her head on the pillow and opened her eyes, awakening in time to hear the echo of her own voice. 'What was I saying?' And then, 'Did Alida hear?' For she was afraid, nowadays, of what she said aloud, foolish things, remarks made to other people, in her dreams, in the past, remarks she repeated now accidentally.

Her curtain blew in the wind and the wind found its way to her face. Cold. December, was it? Or April? No, it had been April then. April. What a sharp, sneering face he had had, though she could not see it, as she had not seen it in the darkness of her dream. Not to believe her, not to believe what everybody knew, what was proven and accepted.

Her hand on the sheet was a little stiff. For a moment, Eleanor Thorne did not recognize it and wondered whose hand it might be. As a girl, she had had beautiful hands: someone had asked to photograph them. *Had* they photographed them? She wondered, until the wind shifted the curtains again and she felt the cold of February, a February morning, for that was what it was, and her room empty.

'Alida,' she said, and then – as she thought – shouted, 'Alida.' I would like a drink, she decided, a hot drink.

The curtain was sucked sharply outwards again. She could not make out the patch of canary-coloured light on the opposite wall, could not make out why the sun was shining and why her brown-stained hand, on the sheet, would not move for cold.

Was it too soon to wear Faith's amethyst brooch? Isabel Lavender was sensitive to propriety but other people would be still more sensitive. Her ears caught the echoes of future remarks. 'And her sister hardly cold . . .'

There had been nothing written, only a long-standing tacit agreement about the brooch. Isabel had always understood Faith to mean that she should have it. And certain other pieces. Kathleen had never been one for jewellery and the amethyst picked up the heather mauve of Isabel's new dress and even, she thought, gave something of a fresh nuance to her mist-blue eyes. Only a week had passed. She was unsure.

She tried it on, high at the neck, to the left side, to the right side. No, it was best dead centre, just as Faith would never have worn it. And why shouldn't she have it? It was little enough to expect.

As a young girl, Isabel Lavender had expected a great deal. She had known hope. She had stood up, full-breasted and straight-spined, in church and sang lustily about the virtues of right. She had assumed that God and goodness, and therefore luck and all earthly and spiritual rewards, were on her side. Unconsciously assumed since her faith necessitated the admission of man's utter unworthiness and the unmerited grace of

God. She had heard and read about the sufferings of innocence, she had observed sorrows and tragedies in those around her. But, for a long time, she had neither the intelligence nor the insight to associate them with herself. Health and strength and a certain robust attractiveness had been hers, good marks in the classroom, an ear for music, parental praise, had been hers. Therefore, hope had been hers, too. Isabel Lavender had never for one moment doubted that everything would somehow, eventually, go her way, though she could accept the idea of temporary setbacks. Not that she had wanted very much: admiration, long-lasting good teeth, a well-placed husband, town rather than country life. She had hoped even more confidently that certain things would *not* come her way.

At the age of twenty-eight she had awakened one morning to the realization, clear as dawn, that to hope for things did not necessarily bring them about, that there was no earthly reason why she should be happy, healthy and husbanded. She had looked out of her bedroom window upon an unjust world, upon undeserved sadness, upon concatenation of ill-luck, upon the at least equal odds of sickness, spinsterhood and narrow horizons. But she had not possessed the capacity to benefit from her revelation, and so bitterness, petulance and self-pity became the only possible responses.

Isabel Lavender, now sixty-eight years old, sat before the mirror, the pretty amethyst brooch at her neck, and felt that she ought to have it, for it was owed to her, it was a little enough thing to covet. She found herself more and more hunting down and making sure of the little things.

Above the mirror, the sunlight danced in a ring, water-pale on the pale wall. She heard the snap of the letterbox and, at once, the opening of Kathleen's door. Kathleen had always rushed for the post, even in the days when their father had laughed at her eagerness and stood above her as she scooped up the white and brown envelopes. As a matter of fact, he hated anyone to get to the post before himself, needed to be the first to turn them over and sort them out. Only he had never minded about Kathleen, the youngest of them. Isabel suspected her still of watching behind the curtains for Blattern. It was an unpleasant, a sneaking habit.

The sunlight showed up a dead fly on its back beneath the window. Isabel started. She did not like to be reminded of dead things, even flies, by the stiff, still bits of leg. She was moving towards it, to sweep it away, when Kathleen opened the door. Isabel's hand shot up to conceal the brooch at her throat.

'A letter has come,' said Kathleen, timidly, 'a letter has come from the solicitor.'

Even the jar looked costly, Alida thought, chalice-shaped, gilt-lidded and made out of what could so easily have been milk-glass. She was a little disappointed in its capacity in relation to its size, for it cheated as a false-bottomed suitcase cheats. But that was the way of things. It had a most elegantly printed label, gilt on grey.

'Crème de framboises,' she read in her governessy accent, 'supernourissante et révenescente. Avec le Vitamin C. Imprimé en France.'

Inside the jar the cream was whipped up, light as a soufflé, and smelled delicately of mimosa.

Alida Thorne was happy. She ranged it beside a dozen other pots and jars and bottles on her dressing-table and it looked well. The sight of them all gave her a feeling of warmth and contentment. So she felt when she allowed herself a journey to London and made like a homing pigeon for the perfumery counters of department stores. They were her Aladdin's caves and, ever since her inheritance, open to her as often as she chose, though for most of the year she contented herself with a reminder of them in the small parcels.

Her belt had come too. The skill and habit of a lifetime refused to desert her altogether now she had no need of it and Alida Thorne still made her own dresses. All save the belts. These she had made up to her exact requirements, with precisely the right number of holes, by an exclusive shop in Knightsbridge. She chose her materials with care. By small things, she had learned, people knew you, by the quality of shoes and gloves and belts. This one was of champagne-coloured şilk. Her plump, spike-nailed hands closed on the little parcel.

'Alida!'

She ignored it. It was ten o'clock and she had been ignoring it for half an hour.

'Alida!'

She dropped the parcel and, pulling the welt of her jumper down to her hips, strode to the door.

'Oh, there you are.'

'Here I am.'

'I had to call and call.'

'I was busy downstairs. The house does not run itself.'

'I'm so cold, dear. My hands are cold.'

'The sun is shining.'

'I couldn't move my fingers for cold.'

Alida banged the window shut. 'The primroses are out,' she said.

'So funny, I was dreaming about Tantamount Hill and those Saturday balls. I wonder why? We often went up the hill from The Gantry, for a stroll, you know. Often.'

'I shall be going to the shops in half an hour.'

The brown eyes, watered to the thin gold colour of whisky, were doubtful on her face. God help me, Alida thought, God help me, it is an indecent age! She would not care to live to such an age.

'I would like a hot drink now.'

'It's bad for your digestion, mother, too much tea.'

'I would like meat extract. Very hot.'

'You burn your mouth – you know you cannot manage it without burning your mouth.'

Alida went round to the far side of the great bed, the unseemly bed, in which her mother's shrunken body was lost as in a great sea. Yet she would not give it up.

'It was very cold.'

'Not cold out, I'm sure. Quite spring-like, in fact.'

'Yes, it was spring then.'

'Then?'

'You weren't listening, you never listen. I was telling you but you never listen. All the best balls were in the spring.'

'Oh.'

Alida hauled up the eiderdown from the floor, threw it over the width of the bed. And I, she thought bitterly, I am not young, not a girl, to bend and stoop and struggle with making and tidying this great bed. I am sixty-one. She does not realize.

'Of course there were winter balls, too,' Eleanor said. 'We wore capes. We had muffs.'

'I'm going to the shops, mother. Is there anything you want?'

'You had a muff, as a child, and matching bonnet, from a sealskin coat of your Aunt Fosters.'

To quieten her, to get away from the dark, lurking forest of the past, she said, 'I'll get you a drink, though for the life of me I can't imagine why you are cold. Enough bedding for a great frost.'

As Alida reached the door, her mother said, 'Will Faith come today? Is it Wednesday?'

Alida Thorne sighed. How could she, how *could* she not remember, there was nothing else to think of, nothing to get in her way, to confuse her.

'Faith Lavender is dead. I have told you so.'

'Faith? Dead?'

'Faith. Dead.'

As she closed the door she glanced back. The old woman, her skin fine-scored as a leaf, was picking at the sheet between two fingers, picking and picking, still uncertain at this news.

Alida went downstairs, stooping a little, not knowing that she stooped, annoyed at the trouble a hot drink caused.

In the bedroom, Eleanor Thorne, Faith Lavender's death forgotten, reminded herself to ask her daughter about The Gantry.

When Dorothea Shottery awoke, she could not remember what day it was, not for several minutes. She had fingered the lamp and slid back an edge of the curtain on to a sun-flecked, eight o'clock day, searching for a clue. She was anxious, for no such thing had ever happened to her before, her memory was always clear and rounded as a bell-note and utterly reliable.

In time, she remembered that it was Tuesday, a week since Faith Lavender's death, pension day, her birthday, as a child 'full of Grace'. But as she washed her breakfast cup and saucer and rinsed them meticulously under the cold tap, she was anxious. She was sixty-six years old. Was this, then, the way it all began?

Beyond her kitchen window, crocuses sprouted up from the grass, bright as doubloons, orange and heliotrope. Banded in sunlight, her cat slid and slunk, stomach-wise, towards a bird.

'Hastings!' her voice commanded through the open window. 'Hastings!'

The cat rolled over on to its back and shadow-boxed with imaginary flies, guileless of face. Dorothea smiled.

'Cats!' She remembered Alida Thorne's voice, soft as fondant, coloured with scorn. 'Uncompanionable things. I don't know what you find in them to admire.' Dorothea always defended Hastings, the most companionable of creatures, when he chose, but she felt no less of a fool. 'Cats!' Alida would say, raising her eyes, a smile pinching her pin-cushion mouth.

Dorothea frowned into the mirror above the sink. I should like Alida, she thought, I should be kind to her – I *will* be kind to her. It did not strike her, for she was a modest and, on the whole, an outward-looking woman, that she had never been anything but kind to Alida Thorne.

Such a life, however eased and softened by money, Dorothea would not wish upon herself. Eleanor Thorne would be ninety in July, and Alida had no memories.

Even after thirty-one years, Dorothea's memories sweetened her days. Even just now, when for a moment she had not been able to remember what day it was, and when Faith Lavender had already been dead a week. Her memories were like a small, locked box of securities and because she knew they were there, safely there, she had no need to open them. Only sometimes, alone with sleeplessness or through one of the long evenings of early dark, Dorothea became afraid. She might open the box and find nothing there, she might be unable to remember the features of his face and the habits of a marriage.

What day is it? she said to herself abruptly, and her heart jerked in alarm. Tuesday? 'Tuesday,' Dorothea said aloud, tapping her right hand with her left forefinger. 'Tuesday, you silly woman.' She laughed. She had shopping to get, a visit to make, a meeting to attend. She began to sing, stabbing a hat pin through her smart, lime-green hat, for wasn't it almost Spring?

Tuesday. A week ago. Perhaps not the lime-green hat, then? Yet why? The sunlight struck her reflection between the eyes. Silly, she thought, you silly woman! And Eleanor Thorne is eighty-nine. God help us!

Chapter Three

'THE whole thing is nonsense. I do not propose to discuss it further.'

Isabel Lavender began to smooth down finger after finger of her gardening gloves, intent upon maintaining appearances, even through domestic tasks.

'But how can it be nonsense? How *can* it be?' There was a whining note to Kathleen Lavender's voice. 'The letter . . .'

'. . . is in error.'

Isabel turned, wanting to end the conversation. Kathleen had always needed a firm voice. But the memory of her sister's surprising her with the amethyst brooch was like a rubbed sore in her mind.

'But responsible people don't make mistakes like that. A business letter cannot be crammed full of lies. How *can* it be?'

As well as being irritating, the refrain was unanswerable. Kathleen Lavender leaned back against the kitchen door, hands behind her in a schoolgirlish pose. Her sister faced her, waiting. They were just of a height.

'How can it be?' Kathleen asked again.

Isabel sighed. 'There was no will,' she said, 'You know it and I know it, so this solicitor clearly has some confusion on his hands. Do not ask me how it can be, I have no idea. A mistake has been made. I shall tell him so.'

'You intend to see him, then?'

'I do.'

'But shouldn't we both . . .'

'Why? Is there something you wish to say to the solicitor which I should not hear or say for you?'

'The letter was jointly addressed.'

Isabel paused. 'Well,' she said eventually, 'you have every right to accompany me. Of course.'

In the further short silence, Kathleen's mobile features sought an expression and, when they had found it, it was one of anxiety. Isabel stood. Beyond the window the sky was a brittle blue.

'Shall you help me in the garden? Chrysanthemum cuttings need to be taken if we are to have any flowers next season. Everyday things go on.'

Kathleen moved slowly from the doorway and shook her head, without speaking. Her sister paused. 'I suppose you had never expected Faith to have any money of her own?' she asked.

Kathleen looked up and moved her hands, bending the long finger experimentally at the joints, turning her wrist.

'She had no secrets,' Isabel Lavender reproved her sister, 'she was never a secretive person. No secrets and no money, that we do not know about and does not belong to all of us.' Because her sister still appeared to hesitate, Isabel took up the refrain. 'How could she?'

'Yes,' said Kathleen, and then, hastily, aware of her sister's eye, 'I mean, no. No, of course not.'

'If you wish to see the solicitor . . .'

'No. Oh, no.' Kathleen opened the larder door. 'No.'

Isabel nodded and went off into the garden. As she carried the clay pots, six at a time, from the greenhouse, a light wind scuttled her skirt. She smiled. Kathleen had always seen the sense of things, once they were explained. She was, after all, several years younger, besides taking after their mother for irresolution as well as for smallness of feature.

In the larder, Kathleen Lavender stared vaguely at various vegetables, at tins of soup, at flour bins and chutney jars, worrying about lunch and not understanding how a solicitor could be mistaken.

'To discuss the will of your sister, the late Miss Faith Margaret Lavender, which has today been brought to my attention.'

How *could* Isabel read any possibility of error into that? How could she?

A badly-balanced packet of tapioca crashed from shelf to floor and burst open like a ripe seed-pot. Kathleen Lavender started and, looking down at the spreading carpet of white beads, felt that it must be her fault.

As far as Gaily could judge, the cards got more and more unsuitable each year. Not to say more and more expensive. He took his time, as always, mostly because he owed it to Ma. And the shop was warm. He had set down the bag of washing on the floor between his feet, for she hadn't been able to manage the washing since last year's fall.

> To you Mother dear,
> On this special day,
> May every blessing
> Come your way.

Nothing to that, nothing out of the ordinary, and the flowers were nastily coloured. He wasn't paying one and sixpence for that. Nor for two pekinese dogs tied up in bows and saying 'Hi, there! Happy Birthday!'

His fingers ranged over mauve condolences and a group of 'Hurray, Hurray, You're One Today!' until they came to one he liked, a carpet of spring flowers beside Lake Windermere, and the writing within plain and tasteful. 'With every good wish for a Happy Birthday.' Gaily sighed. Cold, she'd call that. 'Doesn't say much, does it?'

Someone kicked his washing-bag over and stared down at the spilled shirt sleeve, the maroon-edged handkerchief. Gaily moved it nearer the counter. He knew he must buy what meant something to her, however ugly. He found it. 'To mother dear,' in gilt, hidden among roses.

> It's nothing very new
> But still as dearly meant,
> With my love good and true,
> Is this birthday message sent.

It cost two shillings. Gaily reached into his pocket, and then

27

spotted a long, thin orange and yellow card, decorated with a cartoon. He didn't like the cartoon. It was the words.

'You're only a bird in a gilded cage,' he read. It was Ma's favourite song. Now, if she thought he'd remembered that . . . he opened the card.

So how about me for a mate?

He stuffed it hastily back, afraid someone had seen him reading it, and took 'To Mother Dear' and his two shillings up to the counter.

George was already in the snack bar, a cup of tea and a pork batch on the Formica ledge and his yellow scarf saving Gaily's place. Gaily heaved and hitched himself up on to the high stool, shoving the bag of laundry between his feet once more.

'Sorry, I couldn't manage a table.'

Gaily shook his head. Since George always did the arriving early and the saving of places, it was not for him to complain. George was one of nature's kind men. 'Ham or pork?' he said now, sliding down from his stool, before Gaily could protest, and pottering over to the counter-queue. George was a small man, shaped like a bowling pin and with the same, curious, rocking movement as he walked. His eyes were the milky, undersea colour of green marbles. Gaily was fond of him.

'Now then,' he said, back with the food.

Gaily nodded. 'Yes,' he said.

They sat in silence, eating, drinking, two amiable and contented men. Around them, plates, cups, spoons, came together among the smoke and shopping bags of Saturday morning.

'Washing day again?' George Aspinall said at last, wiping his mouth.

Gaily nodded.

'All right, is she?'

Gaily nodded again. George leaned forward slightly and poked Gaily's arm with his index finger. 'Got a surprise on,' he said, 'do you good, as well.'

'Surprise?'

'For tonight. After a time,' George said, 'the Cross Keys gets boring.'

Gaily had never thought so. Every Saturday night, for a good many years, he and George and George's wife Annie laughed themselves to stitches and talked, glassy-eyed among friends, in the bar of the Cross Keys. Rarely did Hubert Gaily go out anywhere else, on any other night, and never had he failed to enjoy his close, companionable, ale-coloured Saturday night.

'It's what men do,' Ma had always said. 'Go out, of a Saturday. Always have. It's to be expected, it's what men do.'

Her friend came in on Saturdays, on two buses from the Maudslay Road estate, and they had a fish supper. They didn't want him there.

'What's it all about?' said Gaily, frightened at this threat of some unknown change. George pressed the tips of his fingers together. 'It was Annie's idea,' he said, by way of justification. 'She fancies going to a club.'

'A club?'

Microphones floated before Gaily's eyes, and singers with lamé dresses like mermaids' tails, jokey young men and dirt-darkened pianos and mouths rounded in community song.

'No,' he said hastily.

'Now, have you ever been? No. You have not. Then how can you make up your mind, just like that?'

'Have you ever been?'

'I know all about clubs,' George said, 'they're very popular.'

'Yes.'

'You have to keep an open mind.'

'I haven't said anything against them,' Gaily knew himself to be a tolerant man, 'the young . . .'

'No.' George's finger prodded him. 'The average age is forty-three.'

Gaily stared into his cold teacup, anxiously.

'It's comfortable, it's a change. You have a drink, different faces. They have top-class performers, you know, not any of your has-beens. Not now. Two hundred pounds a week, some of them can earn.'

'How do you know all this then?' It seemed to Gaily that his friend was going away from him, penetrating new areas of experience, talking with authority. He was saddened.

'I'm surprised *you* don't know, personally,' George countered, 'very surprised. You're a man who keeps his eyes open, a man aware of things. I'm surprised.'

Gaily sat in silence, the washing lumpy between his ankles, reassuring.

'Well then?' George said.

Gaily shook his head. 'I enjoy the Cross Keys,' he said, 'always have.'

'Well, this won't be all that different.'

Gaily met his eyes. 'Then why,' he asked, 'bother to go?'

George blew his nose.

In his agitation, Gaily carried the brown bag of washing all the way back home. His lunch was ready.

Ada Gaily stared at the spilling-out white shirt and the maroon-bordered handkerchief. 'You've never done a thing like that before,' she said. 'Never.' And peered into his face, as she had done to him as a child, searching for signs of fever.

His dark navy-blue suit lay on the bed, as a man might lie, sleeves folded, legs neatly together. At the foot of the bed, the toe-caps of his shoes shone blackly. It was 7.10 p.m.

Gaily could not decide what to do. What worried him far more than the prospect of change, was the fact that he shied away from it, as a man set in his ways, and that was something he had never considered himself to be. True, his life was ordered and uneventful, and to many would appear monotonous. Gaily's quiet defence had always been that he liked a certain monotony. A man set down roots, and thought. He was even prepared to go so far as to admit that monotony was the most comfortable way.

Now, he stared down at his Saturday suit and was afraid at the new possibility that he had become a man set in his ways, upset by change. When Ma died, he had always planned to break away completely, give up this life and build a new one.

Now, he accepted with distress the possibility that he might finally fail to do so. Suddenly, a world without his present routine, above all a world without Ma, seemed a world without foothold or boundary.

Gaily let in the cat, scratching at the door. Still, he did not know what he should do tonight. The cat leaped lightly on to the bed and padded over the bodiless sleeves. For a second, he watched it absently, and then hauled it off. He had been anxious in case white hairs got on the suit, which must mean that, wherever he decided to go, he would go somewhere.

From the floor, his mother's cat eyed him viciously.

In the kitchen, Ma Gaily buttered bread. 'You're out then?' she said. Gaily nodded. He hovered in the doorway, 'Elsie hasn't come yet?'

'It doesn't look like it does it? You may feel like looking behind the sofa. She maybe floated in.' It was good humoured.

'Don't wait up,' he said.

'Do I ever?'

'No.'

He had reached the living room door before she called after him. 'What about the washing?' she said.

Gaily stopped dead. There was silence, except for a creaking from the gas-meter. Down the stairs came the cat, sullen-eyed.

'Have you heard?'

Gaily returned to the kitchen. Ma bent over the stove, inserted two large plates to warm, slammed the door. 'Am I supposed to take it,' she said, her back to him again, 'or what?'

'You know you're not.'

'Do I?'

'I'll take it Monday evening.'

'You're not in need of a change of underwear then?'

'I can have it on Monday.'

'It has to dry.'

'I can wait.'

'*You* can.' She pushed past him through the doorway, her

hands full of salt cellar, vinegar bottle, sauce bottle and pickle jar.

'You don't have to tell me,' Gaily said, 'that all the clothes either of us has are in the bag or on our backs.'

Ma sat down and picked up her reading glasses.

'I'll take it Monday,' he said.

He reached the door again.

'Have a good time,' he said.

Ma unfolded the evening paper.

'See you in the morning,' he said.

'I see they've caught up with him in Huddersfield,' Ma said, 'that prisoner.'

Gaily went out, smiling to himself. The street was just moist with rain, sweet-smelling. Then he remembered George Aspinall and the change of plan, and that he had not decided what to do. He turned the corner miserably, bumping into Elsie with their fish and chips.

'More haste,' she said.

Gaily nodded. A little further up the street, he realized who she was.

'I cannot do it,' Alida Thorne said, desperately. 'I cannot do it, and there is an end.'

Dorothea sat her down and padded her in with cushions, smiled vaguely and went off to make the tea. She did not understand it. Never had Alida visited her, unannounced and uninvited, before. Dorothea had always wondered if it was because she despised her. But now, she thought, I know that it is not so. Here is proof. She is the sisters' friend and mine, too, she has come to tea on my birthday. Not, of course, that she is to know that, and not, of course, that I shall tell her. Dorothea spooned glistening black gobbets of jam on to a silver dish and wished that she could like Alida Thorne a little more. 'Cannot do what?' she said brightly, returning with the tray. Alida was weeping quietly, snuffling a little, into her floral handkerchief.

'Oh, my dear!' Dorothea disposed of the tray and bent down. 'My dear, what is it? What can I do?'

She hastened to let her concern cover her embarrassment. Alida lifted her head and Dorothea thought how unbecoming tears were, after childhood, how old and ugly and formless they made a face.

'Please tell me,' Dorothea urged. 'If you want to, if I can help.' Although I already know, she said to herself, it is her mother. Eleanor Thorne is eighty-nine years old and Alida is sick and weary. Who would not be? She herself had lost her mother quite early in life, and mourned her still.

Alida, suddenly conscious of company and place, blew her nose wildly, put away her handkerchief and sat up.

'There,' Dorothea said, 'there,' and poured the tea.

'I have never let myself go like that,' Alida said, 'never. It proves to what a point I am brought.'

Dorothea reassured her. 'It is best to cry,' she said, 'I sometimes cry, when nothing else will serve.' It was a harmless lie, for she could see that Alida was a little ashamed.

'If Faith had been here,' Alida Thorne said, biting daintily into a scone, 'I would have asked her advice. Many a time I have wanted to ask her about this, and thought it wrong. At the last minute, I have held it back.'

Jam dripped from her plump, white finger. 'You were closest to her,' she said.

Dorothea looked at the garden, at the sun shining between the apple trees, remembering her friend.

'Dear Faith,' said Alida softly.

No, Dorothea thought, no that is wrong. Alida made her sound a different woman, some pale, sweetly-smiling, malleable soul. In her lifetime, nobody had said dear Faith, though they had loved her. Faith would have had no patience with it. She had been boisterous and sharp, a humorous woman, a woman of decision. Alida would not have called her dear Faith then.

'Isabel . . .' Dorothea began.

'I cannot talk to Isabel,' Alida told her. 'No one can, Isabel is an old woman, the mistress of her own affairs.'

Dorothea wondered why that should preclude her concern in

the affairs of others. But perhaps Alida knew the remaining Misses Lavender best, after all.

'Have another slice of cake?' she said.

'I have made up my mind,' Alida Thorne said, accepting it. 'It's hardly fair I should be required to go on in this way. How many people could have been under such a constant strain, for so long? I have had to make a decision.'

Dorothea nodded. Outside the door, she heard the gentle scratching of the cat Hastings and she dared not, in Alida's company, let him in.

'You must advise me,' Alida said, setting down her plate.

'If you have already decided . . .'

'You must be the one to tell me I am doing the right thing.'

Yes, thought Dorothea, that is it, and that is different. But when the announcement came, she was truly shocked.

'I have made an appointment to see the Matron of The Gantry.'

Outside the door, Hastings scratched and, in her distress and confusion, Dorothea rose and let him in. But Alida was absorbed in herself.

'She is eighty-nine,' she told Dorothea, unnecessarily. 'Senility is known to set in a good deal earlier in many cases.'

Dorothea nodded vaguely. I must not be shocked, she told herself, I must remember that Eleanor is eighty-nine years old and that they are most kind in mental hospitals, these enlightened days. I must remember that she will be cared for and will not suffer. Alida has a right to some freedom, she herself is . . . Dorothea realized that she did not know how old Alida was but it must be around her own age. Not a girl.

'There is an accepted difference between a geriatric ward and a lunatic ward,' Alida was saying, 'people realize that nowadays. I would not like it to be said that I had had my mother put away.'

But what else is it, Dorothea thought anxiously, what else is it that you are wanting to do?

'Come for us at home,' was what George had said, 'we're setting off from there. Come for us about eight o'clock.'

George Aspinall had not doubted that his friend would turn up. Now, Gaily hesitated at the junction with Chapel Street. It was not a question of committing himself. He could go this once, for George's sake, because George was so anxious to show off his new-found club and next Saturday, he could revert to routine and the Cross Keys.

But Gaily knew that he would not go, not even once, to the club, though he did not know of any reason, beyond a feeling, a shrinking-back from an uncongenial world, a novelty, the element of surprise.

He turned back into the town, away from the buses to George's road, towards the public house. There, he was known, there friends would be, and there were, after all, other people besides George Aspinall. And George might easily have changed his mind.

George had not, and the Cross Keys was strangely empty. Gaily sat over his pint of mixed until a quarter past nine, when the barmaid called to him. 'So you haven't gone with them,' she said. Gaily looked up.

'The club,' she said, 'or hadn't you heard?'

'I didn't fancy it.'

'It won't last, can't do. But that's where they've all skipped off to. Like the grave in here tonight. Like a Monday. Oh, they'll be back, they've none of them got that sort of money. You see. Not like a Saturday night at all though, not really.'

'No,' said Gaily. He wished he had the way of talking to women, to individual strangers. He was happy enough, full of ale in the crowd on Saturday nights, listening, laughing. It was not the same. He finished his beer sadly, wondered if he would have been better off, after all, among them at the club.

'You see,' the barmaid said, 'next week, they'll all be in here with their tails between their legs. Habit's hard to beat.'

Because he could think of nothing to say to her in reply, Gaily bought her a drink and left.

'Goodnight,' she said, disappointed, turning back to the empty bar.

Outside, the rain gurgled in shining gutters. Maybe it was only to be expected, a sudden change that tilted your world sideways, slipped the ground from under you a shade. Maybe this was what happened to most people. He was lucky to have led such an ordered life.

The moon rode high, a sixpenny bit of white gold, over the Town Hall tower. Gaily walked home, opened the front door, called out to them not to worry, took the brown leather-cloth bag of washing and left the house again. He might as well save himself a Monday evening. Besides, Ma would be glad of the clean clothes.

Chapter Four

WEDNESDAY afternoon. The first of March. Wind. At the top of Tantamount Hill the sky raced, all shades of grey, so near a hand might reach and take it. At the bottom of the hill, six poplar trees swayed, graceful as girls with their hair long. Wind shaved over the new grass near Faith Lavender's grave, and Dorothea Shottery's cat went mad on the back lawn, leaping, rolling, falling over its own paws.

Upstairs in her room alone, Eleanor Thorne dozed and the wind entered her dreams, confusing her, until the bed was a great sea, and the howling came round the mast of the chimney-pots.

In the town, slates and bin-lids took flight and at the corner of Maxstone Villas, a rheumy old man, blue chinned, bent his back against the blast. Isabel Lavender, emerging from the railway station, was glad of her tight-fitting coat and her well-pinned, tight-fitting hat. She crossed the footbridge that led into the red and grey brick town. Now, she thought, now we shall get things done, sort things out, arrive at a solution. Now, we shall have an end to Kathleen's nonsense. Though, since the day the letter came, Kathleen's nonsense had been all unspoken. Nevertheless.

'Nevertheless,' said Mr Cecil Whittaker, 'I have the will.'

He was a tweedy man, with rough-chopped hair and a blotchy complexion, younger than Miss Lavender liked a professional man to be. She had wanted to argue the matter out, for she had every next sentence there, in her head, only to be followed like a crochet pattern. It had not gone according to plan. The March gale hurled itself against Mr Whittaker's windows.

'I suppose you hadn't bargained for a will?' Mr Whittaker said.

Isabel Lavender inclined her head. She did not intend to commit herself to this man.

'No,' he said, grinning, another thing she did not like. 'Many people don't. It's often the way.'

'I cannot understand why we were not informed.'

'Who knows?'

'Not my sister,' she drew herself up in the chair. 'You, your firm. It is a little late in the day.'

'It might easily have been later. We were not notified of your sister's death. We chanced to find it out.'

'You cannot blame me for that. I knew nothing about any will, I knew nothing about my sister's having consulted you. Nothing that would lead me to inform your firm of her passing.'

'Quite so.'

Isabel Lavender felt uneasy, as though he were mocking and trying to get the better of her, as though she were guilty of something. He lolled back in his swivel chair, one huge thigh thrust over the other, a bright-eyed man. Not his father's son. Isabel noticed a large grease-spot on the carpet.

'So,' he said, 'you'll want to see the will.'

Again she inclined her head. He opened the box file. 'I've had a copy made,' he said, 'you can take it with you, show it to your sister. I shall need to keep the original document. Unless . . .' He took the steel-stemmed pipe out of his mouth and grinned again, 'unless you want to transfer your business?'

Isabel did not speak.

'It's quite straightforward,' he said, fishing out a piece of paper. Isabel scratched her left palm with her right forefinger, anxious. On the soup-coloured wall, above the fireplace, a portrait of Jas. John Whittaker 1801–1880 frowned upon her.

'The sum of two hundred and fifty pounds, invested in Premium Bonds . . .'

Isabel looked up sharply. Premium Bonds, whenever had Faith bought Premium Bonds? But how like her, she allowed herself to think quickly, how like her, without a by-your-leave, without a word, to invest in Premium Bonds, in a lottery. For it was a lottery, no matter how you excused it. Let me not be prim, she thought, let me be sensible, a woman of the world, let me not be unfair. But it was a lottery and lotteries were undesirable. We have always said so, she thought, wanting to cry with annoyance, as a family we have always agreed about it.

'. . . for sick children.'

'What?'

Mr Whittaker sighed. 'To the Great Ormonde Street Hospital for Sick Children,' he repeated.

'What is?'

'I beg your pardon?'

'I did not hear . . .'

'The sum of two hundred and fifty pounds.'

'Is that all?' Meaning, what about us, about us?

'Generous, I'd have thought.'

'No, no, I . . .'

'All she had.'

'*All?*'

'Why, yes.'

Isabel sat mutely, angrily, hands folded on her mushroom leather bag.

'Some personal bits and pieces,' he said dismissively, 'all shares in property, furniture, personal belongings . . . and so on . . . jointly to be shared between my sisters, Isabel May and Kathleen Opal Lavender.'

He looked up, Isabel nodded.

'Jewellery,' he said.

Isabel's hand shot to her throat. A great ball of wind puffed out of the old chimney-place, rocking the portrait of Jas. John Whittaker.

Faith had left all her jewellery, excepting mother's pearl and ruby eternity ring, to Dorothea Shottery.

Mr Whittaker threw the piece of paper down on his desk. His green-lizard-lidded eyes appraised her.

'That's all,' he said, and began to strike a match.

*

She did not begin to think of what she might say to Kathleen. *Had* to say. Though Kathleen was meek and would accept. Isabel Lavender had always been less good than most people at losing face, since she had never learned how to compensate for it, she had never learned to wallow, to conceal partial humiliation in an expression of total defeat.

Thinking of her sister made her impatient. 'But,' Kathleen would say, clasping her hands together, and 'Oh, surely . . .' and 'Why, then . . .' Certainly she would be craven enough to accept the news without comment, or any thought of a fight. Good heavens, she might even be relieved! 'Oh, thank goodness, it is all settled, dear, I never wanted any trouble, I do so hate trouble.' As a child, Isabel had been forever wanting and having to shake her younger sister, shake her out of smiling acceptance, out of vagueness of mind, out of bewilderment, into rebellion and action.

Isabel Lavender stopped dead in the hall of the railway station. Behind the gothic-arch pigeon hole, counting out change, she saw the man in boots, the man who had hung about at Faith's funeral. *Was* it him? Under cover of buying a magazine from the stall opposite, Isabel glanced over, and then stared more persistently, for he had not seen her, was not so much as looking up from his counting. Yes, it was the same man. He had a broad forehead, rather sallow face, and thinning hair. He looked somehow smarter and more formidable now, than at the funeral. Because, of course, this was his place, he knew it, he belonged, and there he had not known where to look or how to fold his hands. He went on counting.

Well, Isabel told herself, putting back the magazine, here is one mystery partially solved, one set of questions answered. Faith could not possibly have known a booking-clerk at a railway station, therefore he had certainly been a stranger, idle and curious, a watcher at the funeral. She stepped on to the train, allowing one minor satisfaction to screen her anxiety at the absence of a major one.

'Three hundred pounds. I think a fair amount. Yes.'

'Fifty up on last year? Surely not.'

'Colonel Baxter . . .?'

'I said, surely not. You can't go on putting it up, year in, year out. It's a struggle as it is.'

'Well . . .'

'I say no.'

'Oh, dear! I had thought we might reach an early agreement on our target. If only to get on to the practical arrangements.'

'Haggling,' put in another voice, 'barefaced haggling.'

'Two hundred and fifty, I say. We managed that all right last year. Comfortably.'

'Which is precisely why we hope to . . .'

'. . . made it a den of thieves.'

'Oh, come, Mrs Marchebanks! Come, now!'

The Reverend George Jocelyn Bottingley sounded deeply upset. And, behind the screen of his catarrh, a little angry.

'Ladies and gentlemen,' he began again, on the downbeat of a sigh.

Dorothea Shottery, her eyes fixed unseeingly on the cream paint of a radiator, heard the sigh and wondered about it. The conversation came from far away, the words like beautiful, meaningless sounds in another language, unspoken, impenetrable, Arabic, perhaps, or Persian. She sat sadly, in her old camel coat and her feathered hat, hearing the words. But she did not see the features of the Reverend Mr Bottingley, broad and bland behind his handkerchief.

Thirty-four years ago, the very first Sunday morning, she had put on her new, spruce-green costume, because that was what her husband liked best, and she and Hallam Shottery had walked through their new-found land to this church. Dorothea remembered little more, though sometimes she would pretend that she did. Not, at least, until after the service. Then, both of them a little awkward, a little shy, not liking to make the first move, the Shotterys had walked together down the path, away from the little group at the church porch.

'Excuse me,' she had said, coming after them, and they had turned gladly.

'Mr and Mrs Shottery? I am so pleased to meet you. My name is Eleanor Thorne.'

'Now there was a woman!' Hallam had said later, though a little puzzled by her. 'Somebody different.'

'Kind,' Dorothea had replied. Or meant to have replied, but perhaps she had not, perhaps the knowledge of later years had imposed itself on that first memory.

Eleanor Thorne had been thin, even then, but an upright woman, straight as a twig, straight in the old way they were all taught, books on heads, stiff-corseted.

'Oh, I have a daughter,' Dorothea remembered her saying, at one of their early meetings, 'she is a teacher. She has an excellent place in a girls' boarding-school in Worcestershire.'

Eleanor Thorne had been proud, blue-eyed, a widow in her late fifties, energetic and generous. Proud, too, of her solemn-faced daughter in the framed photograph. 'You must be of an age,' she had said. 'You must become friends.'

But it had been she and Eleanor who had become the friends, though the distinction was never made in public. When Alida came home, they were polite to one another, no more. Alida had been conscious of Dorothea's married state, hating her for it, burning with scorn at the preoccupations and trivialities of a marriage. Which, Dorothea had often thought, they probably were, and really, she had half-envied Alida, not for her independence but for the responsibility she had, and for the pride and satisfaction she was entitled to feel in her work. Dorothea had never considered the world was a better place for her own existence and activities but surely Alida could feel just that? So many young women educated and developed, and fulfilled, so much knowledge imparted, all because of her efforts.

Dorothea had once tried to tell her this, but Alida Thorne had flushed with anger. 'Stop patronizing me,' she had shouted, 'stop pitying me!' The incident had never been referred to again and Dorothea did not believe that Alida would remember it. But, after that, they had little time to spend together, little to say to one another. It had been Eleanor, quiet, firm, devoted whom Dorothea had loved, and Eleanor had been the only living person whose presence she could bear when Hallam died a year after their coming to Haverstock.

Now, Eleanor Thorne was eighty-nine years old, and her conversation was erratic, but Dorothea still sat with her, and for the odd fifteen or twenty minutes, and sometimes as long as an hour, they would talk, as they had always done and the present world swung temporarily into focus for the old lady, and she held on to it, like a crystal ball, firmly in her hand.

Dorothea did not even mind when she lost her grip and wandered off down the avenues of the past, for sometimes she could accompany her, at any rate part of the way, and Eleanor would talk of Hallam, as if he had been there, in her room, recalling his expressions and conversations more clearly than Dorothea herself ever could.

There was nothing alarming, she decided, about such a life in the past, about such a dependence upon memory. It seemed to her a precious gift, far more than just an alleviation of present discomfort. It proved to her, somehow, that the imagination mattered, that people, events, joys, experiences, visions, had a permanence, and some kind of lasting value. You could leave them behind so much more easily, to get on with the present, if you knew that some day you were going to return.

Eleanor Thorne was returning, her life in the great bed had value. She had been a good woman. And now, Dorothea thought, and now ...

Not in shame, but in confusion and surprise she realized that her eyes were opaque with tears, and that the voices had swayed into the foreground and taken on a meaning.

'The provision stall, Mrs Shottery,' he was saying, 'the provision stall.'

'Yes,' she said hurriedly. 'Oh, yes.'

'I knew we could rely on you.' There was a faint murmur of satisfaction, though only a murmur, for it was what they had all expected. Dorothea wiped her eyes and blew her nose and looked around her, at the overcoated figures, huddled and sneezing about the table-tennis table under the vestry lights. But none of them noticed, they were hunched within themselves, absorbed, waiting to be done with the decisions and get home. The vestry walls shone with damp.

I suppose I have agreed to run the grocery stall, she thought, and with annoyance, for she always ran the grocery stall and tonight she had come determined to ask for a change. Her idea had been rather startling, even silly, but she had wanted to have a black crepe dress and bangles and a tent, and to tell fortunes. Harmless after all, and the Rector was not superstitious but perhaps it was as well, for they would all have laughed. Not that Dorothea minded their laughing at her but she felt protective towards her idea. Madame Claudia, she had wanted to be, Your Guide to the Future. Two Shillings. She would tell the people joyful things, cheer them up, make them happy. Dorothea smiled to herself.

'Then if there is nothing else . . .?' the Rector was saying, and their cold faces were relaxed again, grateful, and they were standing for prayers. Dorothea prayed, very formally and with no hope whatsoever, for Eleanor Thorne. Alida had made up her mind and that was that. Dorothea's heart turned cold and heavy as stone, thinking of it. All the way home, not listening though half-replying to Mrs Marchebanks's chatter, Dorothea worried about it, and in the night she awoke, to find her eyes again thick with tears. She felt helpless. But perhaps it would not come, after all, perhaps they would take one look at Mrs Thorne and refuse her admittance into a ward of lunatic old ladies.

At the foot of her bed, the cat Hastings rose, turned around and around, pushing his paw gently into the eiderdown, and then curling into the soft silk hollow. That, together with the new thought, was a comfort and Dorothea slept.

'But we have always had fish on Fridays. Always.' Kathleen Lavender's hands hovered above the dish of buttered plaice, uncertain what to do. 'You know we have.'

'Well, I cannot imagine why. We are not papists when all's said and done.'

'I don't see what . . .'

'Of course that has something to do with it!'

Kathleen Lavender sighed. Everything was changing now that Isabel was in charge. At least, she supposed that Isabel was in charge. Faith had been of certain mind but easier to please.

'You don't want any, then?' Kathleen replaced the lid of the dish.

'Have we some alternative?'

'Why no, but . . .'

'I do not intend to *starve*,' Isabel said sharply, taking up the serving slice. 'I simply meant that we should not have fish so unfailingly, on a regular day of the week, in future.'

Kathleen began to eat. 'You always were rather against Roman Catholics.' Never mind, she thought, never mind, for it isn't that, she is still upset about the will and still unsure what to do. Kathleen herself saw nothing at all they could, or should, try to do. Faith had disposed of the money and belongings as she chose and everyone had that right, at the very least. And it is not, she thought, sliding the mottled skin deftly off her fish, it is not as though we are starving. No, we are lucky, we live comparatively well. There are so many others who do not have a portion of the things we have, in our state.

Isabel coughed. Her grey hair had a dusty look, as though it had been powdered like a flunkey's wig. She coughed again and looked reproachfully at Kathleen. Bones, the look said.

'They were fillets,' Kathleen countered.

'So I am imagining a bone?'

'I didn't say that, Isabel.'

'You implied it.'

After a short silence, Kathleen took courage, feeling sorry for her sister. 'If you are still anxious about the will . . .' she began.

Isabel stiffened.

'They do need money, you know. For . . . well, I suppose for research and so on. It is a worthy cause.'

'Have I ever suggested that it was otherwise?'

'No.'

'We did not expect Faith to have any money at all. What real difference would £250 make to us? We do not need anything, we have no debts.' Isabel Lavender closed her knife and fork together. 'It is not the money,' she said grandly, 'it is a matter of principle.'

'But . . .'

'Shall we forget it? Your ideas are rather undeveloped and ignorant and, after all, it was I who saw the solicitor. Shall we talk of something else? What pudding have you made us?'

No, Kathleen thought, it is not the money, I am sure of that now. Though she would have liked it. It is partly the very fact that Faith saved and disposed of it without a word to us, but more, it is the jewellery, what little there was. She wondered if Dorothea knew about the money and the will – if anyone knew, she would. They had been quite close.

Without thinking, therefore, Kathleen Lavender said, 'So I suppose we shall see Dorothea soon? Shall I invite her to lunch?'

Oh, but I have said the wrong thing, she thought, for her sister's face had tightened and her eyes burned with a coppery light.

'I hardly think that we need to do that.'

'Oh.'

'She will receive a letter, she will know.'

'And then what happens?'

'Happens?'

'Well – she will have to . . . to collect . . .'

'I have already packed the few things to which she is entitled, in a small box. I shall send it by registered post.'

'Oh, goodness, Isabel, how silly! How childish! We cannot *send* them, by registered or any other post, to a house two hundred yards across the green!'

'I see no good reason why not.'

'It is unkind. I hate unkindness, that is so petty. Dorothea has done nothing wrong.'

'She has insinuated herself.'

'Nonsense! We have known her for years.'

Righteous anger loosened Kathleen's tongue. I am not a mouse, she thought, and I will not stand by and watch this idiocy.

'I will take them to her,' she said. 'You need not come.' She handed Isabel a slice of lemon meringue pie. 'It is the very least one can do.'

'What *right* . . .'

'Every right.'

Kathleen Lavender sat calmly down and picked up her napkin. She would not be taken for a fool, either, not when it mattered so much as this.

Isabel had always known that, with Kathleen, one might, on very rare occasions, go too far. 'This pie is tart,' she said now.

'Oh, I am so sorry,' Kathleen handed her the castor sugar. She did not wish to remain outside of her usual, blameworthy self for longer than was necessary. She had achieved her end, and self-assertiveness was not comfortable for her.

Chapter Five

'GOOD evening,' Gaily said.

This time, she was wearing a hat, which pulled her face back, somehow, and made a line round it, so that she looked older than she had the other night. He wasn't sure he liked the hat but he recognized the gesture in wearing it and was half pleased, half afraid.

'Oh, I didn't think you would come,' she said, and laughed, not at all a confused laugh, but quiet, and at herself rather than at him, looking down at her cupped hands as she did so.

'I'd have to keep a promise.' He stood awkwardly by her table.

'A man of your word,' she said.

'That's it. I hope so.'

'Aren't you going to sit down?' She said that as though she wondered whether it was the correct thing to say.

'I'll get myself a coffee. Will you have another? You'd no need to have bought your own.'

'Oh, I had to, in case you didn't come. You can't just sit here.'

'No,' he said. 'No.'

Standing at the counter waiting for the coffee, he wondered how he could have let it come about, and he felt a stranger to himself. 'Folk don't know where they are with you. I can't understand it,' Ma had said. Because this was a Thursday and he had never thought of going out on a Thursday before, and because of the previous Saturday night, coming back to collect the washing. Routine was the stuff of life to Ada Gaily, had always been so, and now she felt it shifting out of her reach. Yet, Gaily told himself, there is no need for her to worry. She doesn't really know me.

'This is very nice,' she said, when he got back to the table.

'Yes.'

But hadn't it been a mistake though, he thought, wasn't it more pointless than most evenings? For what could he say to her? There seemed nothing at all, no way of climbing back on to the free wheel of conversation they had somehow set going the other night. She was different, after all, he decided, in her hat, and with the grained leather gloves neatly folded, and Gaily hadn't for a moment the wit to see this, prepared self as the false one and her accidental self, in an older coat and head-scarf, of Saturday night, the true one. Neither did he, for the moment, recognize her own diffidence as an indication that she felt in the same way about him. He is diffident, Florence Ames thought, he hasn't anything to say because he is embarrassed to be with me. It was a mistake, then, after all.

'The washing dried all right, did it?' Gaily could think of no other remark.

Mrs Ames looked up. 'Oh, yes. Yes, thank you.'

'They're marvellous inventions, aren't they? The coin-ops? Did you know that in London – because they had them there first, of course, some years ago – in London, the – well, beatniks really, aren't they? They come in during the winter time, and take off their coats and sweaters and put them in the big dryer for a sixpenny warm-up. No, I read it. They've nowhere to sleep you see, having left home and so on. You don't believe me.'

She was smiling. 'Oh, yes,' she said. 'But do you often remember things like that?'

'Like . . .?'

'Well – odd things you read. For no reason. I do. I remember that a spider killed a fifteen stone Rugby player, in Australia.'

'That's it, that's just the kind of thing! Stupid really, because what good can a bit of information like that ever do you? When you think of all the valuable things you ought to remember and never can. No sense in it, is there? I'm full of useless bits of knowledge like that. Well, not even knowledge really, is it? You can't call it knowledge. I must tell Ma about the spider, she'd like that.'

'Is she the same?'

'Yes, but she has a better memory than me, even. Things strike her and she remembers them. She can't ever get over some of the things people do, things that happen, every day. Just casually, you know. She reads them out, never stops being amazed.'

'That is a splendid thing,' Mrs Ames said firmly.

'It is?'

'Oh, yes. To go on and on being surprised by life, however old you are. Most people don't.'

'Don't they?'

'Well – do they?' She laughed.

'I'd have to think about it. I suppose not. I don't know so many people.'

'Oh.'

'You must though. Having been a nurse. New faces all the time.'

'Yes, but too many. You never got time to think about them, you were too busy. Or else you sort of jotted them down at the back of your mind, you know, to think about them later, but you never remembered, or you did but it was too late, they'd gone, your head was full of other things.'

'Like spiders and Rugby players.'

'Yes, that's it. Silly things.'

'Don't you miss the life?'

'Yes. I do.'

But Gaily could not bring himself to ask why she did not return to it. They sat in silence again, in the empty café, and he wondered if the girl behind the counter recognized him from Saturday mornings and would make any future remark. It seemed important that George Aspinall should not know.

'Do you fancy a cake?' he asked suddenly, but she shook her head.

'Perhaps you'd like to go somewhere else? Would you like to . . .' but he did not know what.

Florence Ames relaxed suddenly. Why, she thought, he is so much more uncertain than I am, he has lost touch with the world of women, as I have with the world of men. So she said, 'I am quite happy here, if you are. It's very pleasant.'

'Oh, yes. Right.'

'It was kind of you to ask me.'

'No. No . . .'

'And,' she went on, gathering more courage, 'it's a good deal more comfortable than the launderette.'

'I don't know,' he said. 'It couldn't be warmer than there and you've got chairs and the coffee machine. I'd have said there wasn't much to choose.'

'No tables.'

He looked at her and then grinned. 'No,' he agreed, 'no tables.'

'How is your mother?' she asked.

'All right. Very well,' and, out of politeness, 'How is your son?'

'Very well, thank you.'

I shouldn't have asked that, Florence Ames thought, he doesn't care to be questioned about his mother and it makes me seem too familiar, too prying. And Gaily took her quick reply for unwillingness, too, and decided that they did not know one another well enough yet to ask such questions, such casual, family questions, as between friends.

'She's decided the Empire Road launderette isn't as good as the old one, in Cambridge Street, though,' he told Mrs Ames. 'It mangles up the clothes, she says. Had you noticed that at all?'

'No, I'm happy with it.'

'Yes.'

'They come out very clean.'

'So I thought.'

They paused. 'So you won't be using Empire Road in the future,' she said.

'Oh, yes, I shall. Oh, yes. For one thing, it's a lot nearer, for another, there's no difference but in her imagination. It's just something to say. You know.'

'I see.'

'So I'll certainly be using it.'

'Oh.'

'Shall you?'

'Oh, yes,' Florence Ames smiled at him quickly. 'Yes.'

Gaily nodded, satisfied.

Alida Thorne wore her best suit, a straight-skirted mohair tweed in jewel green. She also wore a new lipstick called Chloe, which took some attention away from the slight sallowness she imagined she saw in her complexion, and a splash of light cologne. The previous afternoon, she had set her hair on small rollers.

She intended to give the best possible impression. They should not think her a woman who had let herself go. And so many did. Dorothea's hips must be all of forty-four inches and Isabel, with that straight figure, Isabel dressed so dully and her face was colourless. None of the Lavenders had ever turned heads. It all came of being so confined, of knowing nothing beyond the village of Haverstock.

But I am well preserved, Alida thought, turning a little to the glass, I have taken care.

'Now I shall not be long,' she said to the old figure in the great bed. 'And Dorothea will be here.'

'What day is it then? Is it Wednesday?'

'It is Friday.'

'Oh. Dorothea is coming.'

'I have said so.'

'I knew it could not be Wednesday, it is Faith Lavender who comes on Wednesdays. Of course, I have not forgotten.'

Dear God, thought Alida, is it any wonder I am going where I am going, is it any wonder? It is more likely to be a wonder I have borne with things so long. She did not bother to say it, again, again, again, that Faith Lavender was dead.

'Are you comfortable, mother?'

'Oh yes, thank you. I shall be pleased to see Dorothea. Are you going out, dear?'

'I am.'

'You didn't say.'

'I told you.'

'Perhaps I did not hear.'

'Most likely you did not.'

'It is a long time since I went outside. Is it a summer's day?'

'A spring day. But cold, I think, much too cold for you.'

'If I were to be wrapped up warmly, and . . .'

'Don't be ridiculous, mother! You cannot go out. And I cannot take you with me.'

'I am sorry for that.'

'I shall be late.'

'Yes, now, I knew there was something, of course I did.' The old lady raised her head a little, her face bright with interest.

'What is it?'

'I knew it and now I have remembered. You must tell me. It all came back into my mind because of the ball, the spring ball, and the partner whose name I could not remember, although I have remembered now. It was Miles. Miles, Miles – what? Never mind that, that will come. But I remembered him and I didn't like him, you know, not really, only I was too well-bred to say so to anyone. That was . . .'

'Mother, have you anything to say that cannot wait? I am already late.'

'Late?'

'For my appointment.'

'You hadn't told me.'

Give me patience, give me a little more patience, Alida thought, for it is soon coming to an end.

'You must have forgotten.'

'I don't forget the important things.'

'What did you want to ask me?'

Eleanor Thorne lay back again on the high pillows, and her nut-brown face was petulant. 'I don't know,' she muttered. 'You have interrupted me. You made me forget. You were not listening and now I have forgotten.'

'It's time you had your sleep.'

Alida shut the door and leaned on it, breathless for a second. Then, she had to return and re-powder her forehead and compose herself and try not to be anxious that she was already late.

At least it would give them some idea, at least they would now understand how things were. Her life could not be called her own.

'My life cannot be called my own.'

The Matron pursed her lips, in what Alida took to be sympathy, but she did not comment.

'She has lost all sense of time. One moment she is here, the next she is thirty years or so ago, and then again, she is a young girl and cannot remember who I am. It is *mentally* so exhausting, that is perhaps the worst. I am under such a constant mental and emotional strain. Why just today, you see, before I came out, she insisted a friend would be coming to see her, a friend who died – so sad – a few weeks ago. I have told her, as gently as I can, but quite firmly. 'Faith is dead, mother,' I have said, 'Faith is dead. She will not be coming to see you.' I cannot repeat myself indefinitely. It is like talking to a child. She does not take it in – you will understand this, with your experience.'

The Matron's office was papered with light blue flowers on white and there were canary-yellow curtains. It had none of the institutional smell Alida had prepared herself for. There was a silence, the Matron, who was a Miss Cress, tapping her fountain pen lightly on the blotter. Beyond the window, Alida could see Tantamount Hill, poplars at the foot, banks thick with daffodils, climbing out of sight.

'She would enjoy this view. We have nothing like it, only a view across the green. When The Gantry was a private house, many years ago now, she came here, to balls and parties, it was quite the social centre of the county. Oh, she talks about it so much, just as though it were yesterday. The house is in her bones. She was so fond of it. It would please her to come back here.'

Miss Cress had periwinkle-blue eyes, small and clear as stars. They were on Alida's face and Alida felt a chill and shifted in her chair, as though Miss Cress, in her navy uniform and bib, were one of the old headmistresses.

'Have you a doctor's report? A recent one. I mean ...' she

stressed, as Alida opened her mouth, 'on her physical health.'

'Oh, she is very weak, she cannot get out of bed without assistance.'

'It was a medical opinion I wanted.'

'Doctor Sparrow calls perhaps once every month. He came last week,' Alida said, annoyed at not being believed.

'And?'

'And – well, the situation had not changed, it cannot change. It was I who needed to see him because of the broken nights, the strain involved in loss of sleep.'

'You sleep badly, Miss Thorne?'

'I sleep perfectly, I have always been an untroubled sleeper. But my mother wakes and calls, two, three times and even more, although there is never anything wrong. I cannot very well lie and ignore her.'

'Do you mind telling me how old you are, Miss Thorne?'

Alida did mind. In front of this woman, under any normal circumstances, she would have dropped half a dozen years, for she knew she did not look her age. But it occurred to her that today, it might matter.

'I am sixty-five,' she lied, and was gratified to see the Matron's eyebrows raised. 'You do not look it. You could well give me ten years.'

Alida bowed slightly.

'Now, there are several things that must be done.'

At last, Alida thought, at last we are getting down to business, to the signing of papers, the question of money. Soon, it will all be settled.

'I shall ask Doctor Sparrow to come and see your mother and give her a complete medical check.'

'Oh, but . . .'

'Yes, I know we are primarily a mental hospital, but you must understand how important it is. With old people, the physical condition has so much bearing on the mental state. And frequently, I am prepared to take patients who are only physically ailing and frail, but whose mental faculties remain unimpaired.'

55

Alida was silent. She had never liked Doctor Sparrow, who was too young and wore a constant air of disbelief. Old Doctor Tinsley had been so much more sympathetic.

'Then, with your permission, I should like to come and see Mrs Thorne myself.'

'Oh?'

'You have no objection?'

'I suppose not, if it is necessary.'

'I think it is.'

'And when can she – be admitted?'

'I have to decide first if I will have her! If she needs to come. I have a waiting list, Miss Thorne, and I am overcrowded as it is. There are plenty of people without the benefit of a home and a relative, who must be taken.'

'If it is a question of money . . .'

The blue eyes were hard as diamonds. 'It is not a question of money. Some people here pay nothing at all. They, or their families, cannot afford to do so. Others pay high fees. They can afford them. You will see I am something of a democrat.'

She rose and the apron made a tissue-paper sound. 'And we have to bear in mind, Miss Thorne, that for many people a hospital of this kind is not the answer. It would be positively a bad thing for them. They are better at home.'

'Do you not think of those who must be responsible for them, who bear the burden and strain without training, and without help of any kind? Surely they need to be considered?'

'Oh, they are, I assure you, they are. Now – perhaps you would care to look round?'

Alida shrank back. 'Oh, no, thank you, but I am afraid I have to hurry home.'

'Are you sure? It is . . .'

'Yes, quite sure, thank you. I cannot look round today.'

'Just as you wish.'

They shook hands in the light-filled hall, and Miss Cress stood to watch Alida Thorne walk smartly away down the drive. Alida was breathless. But, she thought, I might be called back and I would not know what to say, I do not want to go amongst mad people, to have them stare at me, to see the unpleasantness of a lot of geriatric cases. I have enough. The thoughts of madness and senility frightened her. As she turned away from the house, into the lane, she gave a shudder of relief.

Miss Cress rested in the sunshine at the top of the steps for a moment or two, saddened. And she did not even want to see, she thought, she had not enough interest to see round the place to which she was so anxious to consign her mother.

Dorothea Shottery sang. She sang because she was miserable and hoped that it might cheer her up. That was all, there didn't seem to be much to sing for. The arthritis, an inherited complaint, was painful in both knees, she had slept fitfully, disturbed by nightmares, and now she was to go and spend a distressing afternoon with Eleanor. For it would be distressing, if Dorothea was to sit there and know the future and be forced to act as though she did not.

Two or three times, during the past few days, she had caught herself blaming Alida Thorne bitterly, but had pulled herself up short, for she had no experience of life alone with an elderly and ailing dependent, she could not say, I would never do such a thing, because how did anyone know? It was hard to imagine Eleanor's contrariness, since she rarely saw it, but even, Dorothea told herself, were she the dearest, most unselfish soul in the world, she is old, nevertheless. Alida has to carry heavy trays up and down stairs and see the food being left uneaten, to get up in the middle of night after night, to listen to the rambling memories, to put up with incoherence and with having to repeat everything because her mother did not remember. I cannot imagine what it must be like, but of course facts have to be faced, one's own life has some kind of vestigial importance, the question of cruelty really does not arise.

All this Dorothea Shottery told herself. And told the cat Hastings, to whom she talked, because cats liked to be talked to, it comforted them, and because it comforted her, too, helped her marshal her thoughts. None of it removed the nagging misery from her mind, the horror at the thought of Eleanor Thorne, sweet-natured as she was, being consigned to a mental hospital for geriatrics, to a public ward in a public bed, her possessions named with white tapes, her false teeth removed, her talk and actions, perhaps even her death, made common property. Nobody deserved that, and Eleanor perhaps less than most people. But, she said to herself, if Alida were not here, or if anything happened to the daughter before the mother, then Eleanor would have to go away. But no, that was not true, she would not go, for she herself would gladly look after her.

'That is an easy thing to say,' she observed to Hastings, who lay sleek in the sun, 'when I know how unlikely I am to fulfil it.'

Hastings extended his back legs slowly. The clock struck two. The front door bell rang.

'I did so want Isabel to come, too. You must forgive her, but she is still not herself. She would not come, she would not.'

Now here is another unhappy woman, Dorothea thought, and they all come to me, though goodness knows why, for I am surely no inspiration?

'Shock treats people so badly, Kathleen,' she said now. 'Do not worry at all on my account.'

'Oh, I do hope you are right, Dorothea! But perhaps I shouldn't have come, now, you were just going out.'

'Only to see Eleanor Thorne. I can be a little late.'

Kathleen Lavender held out a cardboard box between her hands, speechlessly, so that it looked like some kind of dumb offering and Dorothea at once remembered the solicitor's stiff letter, her own shamed surprise and then her agitation. Almost at once, she knew what she must do.

'I have always wanted Isabel to like me,' she said sadly, looking down at the box, 'but she never has.'

Kathleen sat still, the box outheld.

'Perhaps because I was so friendly with Faith and never with her. Though I have always been willing. Faith did not tell me about this, you know, she would have realized how angry I should be. When I got the letter, I knew how angry Isabel would be, too, and perhaps *you* are angry – you have every right.'

Kathleen Lavender shook her head mutely.

'In any case, whatever you both felt, I decided that I could not possibly accept these things. I was going to come and see you, or write a note about it.'

Kathleen gave a little cry and put the cardboard box down on the table in front of her, as if afraid of it.

'Do say something,' Dorothea said, standing over and smiling a little. How cowed Kathleen Lavender has become!

'There was nothing I wanted,' she said, 'I was quite happy for you to have them, Dorothea. They are of no great value, you know.'

'I know.'

'You might have had them . . .'

'But I am sure Isabel did not like the idea?'

Kathleen looked up. 'There is so much Isabel does not like,' she said, a note of real scorn in her voice that threw Dorothea into confusion, and she fidgeted, avoiding Kathleen's eye. Anyone acting out of character worried her in this way, until she had had a silent time alone, to work it out and grow used to the change. Though when she did so, she knew she would be pleased at the small show of spirit.

'So take the box back with you,' she said gently, 'and say I would not dream of accepting anything, because of course they are family things. But I will always appreciate Faith's kindness.'

It was a stiff, formal speech, not at all what she had wanted to say. Kathleen rose. 'You will be late,' she said, 'I mustn't keep you longer.'

'But Eleanor has lost all sense of the present. She will expect me when she sees me. Indeed, why not you, too? Perhaps you would care to come with me?'

'Oh, no. I . . . there is so much to do. Another day.'

But there would not be another day. Faith had been the only sister to visit regularly, for Isabel and Kathleen were afraid, afraid of sickness and infirmity, of germs and ill-health and old age and death. Kathleen was kind but she would not bring herself to visit and Dorothea knew she ought not to have asked.

She had expected to get satisfaction from refusing Faith's jewellery, because it seemed an action on principle, and because there was always a surreptitious pleasure to be gained from snubbing Isabel. Now, Dorothea felt justly punished, for she was merely sad, and Isabel would in any case consider it as inevitable good manners to have refused. She would have expected it.

Dorothea put on her coat and went out into the garden to cut some flowers for Eleanor. The cat followed her. 'Now I shall be late,' she told him, 'and Eleanor will have been alone, I must hurry.'

The cat began to stalk her through the blade-broad iris leaves with such solemnity that she laughed and paused even longer, to play with him, and was cheered.

Chapter Six

'THEN we will bury them,' her sister said. 'We will bury them in the garden.'

Kathleen Lavender stared. She is referring to something else, she told herself, I have been dreaming and have not followed the conversation.

'What?'

Isabel's eyes were suddenly opaque, you could no longer see into them and Kathleen shook her head. Across the card-table, they faced one another and, between them, the careful pattern of red and black. Spades 2, 3, 4, 5 and Jack of Hearts, Queen, King, Ace. Isabel had the pack in her hand but she kept her fingers still.

'What?' she mimicked, like a schoolmistress, 'What? What? What?'

Kathleen flushed and was angry with herself for it and for allowing her sister to get the better of her again.

'I mistook what you said, Isabel.'

'You did?'

Isabel removed the seven of diamonds from the third row, placed it over the six, on the seventh row, and turned up a new card, the four of hearts. She shook her head, while Kathleen stood, uncertainly, watching, still in her coat and hat.

'She was just on her way to see Eleanor Thorne,' she ventured.

'Oh.'

'She wanted me to go with her.'

Isabel shot her a sharp glance over the cards and there was still that curious opaqueness, that veil over her eyes.

'But you did not.'

'No.'

'No.'

'Well – well, then, I will get us some tea.'

'Already?'

'I thought I would bake some scones.'

'Before you bake anything, you can help me.'

'With the game?'

'No, not with the game.' Isabel laid down her cards. 'As a child, you never listened to anything properly. Always half an ear, half a mind. I can remember our mother complaining about it.'

'What is it that you want me to do, Isabel?'

'We will bury it in the garden. Have I not said so?'

'Bury *what*?'

'The box, girl, the box.'

Kathleen looked over at the square cardboard box she had just brought back from Dorothea. 'But it is such a useful box,' she said, 'I have been looking about for one like it. I could make a hole in the lid and feed balls of string through. It's too handy to be thrown away.'

'I was not talking about the box alone. Very well, keep that if you are so parsimonious, and we will find something else for them.'

'Something else? For what?'

'Kathleen?'

'Yes?'

'Do you not know what we are going to do? Have you no idea? Are you now unable to fit two sentences together, form an idea? Have you not listened at *all*?'

'I wish you would not speak to me like that. I am not a child, Isabel.'

'We will bury the jewellery in the garden in whatever container you prefer. You shall choose.'

'*Bury* . . . but we . . .'

'Yes?'

'Oh, what nonsense! What a silly, petty, childish idea, Isabel! How can you? "She did not leave them to me, so nobody shall have them." Oh, how ridiculous! I fear you may be ill. Are you ill? And if Dorothea is too good to accept a few semi-precious brooches and earrings, if you are too sensitive to wear them, very well, I will have them and *I* will wear them. They will be of use to somebody.'

Kathleen took off her hat carefully in the big fireplace mirror, noting the two pin-points of scarlet anger on her own cheek-bones. Isabel sat at the card-table, her hands folded calmly. 'You will not help me? Is that what you are saying?'

'Help? I won't hear of such idiocy. I wonder what has got into you.'

'I see. Are we then, at our age, to have a fight, to come to scratches and blows? Two sisters, two elderly women, clawing at one another? Is that it?'

'Isabel, do you feel unwell? I am really worried . . .'

'I am perfectly fit. You have not answered me.'

'No.'

'Well?'

'It is hardly a question a sane person can answer. You always were spoiled, and petty, if you did not get your own way. I am going to make the scones now. Perhaps you should have a rest.'

'Very well. If you prefer not to have anything to do with it, if you prefer not to sully your hands . . .' her voice was heavily sarcastic, 'I will do the job myself. I will bury the wretched box.'

Kathleen Lavender stared at her sister. And realized, her heart churning a little as she did so, that this was no joke, that it was not an angry expression of Isabel's pride. She was quite calm and serious and, for reasons of her own, she intended to bury the jewel box. She is mad, Kathleen thought, she is surely mad. We say these things, we accuse others of madness so lightly. But my sister is unbalanced. At three-thirty on a Monday afternoon in March, she has become unbalanced in her mind. Kathleen went into the safety of the big kitchen, and shut the door. She had no idea what to do, less than if her sister had become violent and raved and attacked her, or claimed to

63

be Lady Hamilton. That was how insanity had always presented itself to Kathleen Lavender's imagination. And now, here it was, calm and quiet and peculiar. She glanced out of the kitchen window.

Isabel was walking towards the bottom of the garden, where the apple and cherry trees grew, where the compost heap was kept. She wore her old green and brown tweed coat, and her gardening gloves and, in her left hand, she carried the cardboard box. In her right hand was a spade.

Kathleen turned away from the window, hastily, for fear her sister should see her watching and began to get out the mixing bowl and pastry board, the flour and the milk.

Above all, Alida Thorne said to herself, she must not receive the impression of neglect. The way to convince this Matron of my mother's extreme need of a hospital bed is not through any show of carelessness on my part. She would rightly suspect something. And, in any case, I have always cared. I have run upstairs and downstairs, ironed huge sheets and four pillowcases at a time, spent a good deal of money on nourishing and delicate foods and extra milk. There can be no question of her discomfort. That is not the way.

Alida Thorne took a china bowl and rose-patterned jug into her mother's room. I have a logical mind, she decided.

'Now let me prop you up,' she told her briskly. 'Let me have you sitting up straight and firm against the pillows, please. I have come to wash your hands and face and do your hair. There is some new, scented soap.'

Never let me have this humiliation, she thought, looking at the drowsing face. Let me be able to wash and dress myself to the last.

'Come along. You are to have a visitor.'

'Oh no, dear. You are quite mistaken. Faith Lavender is dead, that you have told me. I do remember that. Faith Lavender is dead and there will be no visitors.'

Alida slid the blue crotcheted sleeves deftly up the stick-thin arms. At least that is something to be thankful for, something I shall not have to explain a tenth or fifteenth or hundredth time, one worry off my mind.

'Other people have been known to visit you, haven't they? You cannot say that you are a neglected invalid. Indeed not.'

'Dorothea?' The old hands slipped ruminatively over the oval soap. 'Do I have a wash especially for Dorothea,' she glanced up sharply, 'with the scented soap?'

'You have a wash every day, as well you know. Oh, now be careful, I cannot be changing sheets again, not at this time.'

And the water is splashing over my dress, Alida noted, to herself. She wore a soft, hyacinth-coloured jersey, for she had summed up Miss Cress as a rival and as a woman who took everything in, clothes, manners, appearances, weighed and judged them. Besides, the hyacinth jersey was an older woman's dress, adding just a little frailty. On the bathroom shelf, Alida's special salts for rheumatism were prominently displayed. She hoped Miss Cress would ask to use the bathroom. In any case, Alida intended to make a clear point of lifting. Her previous doctor, the understanding Tinsley, had been firm about it.

'Do not lift things, Miss Thorne – no heavy lifting. The consequences for someone in your condition can be quite serious.' He had confided to her that he himself suffered with back trouble. 'Surely you can organize your life so as to avoid lifting?'

He would unquestionably have recommended that her mother be given a hospital bed, and long before this. Indeed, the suggestion might well have come from him in the first place, which would have been so much better for everyone. But how can I change my life? Do I allow her to slide further and further down into that great, that unseemly bed, to smother and suffocate? For she cannot raise herself, her limbs are no longer able to do their work. She is old and she is helpless. A hospital would be a kindness to her.

'It doesn't lather,' Eleanor Thorne said, 'it is a cheap soap.'

'You know nothing of modern soaps.'

'Soap is soap, has always been soap. And cheap soap is hard and does not lather.'

'I have to economize where best I can, you must realize that, mother. We are not *rich* people, I cannot afford to buy the costliest brands of this or that. It is an extravagance. You are not denied the best of foods, chicken breasts, cream, fresh vegetables, asparagus.'

She lifted the bowl of scummed water. 'In any case,' Alida said, 'the argument is spurious, for it is not a cheap brand of soap.'

She left the room.

Eleanor Thorne moved her head about uneasily on the pillow for a moment or two, wishing she had not complained about the soap, for now Alida might change the brand, keep that tablet to herself. And if it did not lather well, it had such a distinctive scent, a scent Eleanor liked. She lifted her left hand to her face and sniffed. It would be pleasant to use that soap every day.

Aunt Harriet Craven had been married to a politician, a Cabinet Minister, so that always their Surrey house was full of week-end guests, men strolling in twos and threes about the lawn before luncheon, tall and important, and their lady wives, as Eleanor must learn to call them, in drooping hats. She had gone about in awe of these adults, to whom she must not chatter, before whom she must be silent and polite and smiling. Though sometimes, the gentlemen chucked her beneath the chin absently, or gave her a sixpence, and one, even, pushed her for a whole quarter-hour on the swing. Afterwards, she had learned that he was an important man, more important than any of the visitors, who seemed to smile and bob to him, and sidle up to take his attention. He took care of the nation's finances, Aunt Harriet had said, you might call him the Keeper of the Purse.

Eleanor remembered the swing, up and down, high into the cherry trees, and laughing with delight, and saying, Oh, thank you, thank you, as he pushed her higher and higher. She wore a white muslin dress because, with her long black hair, white was thought so striking on her. Aunt Harriet would have been cross, normally, for the seat of the swing made green press-marks on her skirt, but the visitors had spoken up for her, taken whatever blame there was and Aunt Harriet had led Eleanor away to wash her hands before tea, telling her how very, very lucky she was, and how she must always be grateful to the Minister and remember this occasion in future years. And in the bathroom, she had been allowed to use one of the tiny, individual soap shells especially provided for the guests, and to keep it afterwards. It had smelled like this soap today, a light, entirely distinctive smell, a little like – what flower? Any flower? Eleanor had known so many flowers as a child, each by its botanical and by its common name. Though she had not pressed them, as her friend Lois pressed them in between the pages of her Bible. That seemed in some way cruel, a form of burying.

Burying. Yes, Faith Lavender was dead, and so young. When Faith Lavender was born, Eleanor thought, I was already a married woman, far from Uncle Arthur and Aunt Harriet Craven, both dead, and from the Surrey house, sold; with its lake and cherry trees. The Gantry had become so much more important, a house of enchantment and adult delights, not one of childhood pleasures. For there she had met her husband. Eleanor Thorne lifted her hand to her face again, happily.

'She will be delighted,' Alida Thorne said, 'she's so looking forward to a visitor. I cannot spend all day with her, I have the house to run, things to do.'

'Your own life to lead,' said the Matron, Miss Cress, startlingly smart in navy blue, with a chiffon blouse.

'Oh, dear. I cannot be said to have a life outside these four walls. With my mother . . .'

'You should try. You will not always have her company.'

Miss Cress examined a photograph on the bureau. 'Your father?'

Alida nodded. She herself would not have peered so openly at personal photographs.

'Yes, I see there is a resemblance. A firm face.'

Alida turned away, to the tea trolley, impeccably laid out with the Worcester china, for she intended to give the impression of perfect comfort, and a good background, of genteel upbringing and attention to detail. Miss Cress should not think she had let things go.

'I have received Doctor Sparrow's report,' the Matron said, accepting a cup of tea but refusing anything to eat. Alida frowned. She had hoped to guide the early conversation along vaguer, more social channels, not to have this immediate plunge into medical details, definite decisions, not to face a situation already cut and dried by her opponent.

'Doctor Sparrow was concerned about the lifting,' she said.

'Lifting?'

'My mother is a small woman, I grant that, but it is none-theless a considerable strain. I have had a long history of mus-cular trouble, of a weak back. Doctor Tinsley, my old medical man, absolutely forbade me to lift any kind of weight, not so much as a shopping basket.'

'Yes, quite . . .' said the Matron, and to Alida's ears it was a firm interruption.

'What an attractive garden you have here! Are you a gar-dener, Miss Thorne?'

The woman is looking me straight in the eyes, Alida thought, she does not know even the basic elements of courtesy, she has paid no attention at all to the very relevant account of my con-dition.

'I can hardly be expected to have a great deal of time for gardening,' she said, 'I am forced to pay out money for gar-dening help.'

'Quite clearly money well spent,' Miss Cress smiled, a sharp-eyed smile, and set down her tea-cup. 'Perhaps I may now see Mrs Thorne?' she asked, and Alida was forced to rise.

'Ah, now that you will not remember,' Eleanor said, wagging her finger, 'for I was just twenty and you cannot have been born. But they would roll back the great doors that divided the hall from the morning room, and carpets would have been lifted and floors polished, earlier in the day. Such a simple idea, I always thought to have a wall of panelled doors that folded back. Perhaps it is no longer there?'

'No, the wall has been made a permanent fixture, I'm afraid.'

'Oh, but things change, I understand that. I am not too old to accept the difference in life, Miss Cress, and nowadays, people do not dance, they lead such serious, earnest lives. Well, at the morning room end, there would be a small orchestra, on a specially built, movable dais. And we were all around and below them. And how we would dance! Dance until we nearly dropped.'

The Matron smiled. 'But you did not drop,' she said.

'Oh, no!' Eleanor Thorne shook her head, laughing, for this visitor of hers understood so well. 'No, we walked out of the French windows – they are still there?'

Miss Cress nodded.

'Ah! Yes, down the lawn and through the orchard and then, if it were a really fine evening, out, up the hill. Looking back, we could see the orchestra and everyone swaying and whirling round, and the room lights glittering. Oh, it is a splendid house!'

'You knew it in its best days, Mrs Thorne.'

'Yes, but how lucky you are to *live* there!'

How can I begin to tell her for what reason, in what capacity I live there, the Matron thought. If ever I have to do so.

'Your husband was a visitor to the house, you tell me.'

Eleanor smiled. She could not have guessed how much she would enjoy herself with a stranger, how completely this woman was in sympathy with her, could not have hoped for a new friend to come out, at this stage in her life, and give her so much pleasure.

'My husband was a cousin of the young lady to whom the son of the house was engaged. He was in the Royal Navy – my husband, you see. So for eighteen months we only met three times, when he visited during his leaves. Oh, what a time there seemed between those visits!' Eleanor Thorne laughed at her young self.

'I have seen a photograph of your husband today.'

'A photograph?'

'Your daughter has one in the sitting-room, on the bureau.'

'Alida? Alida has a photograph?' Eleanor Thorne shook her

head. 'She was barely three when her father died, she will not remember anything of him. I wonder that she keeps a photograph.'

'There is a close resemblance between them.'

'You could tell that? I can see it, of course, even now. But for a stranger to see it . . .' She stopped and lay silent. Then she said, 'Alida is very good,' the tone of her voice a little vague, 'she is . . .'

Miss Cress watched her, not for any signs of betrayal but wondering if this might be the vague mind, the senility that her daughter had stressed, this symptomatic breaking-off of sentences. Eleanor Thorne was resting, her eyes looking beyond the window and into the distance.

'In August,' she said suddenly, without changing the direction of her gaze, 'next August, I shall be ninety years old.'

'For ninety,' the Matron said, 'you have a most agile mind.'

The old woman looked at her speculatively, 'I have a long memory. That can often be mistaken for agility of mind. I have almost ninety years of memories.'

No, Miss Cress told herself, and wanted to tell the daughter, angrily, no, this woman is not senile, she is not in need of a geriatric bed in a hospital, I could not take her, it would be morally wrong, a sin. She is happy. For her age, she is remarkable.

'My daughter does not have patience with memories. I wonder if it is because she has so few of her own. I am guilty in that respect. Perhaps I sheltered her from experience. But she did not seem to want to see it.'

'You cannot accept responsibility for the life of another.'

'That is a wise remark.'

'No, a common truth.'

Mrs Thorne turned her head. The eyes are a young woman's eyes, Miss Cress observed, bright, shrewd. 'Now,' she went on, 'now I would so like to hear about this Uncle you talk of, the Cabinet Minister. I have long taken an interest in nineteenth-century history.'

'My Uncle Arthur Craven, Member of Parliament.'

'Oh, that is a familiar name! One of Mr Gladstone's Liberal ministers.'

She watched the old face overspread with brightness, began to listen to the clearly-presented, carefully-recalled recital of the past.

In the sitting-room, Alida Thorne sat and fidgeted, like a parlourmaid banished below-stairs. She was anxious at the long absence of her visitor, and at the voices, her mother's voice in particular, sounding on and on through the afternoon. Yet she dared not interrupt, and show the woman rudely out, for fear of an influence upon her decision.

Above the photograph of her forgotten father, full-bearded and with the braid and sword of a naval officer, the clock struck five.

It is becoming a habit, Dorothea thought with a shock. I must not give way to it, because it is so unlike me and quite causeless. I must guard against the habit of depression.

For, when she had woken up, rather late that morning, her usual brightness had been replaced by a quiet, sinking unhappiness, and instead of getting straight out of bed and opening the curtains to see what kind of weather was there, she had huddled down between the sheets, reluctant to face anything.

Dorothea had always believed in the idea of a new day, a new start, and always looked forward to something pleasurable in it. Something pleasurable had, therefore, generally happened.

In the face of misfortunes and petty irritations, of death and daily pain, and the loss of love, she had held to her expectations and they had never let her down. Yet now, she thought, when nothing is wrong, there are no misfortunes to speak of, now I am lying here loath to admit the weariness of getting up. It was only because she was a Christian woman, with a clear view of the seven deadly sins, that she pushed the bedclothes back firmly. Sloth was much on her mind. And what an ugly word that was, sloth, fat and white and slow, like slug and slither, so expressive. She herself, this morning, felt fat and white and slow.

Down the stairs, followed by the cat, was a long way, and the mirror on the landing showed up in full light the pouches beneath her eyes. Dorothea allowed herself to make a pot of tea, in her dressing gown, and carry it back upstairs, to enjoy over the newspaper and any letters there might be, though she did not allow herself to return to bed. From girlhood she had always risen early. Now, she felt, I am suddenly old, and I would like to crawl back into my cocoon of bedclothes and sleep and sleep, for what else is there? Only, of course, there were the plans to make for her grocery stall, people to see, the same plans as last year, and year upon year before that, the same people, the same questions, the anticipated replies for help.

'Mrs Day, how very kind! How reliable you are.'

'Mrs Lucas, your chutney is so much in demand each year, could I prevail upon you . . .?'

'Miss Brotherton, the date now, is 10 August, Saturday, 10 August. If I asked you to give your usual willing hand, would . . .?'

'Kathleen, it would be so kind of you to bake the cake again, for the guessing competition – a different weight, of course – have you your record book? how *very* . . .'

Dorothea shook her head, angry with herself, for everyone expected her, rushed to help her, everyone, truly, was so kind and the Rector relied upon her industry. Besides, Madame Claudia had been a foolish idea.

The cat Hastings was at the kitchen door, alert, a shaft of sunlight dappling the stripes of his back. Dorothea saw herself, barefooted on the plastic mat, dressing gown wrapped round her and staring into space, towards nothing, half-thinking, unaware.

For company, and a reminder of where she was and how much she had to do, she switched on the radio, let the cat out, filled the kettle and began to plan her morning's round of visiting. After that, she decided, I will clean every window in this house. And then, she had a recollection of a letter on the mat.

'My dear Dorothea.'

Florence Ames had written after all this time, four or was it six months? Florence Ames, with her new address, a welcome friend. Dorothea stayed in the sunlit kitchen with her tea, happy at the letter, her loss of purpose, her anxiety dissipated like a past illness, already wondered at, the symptoms forgotten.

'My dear Dorothea.'

Florence Ames wanted them to meet, as they had always met so regularly, sharing a common isolation never expressed. Dorothea smiled. She was to travel the twenty miles by train, into the city, and they were to meet, in the restaurant of Marshall and Snelgrove, to have coffee and talk, to shop together for this and that, a new spring suit, some curtain material, a lampshade and the Ceylon tea nobody would stock in the village, and back for lunch, and then for tea, with aching feet and happy conversation, until their trains home. She may even be persuaded to come back with me, to stay a week or longer, Dorothea decided, for she had no reason to live in that ugly little town house alone now that her father was dead. She had always been too conscientious, never spared herself, been afraid to leave him for longer than a day, she deserved a rest, a holiday. I can look after her, Dorothea thought, and we will do the garden together, I shall take on a new lease of life.

She rebuked herself, feeling deeply ashamed, for having given way earlier to despair and self-pity. How good Florence Ames will be for me, she thought. The tea streamed, honey-gold, from a blue pot, and round the door came the cat Hastings, pert of face, in search of cream.

'Oh, you should have brought her to me long before, long before, Alida. Such a kind, charming woman. I cannot think when I have enjoyed a visitor so much.'

Alida hauled her up by the arms, plumped up the pillows, and shook them hard, until the dust soared. 'You have talked your head off,' she said, 'I heard you.'

'I talked and she talked. She was so interested, she wanted to hear.'

'She was being polite.'

'That is real politeness, then, to stay for two and a half hours, in an old woman's bedroom, listening and asking questions. That is courtesy of a rare kind.'

'Miss Cress is a busy woman, I am astonished she would waste a whole afternoon in such a way. I do not have afternoons to waste.'

'I felt I wanted to keep her, to have her back day after day.'

Alida did not speak. Miss Cress had left, smiling, had not committed herself, nor had she asked to use the bathroom. She must have some complaint, Alida decided, to stay in this house two and a half, three hours, and not ask for the bathroom, it is unnatural.

'She will come again.'

'No, she has too many other people to visit.'

'Oh, but it was a firm promise! And so very clearly to be trusted. A firm promise to spend an afternoon with me again.'

'We shall see.'

'What have you for my supper? I would like some soup – cream of mushroom soup.'

'You have clean sheets. Soup is out of the question.'

'I am very fond of soup.'

'I have made a shepherd's pie and there are fresh runner beans. It is not everyone who can enjoy such home cooking.'

The door clicked shut. Eleanor Thorne would have enjoyed a bowl of soup. But she was too bright and restless with happiness, the newly-stirred memories, to be gone over, noted and enjoyed, for any unhappiness merely because soup was denied her. Miss Cress had a well-bred, kindly face, tasteful calf handbag and gloves. She had made a firm promise. She would come again.

'I will come again,' Miss Cress had told – *told*, not asked – Alida, on the doorstep. 'I have so enjoyed this afternoon. Your mother is a remarkable woman and I have promised to come again.'

Alida dared not ask, could say nothing, though she had shut the front door quickly on the Matron's moygashel back. In her

74

heart, Alida Thorne knew both the future and the truth, and she was both oppressed and afraid.

'Such a good woman,' her mother began, as she took up her supper tray, 'such an understanding woman.'

'She did not seem to me to have very much insight,' Alida said bitterly, 'I doubt if she could assess a human situation very accurately, I doubt if she would know where the truth of a matter lay.'

Eleanor Thorne dropped a forkful of meat and gravy on to the clean sheet.

Chapter Seven

'WHAT is it? I am busy. I am changing.'

The knocking stopped and Isabel Lavender, who had turned the key in her door, went back to trying on the old, brown skirt. She had discarded it several years ago, as being much fuller than she really liked, but everything came into its own, she reflected, for every article purchased she took pride in finding an eventual use.

On the landing outside, Kathleen Lavender turned the corner of her apron anxiously between her hands. 'It is the butcher,' she said, 'I have to know what you will want. You asked me to consult you, not to buy at my own discretion, as before. You have complained about the toughness and the cut of meat, you will no longer eat liver and pork. The butcher is on the back doorstep for the order.'

She hesitated, and then said lamely, 'That is all.'

There was a silence. Downstairs, the butcher stood, waiting, curious, impatient, and through the open door, he saw fresh pies, a wire rack full of small cakes, a chocolate sponge.

'Isabel . . .'

'He must call back. I am busy, can you not understand?'

'The butcher has better things to do than make journey upon journey, until we are ready for him.'

'Nobody has mentioned journey upon journey. Have they?'

'You can at least decide and call to me through the door, whatever you are busy with.'

'That is my affair.'

'Isabel, I do not wish to know, I am not interested and there is pastry burning in the oven. I simply wish . . .'

'Lamb chops.'

'And what else? A joint of beef for the week-end?'

'Beef? I hardly think we can afford beef, particularly uneatable beef, such as the piece you cooked for us yesterday.'

'I cannot simply order lamb chops.'

'Why?'

'That is a single meal. I am ordering for the week.'

'Are you quite at the end of your resources, that you cannot provide a meal of fish, or eggs or cheese? Is it vital for us to eat meat daily, meat which is both costly and tasteless.'

Kathleen Lavender sighed in her confusion. She no longer looked forward to each day, so much had she come to dread her sister's peremptory orders, the changes of routine, the explanatory telephone calls. To nobody else did she appear ill and unbalanced, because before nobody else would she now appear. Isabel remained indoors, taking fresh air at night, in a solitary walk to the bottom of the garden and back, in her old tweed coat. Kathleen Lavender lay awake and feared for her own sanity.

'I am tired of lamb chops,' she said at last.

Isabel was pleased with the fit of her skirt. It would do nicely, the fullness would give her ease of movement. There were so many trunks and piled boxes in the attic, and she would have to make dozens of journeys up those narrow stairs. She heard her sister's complaint and paid no attention. Lamb chops were both nourishing and cheap. The butcher had lined his pockets too thickly in the past at their expense, and Faith's will had been a warning, a pointer to their future.

Kathleen went heavily down the stairs. The smell of sweet, warm pastry, of fruit and yeast, comforted her, gave her a sense of direction and purpose. She would make herself a pot of tea, put the confusion to the back of her mind.

'Lamb chops,' she said. 'Yes, I think four lamb chops.'

The butcher had gone.

Dorothea drank Russian tea in a tall glass, with one of the silver holders. Florence Ames ate two chocolate éclairs. But the waitresses in Marshall and Snelgrove had new uniforms, dark purple instead of the old coffee-cream shade, and a different style of cap, more up to date and less obtrusive. Dorothea supposed that change must affect even such trivialities as the uniform of waitresses, although she did not quite see why, and it was a note of uncertainty in an otherwise happy day.

There was nothing uncertain about Florence Ames. Her friend had not changed in looks or in firmness of purpose.

'Now what is there,' Dorothea asked, stirring her lemon tea with the elegant long spoon, 'what is there to prevent your coming? You have no longer any excuse.'

'But I have not said I will not come! I should enjoy staying with you, Dorothea.'

'Oh, a week-end, but what is a week-end? It is hardly worth your while bringing a suitcase all that way, just for a week-end.'

'Twenty-three miles.'

'A week-end is nothing.'

'I think you are lonely, Dorothea.'

'And are you never lonely? Your father was company.'

'Yes.'

'We could cheer one another up. You would cheer me up, for you are ten years younger and at my age the years once again begin to tell.'

'Nonsense!'

'No.'

'You have always been the soul of industry and cheerfulness.'

'Oh, how like a fussy old woman you make me sound, an embroiderer, a jam-maker, a do-gooder.'

Florence Ames smiled. Yes, Dorothea thought, I would enjoy her company, she would take me out of myself, for she has never for one moment lost her grip upon life, her grasp of a situation, her confidence. Not that, until very recently, I have begun to do so. How sudden it all is, leaving us no time to make adjustments and to learn acceptance.

'A week,' Dorothea said. 'What is there to stop your visiting me for a week? Nothing at all.'

Florence Ames ate the last half of her second chocolate éclair, laid down her fork, wiped her mouth, finished her coffee, wiped her mouth again. At the adjacent table, a loud, powdered woman in a cyclamen hat slipped her shoes off under the table.

'Very well,' Florence Ames said. 'A week. I should enjoy that.'

'Do not let me persuade you against your will, now. Nothing is worse. Haverstock is very quiet.'

For Dorothea suddenly saw herself as an old woman badgering a friend into giving up her time and company, and, self-sufficient as she had always been, the picture repelled her.

'There is nothing I should enjoy more. I have always liked your house.'

'Yes, it is a comfortable house. I am a lucky woman.'

'And you miss Faith Lavender?'

Dorothea nodded.

'I have a new friend,' Mrs Ames said, 'I should not like to stay away from home too long, just because of that. It is a question of companionship.'

'Oh, but why can you not bring your friend to stay with me, too? That is an idea? We should be three very gay companions, we could make excursions, the sort one never ventures upon alone. We could visit a theatre, and there would be an extra pair of hands in the garden. What a selfish thought! Oh, but yes, of course, your friend would have to like cats. Hastings is very unobtrusive, you know, but he is a cat. Does your friend like cats?'

'My friend's name is Hubert – Hubert Gaily, and I think his mother has a cat. But that, as you see, is not altogether the point!'

Florence Ames smiled. After a moment, Dorothea smiled too. 'No,' she said.

'No.'

And they suddenly began to laugh, the joke toppling over them like a wave, until they wept tears of laughter, stared at by the loud, powdered woman, and by the waitresses newly attired.

'Oh,' said Dorothea Shottery, 'Oh, oh, I am so enjoying myself! Oh, I have not enjoyed myself so well for years. I must have another glass of tea.'

Florence Ames was too overcome with laughter to trust herself to speak.

Dear Miss Thorne,

I so much enjoyed coming to see your mother. I do understand that the burden of an elderly, dependent relative, even of one so sprightly as your mother, can be great. However, there is no doubt in my mind that it would be quite wrong to confine her in a geriatric home among seriously deranged patients. Her physical and mental condition would deteriorate. Moreover, as I explained to you, I have a waiting list of really deserving cases.

I will visit Mrs Thorne again, as I promised. I found her company most entertaining. Meanwhile, Doctor Sparrow recommends that she be allowed to sit out of bed, in a chair, for an hour a day, during the summer months. And that, if a wheelchair can be obtained, a breath of fresh air would do her no harm.

Alida Thorne read the letter again, and then tore it into forty or fifty tiny squares, her hand shaking with anger. But I am not so much angry, she decided, as upset at being misunderstood, at this complete and utter disregard of my situation. I am sixty-two and what life have I had, what opportunities? Even Dorothea Shottery had the comfort of a home and money left by her husband, even Dorothea who has contributed nothing to life, has a married name and her freedom. Who has the right to ordain that I should be the one to go mad in this house, with a senile old woman of almost ninety years?

'Even one so sprightly . . .'

'. . . her company most entertaining . . .'

And all this nonsense about getting up and going out. I am now expected to lift her, helpless as a fool that she is, out of that great bed, daily, across the room, into a chair, and back again, and to run up and down when she catches a chill, when her back aches from being pressed against the chair. The village is to enjoy the spectacle of me, pushing an old woman in a bath-chair. For I cannot expect to be offered help, nobody else will care to take a turn at the heavy work of pushing. Besides, she is to be got downstairs, and how is that to be managed? Am I to sling her across my shoulders in a fireman's lift? Alida almost laughed aloud at the picture this presented to her mind, except that it was scarcely an occasion for laughter.

'Oh, it is unfair, the hard-heartedness, the blindness! How can they *know?*'

Alida Thorne allowed herself to weep.

In her yellow-curtained office, the Matron, Miss Cress, picked up her pen to record a death and, as she did so, thought momentarily of Alida Thorne. She'll be back, she nodded, she will undoubtedly be back. But, poor woman, tied to a mother she can no longer love, with whom she has no patience, because of her resentment, her lonely guilt. In truth, Mrs Thorne has the best of it. She is not an unhappy woman, by comparison.

Kathleen Lavender stared down once again at the shopping list in her hand. It was divided into two parts, her own list of household requirements, and the list that Isabel had given to her, which read:

One ball stout string
One packet economy labels
One small reel adhesive tape
One indelible marking pen – permanent black
A large quantity of brown wrapping paper, obtainable free from shopkeepers.

So Isabel intended to pack a parcel – several parcels. Of what or to whom, Kathleen did not know and dared not ask.

She hoped very much to meet someone this morning, Dorothea perhaps, or Alida Thorne, or Mrs Bottingley, wife of the Rector, for they might invite her home to coffee and she could confide in them. She needed to confide in someone, to present the situation as clearly as she could, to ask for advice about her sister's condition. She is surely not herself, this cannot be normal behaviour, Kathleen Lavender said to herself, day after day, night after night. Chopping onion for a casserole, mopping the kitchen floor, her hands would pause and she would be overwhelmed with fear and confusion, not knowing what to do. A doctor was out of the question, Isabel would never see doctors, had always been in rude health, had not, indeed, wanted to call the doctor to Faith, until her colour had changed and, by her breathing, they had known that the illness was grave. Kathleen had several times suppressed the thought that if they had telephoned to the doctor half a day earlier, Faith might ... But no, for he had said her heart was badly damaged, death might have come at any time. Kathleen Lavender had a respect for death, for the propriety of letting it take its due, as and when it required. I would not like to be kept alive by a machine, like a vegetable, day in day out, she had once decided, I would prefer to accept my appointed day.

The house was silent. Isabel sat in her room, behind a locked door, and her sister knew neither what she did there or what she was planning to do and least of all did she know why. Kathleen buttoned her coat. If she could only persuade Isabel to come downstairs, other than for meals, to talk to her, to listen to the radio, not to be afraid of meeting the butcher or the postman or whatever visitor might call. No, Kathleen thought, looking at herself in the mirror at her own, pale face, no, she is not afraid, that is not it, Isabel has never known fear. It is something else, I cannot understand. She shook her head.

Isabel Lavender heard the click of the door, her sister's sharp footsteps, the latch of the gate. She breathed out in relief, at the silent house. There was so much to be done. And she will forget the shopping list, she said, she will return with a basketful of trivialities, domestic purchases, and everything I require will have been forgotten. I have had to bear with a stupid younger sister for too many years.

Wearing her full brown skirt and white gloves, Isabel Lavender went upstairs to the attic, oiling the lock and shifting cases to make a passage for herself. Whether Kathleen remembered the list of requirements or not, things might as well be got ready, the sorting out begun. The attic stairs were rather narrow. If I fall, Isabel thought suddenly, I am alone in the house, there will be nobody to hear me cry out, Kathleen will be delayed, she wanders around the shops, gossiping everywhere. Not that I am old or likely to fall, not that I have ever for one moment been unsteady on my feet. But if I should fall ... No, I have thought of that, I shall have to waste time, to sit about until she returns, and what help can she ever be?

Isabel Lavender went back to her own room. Outside, a thin rain fell, staining the newly-turned soil. It was Faith's fault, after all, and speaking ill of the dead was one thing, making correct, clear-minded private judgements about them quite another. Faith had behaved without thought, without foresight, and now, all this work must be done, risks must be undergone, trouble taken, because of one secret and foolish action. At the bottom of the garden, under the cherry trees, Isabel saw the low mound of earth, below which, two or three feet below, was the cardboard box, containing Faith's pieces of jewellery. The mound satisfied her, it was the visible result of a correct decision.

And why should we not think ill of the dead, she wondered suddenly, for they cannot hear, word cannot be passed to them, they cannot be hurt. Surely it is better to speak ill of the dead than of the living. The idea was a novelty, it illumined a new area of thought in Isabel Lavender's mind, and she felt a little daring, a little afraid, at bringing up for scrutiny something she had so long taken for granted. It had been part of the creed of childhood, indeed, the whole of life, unquestioned as so many other maxims were unquestioned, respect for parents and elders, the courtesy of men towards women and the inferiority of women to men, and original sin.

Isabel was proud of herself, proud of her incisive mind. I am able to examine concepts, she thought, to test values, for I have thought things out, I am not like my sister who bakes and cleans and shops and irons, and goes from day to day, never realizing what her mind might discover, content to accept what has always been told her, without a doubt. In the end, I am a better woman, for my values are secure, they have been tried and not found wanting. There is good reason why we should not speak ill of the dead but no good reason why we should not think it, if it seems to be necessary.

She was comforted, being able to lay the full quota of blame at her dead sister's door. Beyond the window, the rain ceased, giving way to sunshine.

Chapter Eight

'I DON'T understand you. I do not.'

'So you say.'

'Change like the moon.'

'Very likely.'

'It used to be Saturday nights, and that was all, bar taking the laundry, an hour Wednesdays. And then those jaunts, on and off. That was how I'd got used to it, at any rate.'

'I know.'

'I'm seventy-four. I'm too old for all this shifting and altering.'

Gaily put a brief arm around Ma and grinned into her face. 'Get on,' he said, 'you're young yet.'

Ma's face remained blank.

'Look,' he said, 'why don't you sit out, while it's like this. You don't know when we'll get a day like this again. Why do you stay cooped up in here? I don't know.'

Beyond the back sitting-room was the conservatory, full of geranium pots, and piles of old magazines, and thick with dusty heat, and beyond its glass windows, the garden lay.

'I'll get you out a deckchair,' Gaily said, lacing his shoe.

'I've more to do than sit about.'

'What?'

'How do you mean, what?'

'What more have you to do? Tell me. You invent jobs, that's your trouble, you can't bear to think of being idle.'

'A house runs itself, does it? A house with a great man in it and an old woman and a cat, that runs itself?'

'The sun's out.'

Ma heaved herself into the armchair. 'I get blisters in the sun. My arms come up in great red weals.'

'Sit in the shade.'

'Well where's the point of that? I can't see it myself sitting outside, in the shade when I can sit in here and be comfortable.'

'It's comfortable there.'

'There's midges.'

'Not till the evening.'

'I'm not having her next door peering at me all day.'

'She has better things to do, as well.'

'*And* I have.'

Gaily went to the door. 'Right then,' he said, 'don't go out. Stop in.'

'Not like some. Always off, these days, every free minute.'

'No.'

'Just off out, the moment you've eaten.'

'I stay in Monday and Tuesday, Wednesday I take the washing, Thursday I stay in.'

'That's another thing,' Ma said, to the centre tile of the fireplace. 'Washing never used to take you the whole night, two hours or more.'

'There's a queue.'

'There is?'

'Yes. Are you all right, then? I'll be off.'

'I'll have those conservatory doors shut and locked before you go.'

'You'll grill in here, you will.'

'That's my lookout.'

Gaily shut and locked the conservatory doors. The cat shot up behind the panes, waving its tail and glared at him. Gaily opened the doors, let it in, closed the doors, and locked them.

'I don't want that cat in here,' Ma said, 'I might want to do all sorts of jobs and a cat gets under my feet. Outside's the place for a cat in the afternoons.'

Gaily picked the cat up, pushed it out, shut and locked the conservatory doors again. On the lawn, the cat arched its back and spat at Gaily through the glass.

'Right,' he said.

Ma did not glance from behind the paper.

'I'm off.'

She turned a page noisily. Gaily went out, grinning to himself.

'And you can leave that door open. It gets like an oven in here.'

'Right,' said Hubert Gaily, pushing open the door.

'It won't last,' he said. 'Not for April. It's too soon.'

'Then we shall have to enjoy it while we can,' Florence Ames said. And that was an end of it. Gaily always felt that she decided things, signed them and sealed them and delivered a verdict. 'We shall have to enjoy it while we can.' Of course, it was as easy as that.

'You've a very reassuring nature,' he told her. That was how he felt. There was no blurring of the edges with her, no worrying round in circles, no temporizing. With Ma, there was decisiveness, but somehow, the two things were not related. Florence Ames was quieter about it, as though she had the measure of things because she had spent a long time in looking at them.

The sides of the pond were flat, slabbed with grey stone, and in and out of the water lilies, also flat, great goldfish, thick as your fist, slid underwater. Gaily watched.

'Placid,' he said.

'The fish?'

'Yes.'

'Do you suppose they find it monotonous?'

'Well – they don't know any different, I suppose.'

'No.'

Gaily relaxed in the sun. Behind the hedges and plane-trees, the town traffic. He could see the clock tower.

'I'm going away,' said Florence Ames.

Gaily opened his eyes. You could never expect things to last, after all, could not plan more than a few days ahead. A goldfish lay low in the water, coloured like a slice of tinned peach.

'I see,' Gaily said. He would have liked to say I'd rather you stayed, except that he had no real reason, or no reason he could give her easily. He was still wary of her taking things amiss. He scarcely knew her.

'Only for a week,' she said, folding her hands on her bag. 'A week in the country.'

'A week?' Oh, a week was different, a *week* was all right, he had not understood. Gaily was surprised at himself, at his own reactions.

'Well, that's all right,' he said expansively, 'that'll do you good, a week in the country. You'll enjoy that.'

'I'm to stay with my friend, you remember, I told you I'd met her last week? Perhaps you don't remember?'

'Yes,' Gaily said. 'Oh, yes, I do.' For, ever since, he had been turning the name over and over in his mind, puzzling over its light familiarity. Dorothea Shottery.

'Dorothea Shottery,' she said.

'That was it.'

'We were friends a long time ago, during the war.'

The Town Hall clock struck three, and still it was warm, April sunlight lying across the pool, lacing over the backs of fish.

'Haverstock,' Gaily said suddenly, 'Haverstock.'

'Yes,' she said, and looked at him. Gaily began to tell Florence Ames about the funeral, about the snowdrops and Faith Lavender's coffin, about Dorothea Shottery's name on the wreath and his own confusion among the female mourners.

'Then you must meet her,' Mrs Ames said, 'I must bring you together. Two friends.'

'I'm not very good with people – new people,' Gaily said.

'Oh . . .'

'Unless it's what you'd like, for me to meet her.'

The fish darted, gold in the dark water. Gaily looked at her. 'Any friend of yours . . .' he said.

Today, she wore no hat and her face looked younger and a different shape. He wanted very much to do something to please her, and it was hard, for he had never had any kind of a way with women, did not know their minds or their tastes, except for Ma. Only what he'd read. Now, here seemed to be something.

'Perhaps I'd surprise myself,' he said at last, 'if I met your friend.'

Florence Ames turned her head and smiled. 'Are you trying to talk yourself into it? I wouldn't want you to do that.'

'I'd like to meet anyone – if you say so.'

'Then you shall. She is a good person.'

'Good?'

Nobody ever said a person was good, like that. They were nice, or all right, kind or likeable or easy to get on with. Not good, right out like that.

'I can't say I know any of what you'd call *good* people.'

She turned to him in surprise.

'Not,' Gaily said, worried, 'not that I meet bad people. No, it's just – well, it's not a word you tend to apply, is it? You know . . .' He began to confuse himself. 'I'm not sure what it means,' he finished up, 'a good person.'

'Why,' she said, '*you* are a good person! It is quite easy. That is what it means.'

Gaily did not disclaim it. He opened his eyes wider, struck with the forceful novelty of this application of such a difficult word, to himself. He could not ask her to define it further, that would be asking for flattery. Yet Gaily knew flattery and this had not been it. She had said it, just in the way she said all things, as she might say, it is cold, your hair is brown, the sky is cloudy, and Gaily had come to accept her words implicitly. So he would accept that she thought him good, whatever she meant by it, and he at once felt a curious sense of relief and surprise within himself.

The goldfish shuttled to and fro, beneath the flat leaves, and there was an hour longer for them to sit there. Gaily smiled at Florence Ames.

Kathleen Lavender did not have her mind on what she said to her sister. It seemed that she should say something, for Isabel would let the meal run on in total silence, as every meal now ran, until Kathleen feared that she might scream. And so, she said, 'You seem to have been busy this morning, Isabel,' but absently remembering the bumping noises from above and the journeys her sister had made to the front sitting-room (locking the door after her) and back again to the attic (locking the door).

Isabel Lavender laid down her dessert spoon. 'So I am to have no privacy?' she said flatly. Kathleen looked up. 'Privacy?'

'I am to be questioned and interfered with and hounded, not to be left doing a job of work the way I choose, a necessary job, a job our sister has made tediously inevitable, a job the result of which may save us from potential disgrace, even if we cannot go so far as to expect it to improve our situation out of all recognition. I am to be given no privacy.'

Kathleen Lavender sighed, her mouth full of baked apple, cold and solid, her appetite gone. It was not even easy to remember exactly what she had said, so lightly had she said it, that had offended her sister. And now, Isabel had spoken the first words for a day or more, only to make them aggrieved, angry words, and incomprehensible too. Kathleen sighed again, not daring to look up. I am afraid of my sister, she thought, and why? What can her words do to me? But it was as much her actions, now, that Kathleen Lavender feared.

'The garden is in a state of wanton neglect,' she said. 'I shall go out this afternoon and make a start on the borders. The sun is shining, things need to be done.'

'Your mind is wandering.'

'There is nothing wrong with my mind! Why should there be?'

'Your mind is wandering in line with your conversation. One moment, you are prying into my affairs, the next you are burbling about the garden.'

'Will you have some custard?'

'And the next,' Isabel shot triumphantly, 'about food.'

'Isabel . . .'

'It is trying, to keep up with you.'

'Whatever the fact of the matter is, I intend to do the garden.'

'Oh, I believe you!'

'The sun is shining.'

'So I see.'

'Then if it is all right . . .'

'Why should it not be all right? I am not interested in the way my sister spends her afternoons. Am I my sister's keeper?' A small smile played about Isabel Lavender's mouth, a smile of delight.

'And will you help me?'

'No.'

'But it would not . . .'

'No.'

'Very well, Isabel.'

'I should like some more custard.'

'There is plenty.'

'I am glad to hear it.'

'I do wish you would not laugh at me, Isabel. Smirk is more the word.'

'Perhaps you would prefer my room to my company? You are welcome to serve my meals in my room, there is plenty for me to do alone upstairs.'

'I am quite happy with your company. And why do I talk in this way? Your way. It is your fault, Isabel. I enjoy your company, this is where we should eat our meals, together, of course it is. That is what I was trying to say.'

'Then you have succeeded.'

'Isabel . . .'

'Kathleen?'

'This job you have to do . . .'

Isabel Lavender laid down her spoon.

'Oh, nothing, dear . . . nothing at all.'

'Then your mind is wandering,' Isabel said, and attacked her second helping of the pudding. Kathleen Lavender lowered her head, in tears of distress. I believe that it is, she thought, I truly believe that it is my mind, for Isabel has always been so firm, so clearly in control. I have been the weaker vessel. Perhaps this is the way of it.

'Eat up,' Isabel said, 'we cannot afford to let things go to waste. Isn't that the very thing I am trying to prevent?'

Kathleen Lavender did not know.

That afternoon, Isabel finished packing her parcels, upstairs in the attic. She labelled them neatly, writing the addresses in ball point pen and capital letters. It had taken her three full days and now they were to be carried downstairs and arranged in the hall, after which her sister would take them to the post office. Isabel felt a great calm, a satisfaction, for all this would surely go some way towards cancelling out the effects of her sister Faith's thoughtlessness. In all, there were sixteen parcels. She went to her room, changed out of the full brown skirt and the old twin set, and lay, full in a patch of late afternoon sunshine, on her bed, smiling a little.

In the garden, her sister drove ferociously at the root of a weed clump with her fork, allowing her aching back and legs to take the place of thought. That was the best way. For, she said to herself, standing momentarily, I am going out of my mind. It is not my sister, it is I who am going out of my mind, and that is a terrible thing.

I am dying, Alida Thorne said, I am surely dying. Her heart-beats came in great, straining jerks, she could feel the blood squeezing through. I am dying. For a second, she lay back and the pillows and the nightmare took her, sweat ran from her pores, and she felt herself falling and the great straining of her heart. I am dying.

Alida flailed upwards, tearing off the bedclothes, and switched on the light. I am not dying, no, I have suffered a terrible nightmare, but I am here, in my room, and the night must be far gone, it must be almost morning, I shall go downstairs and make myself a first pot of tea.

But her legs shook and she clutched at the bed, which seemed to recede and there was a strange, fizzing sensation in her head. The house was silent. The clock gleamed a phosphorescent midnight.

What is happening to me, she asked, sitting on the bed and holding out a shaking hand, what is wrong? I do not wake in the night, I am a sound sleeper. My mother did not call. Then why is this happening, if I am not ill, what is wrong with me? For answer, she put her right hand on her heart and could feel nothing. My heart has stopped, Alida Thorne said. She put her finger to her pulse. Nothing. I am dying, oh, dear God! And then a great lurch and pit-pat pit-pat pat-pat-pat-pat-pat-pat-pat, racing until she wanted to hold it, rein it in, for this was surely worse, this would overtax the heart muscles, until it fell, exhausted, this was a race to death. Downstairs in the hall, midnight struck, so that her own clock had been slow and she had seven hours and three minutes before morning and the sound of the milk bottles on the step, of Eleanor's waking movements.

If I were to die, she thought, there is nobody to find me, perhaps for days and weeks, for we do not have visitors, and my mother would die too, of fright or starvation or a broken limb, after her voice gave out in screaming, and she tried to struggle from the bed. I might not reach the telephone, or I might be unable to dial a number, the doctor might be out ... Alida Thorne clutched at her wrist with its thudding pulse. As long as my hand is here, she thought, I cannot die. Well, then, she would sit here, conserve her strength, not move until morning, nor sleep either, for fear of slipping away without warning into unconsciousness and death. If I watch, if I am awake and aware, I cannot die, I shall not allow myself to die.

Far away in the darkness, a train sounded a horn, and it was a small proof of human existence, even at such a distance from her, even flashing past across the countryside powerless to assist to her. If I sit here, she thought, my hand guarding the pulse, if I sit here and do not move, I shall not die.

'Alida! Alida!'

I cannot go to her, she does not realize, she can never understand.

'Alida!'

I know what it is to be alone, to fear death, I know and she is unaware that I know, and yet I have to go to her, I have to leave the safety of my room. But I cannot do so.

Alida Thorne sat rigid until the calling ceased and the house folded back into silence, and her clock showed twenty minutes past twelve. I shall not sleep, she told herself, I must not sleep, and shivered in her nightdress on the edge of the single bed, afraid to reach up to the hook for her dressing-gown. I may not sleep. And slept, half crouched, falling at last across the pillow, her right hand over the left wrist with its quiet pulse.

It began early in the morning, with the milk boy.
'Seventeen and fourpence, Miss Thorne.'
'Nonsense.'
'Seventeen and ...'
'Sixteen shillings and one halfpenny. I keep a most accurate record. I am surprised at you. You must not expect to deceive *me*, no matter how many others you manage to deceive.'
'Now just a ...'
'There are sixteen shillings, and there is one halfpenny.'
'Seventeen and four.'
'I do not propose to argue with you, I propose to give you sixteen shillings and a halfpenny. It is up to you, either to take it and go away, or go away and return when you are in a less deceitful frame of mind. I cannot stand here chattering, it is a cold morning. I am ill.'
'Suit yourself, suit yourself. Seventeen and four it is, you owe me one and threepence halfpenny, and it'll go down in the book. Don't blame me.'
Eleanor Thorne would not eat, she felt sick, her breakfast, a carefully boiled egg, the brown toast thinly cut and allowed to cool before buttering, all was left for Alida to clear away and waste.
Blattern the postman walked slowly across the green, more slowly than ever, whilst Alida waited, twitching at the curtains, and then he paused at their gate before walking past. Alida went out and stared at the empty letter cage in the hall, called sharply after the man, that there had been some mistake.
'I expect an important letter. Kindly go through the mail that remains in your hand.'
But Blattern muttered and walked away and there were no letters that morning. Not, in truth, that she expected any, important or otherwise, but it would have made a difference to the

day. It was as though she had been swept aside, neglected, and Blattern took note of these things, and would rejoice because Alida Thorne had received no letter, was an unwanted woman.

She touched her fingers to her pulse and drew her breath hard. Within the cage of bone, her heart turned over, packed two beats into the space of one. I am dying, she thought, as her forehead broke out into a fine sweat, I do not even have to think of it, my mind is on other things, but there is a disturbance, quite plainly to be felt, in the mechanism of my heart. And I am alone, I can talk to no one. I shall die alone.

'Perhaps I shall not be alone. Perhaps my new friend will come. Miss Cress.'

'I doubt it very much. Do not lie here all afternoon in hopes of that. She is a busy woman, as I have said before.'

'She promised me that she would come.'

'I would not trust her promises.'

'So you are leaving me alone.'

Alida clenched her hands, until the nails bit into the soft palms.

'Will Dorothea come today?'

'Possibly. I do not know her plans.'

'Well, I shall lie here and think, as usual. There are always my thoughts.'

'What have you to complain of?' Alida asked her, very quietly. 'What have I ever done to give you grounds for fault-finding and self-pity? You are old, you are bed-ridden, the work falls to me, you do not think or care, lying here day after day, waited upon and given in to, without worries or anxiety. You know nothing of me, of what I suffer.'

Alida listened to her own voice, soft in the chilly room, watching her own hands, plump, well-creased and polished, banded with rings, twisting together.

Eleanor Thorne moved her head on the pillow. 'Do you suffer?' she asked. 'I would not have it so, Alida. I do not complain, I am content.'

'You are an old woman.'

94

'And you will be late for whatever appointment you have made.'

Alida stared at her. She is not hurt by what I have said, she thought, she is neither hurt nor angry, she does not understand what I have said, her mind is losing the powers of comprehension and she has no longer an emotional response.

'You must accept things, Alida,' her mother said. 'You have never learned to accept. Acceptance of things is so necessary, it leaves one free.'

'What do you know of that? What have you to accept? What do you understand of my situation or my mind? *Accept!*'

'Yes.'

'I am ill.'

'Then why do you not go to bed?'

'And who is to run up and down after you, in that event? Who is to answer your demands and cook for you and carry your meals?'

'Someone would come in.'

'No one would come. We have no friends.'

'*I* have friends, Alida, you have forgotten that. Do not confuse yourself. I have visitors, people come to see me. Miss Cress came to see me.'

'Miss Cress! What do you know of Miss Cress?'

'And Dorothea and Faith Lavender.'

'Faith Lavender is dead, can you not hear, can you not understand? Faith Lavender is DEAD.'

'Faith? Dead?'

Alida slammed the door and stood trembling on the landing, listening to her heart like the sound of the sea rushing through her ears. I am a wicked woman, she thought, to speak to my mother, who is eighty-nine years old and cannot help herself, in that way. I am a wicked woman and it is a punishment that I am also ill. There is no forgiveness for me, none.

She pushed open the bedroom door again. 'Have you everything you want before I go?' she asked.

But Eleanor Thorne slept.

*

The soft, tight band strapped around her arm was nevertheless a comfort, as the pointer pushing up the dial, achieving a number, was a comfort, too, for now something was being done, someone would give her treatment to ward off the attacks of death.

'Well,' said Doctor Sparrow, young and arrogant.

'I was quite unable to get my breath.'

'But you managed it eventually.'

He had a dark line of beard beneath his pale skin, and a mephistophelian smile. Alida hesitated.

'Well, if you hadn't, you would not be here to tell the tale, Miss Thorne?'

'I was afraid. I was alone and it was late at night. There was nothing amusing about it then.'

'Oh, these things always look better in the cold light of day. Smaller. Less significant. The shadows are always long at night.'

'It is all one, by day or by night.'

'What is all one?'

'Heart disease.'

'I daresay that it is.'

'What will be done? Clearly, I can no longer be expected to run up and down stairs, the very thing all heart patients must beware of, and clearly my mother must be moved. I can no longer be responsible for her.'

'Why is that?'

'Why? But I have just explained, surely you do not need me to tell you. I have just stated the relevant facts.'

'You have just told me what patients with heart disease may or may not do. I am grateful to you for the information. That is all.'

'Quite.'

'You have no heart disease.'

'Perhaps *disease* is not the correct medical term, I would not know. Perhaps you prefer failure, or weakness? Nevertheless . . .'

'Neither weakness nor failure. Your heart is as sound as any heart, as a healthy young man's heart, as a new-born heart, Miss

Thorne. Your heart will give you another thirty years of sound service. I would not have you worry about the stairs.'

'You do not know what you are saying, you have clearly misunderstood my symptoms! Well, you are a young man, Doctor Sparrow, without sufficient experience.'

'I am also a remarkably tolerant man, Miss Thorne, and is not *that* a very good thing?'

He swivelled round in his chair, lifting his feet from the floor. He is an irresponsible boy, Alida thought, making malicious fun of a woman's anxiety, not understanding symptoms, uncaring.

'I require a second opinion,' she said.

'Oh, my opinion is a very sound one, you may rely upon it.'

'I have said that I require a second opinion.'

Alida noticed that Doctor Sparrow had no lobes to his ears. Aunt Fosters had always seen, in the lack of ear lobes, a lack of character, a trait of unreliability and of deceitfulness.

'Miss Thorne,' he leaned forward, no longer good-humoured, but patient, quiet-spoken. 'If you are not satisfied with my treatment, you are at liberty to find another doctor. That is your privilege. While you are a patient of mine, however, you must accept my professional judgement. I have no reason for acceding to your request for a second opinion. Doctors are not idle men, Miss Thorne, and you are a fit woman. It would be a criminal waste of someone's time.'

'So, nothing is to be done. I am to remain ill and without treatment, I am to carry on with the exhausting task of caring for an old and senile woman.'

'Ah, that is the crux of the matter, is it not?'

'I do not understand you.'

'Think about it, Miss Thorne, think about it. Do not think about your heart, that can look after itself.'

'Can you offer me no explanation of such clear symptoms, or are you ignoring these, are you telling me that such suffering is a figment of my imagination?'

'Your symptoms are real enough, I have no doubt, Miss Thorne. And common enough. You are merely a little anxious – perhaps you have a problem on your mind, some emotional conflict? Ignore your symptoms and sort out that conflict. Relax. Get out in the fresh air.' Doctor Sparrow waved his arms.

'What chance have I to rest, to take walks?'

'I said relax, not rest. As for the walks – did not Miss Cress tell you – but I am sure she did – that you should take your mother out occasionally? Good for both of you. If you need help in acquiring a chair, that can be arranged.'

Alida rose. 'You need not trouble yourself, Doctor Sparrow, you need have no anxiety about the question of a wheelchair.'

After she had gone, Doctor Sparrow swung round slowly in the chair, hands behind his head, annoyed, angry, concerned. And wrote, then, a single sentence on a line of Miss Thorne's medical record card.

Alida stepped from the surgery door into sudden sunlight, and beneath the contempt and the anger was a seed of relief, of new hope, of freedom, for the instrument did not lie, the sounds must have been clear, she had no heart disease, no weakness, no need to accept the fact of death.

Chapter Nine

Is it only a fortnight ago, Dorothea asked herself in amazement? Is it only two weeks since that bleak morning when I had nothing for a future and everything seemed too late, when I dragged myself about the house, alone and miserable and weighed down by self-pity? Yes, on the calendar it is only two weeks.

But it might be months, or even years away, for it seemed to belong to another person, a different life. Above Dorothea's head, six new, blue mugs hung on six newly-erected hooks, for Florence Ames thought of all things and was constantly suggesting improvements – not that she insisted upon them or took anything in hand, only looked and suggested and then left the idea to be considered, accepted or rejected. And the pretty new mugs were a symbol, something Dorothea would never have found or thought of for herself, for they were hand-thrown pottery, and she had always been brought up to fine-spun china. Florence Ames opened new doors upon life, it was a quality Dorothea had always been grateful for.

I am happy, she said, smiling at herself a little. From the window, she could see her friend, Florence Ames, filling the freshly-turned beds with rows of small green plants from the boxes by her side. We will go and buy some bedding plants, she had said yesterday, only an hour after her arrival. There is just time and I will make a start. When they come up, *there* will be something to remember me by. But Dorothea needed nothing to remember her friend by.

She rinsed flour from her hands, dried them, crimped the edges of her two pies and remembered Kathleen Lavender, hurrying away from the nursery garden.

'Oh,' she had said as they came towards her, distraught, her face and neck colouring as though with guilt. 'I have to be home, I am so late, I dare not stop.' All before Dorothea had a chance to ask if she would come to tea to meet Florence Ames again.

'But,' she had said suddenly, 'I have only been ordering a dozen geranium plants.'

Dorothea had been puzzled, and then, recalling the silly, embarrassing episode over the box of Faith's jewellery, thought that she understood. Today, lighting the oven, she was sure that she did not understand. Why should Kathleen not visit the nursery garden, why had it been necessary to make the explanation about the geranium plants, why had she flushed with guilt, and fear and concealment? Surely not over the box of jewellery, surely not, Kathleen Lavender who bore nobody a grudge. No. Dorothea shook her head.

'Now, that is pansies, fuchsias, geraniums – but you must speak very severely to Hastings. He digs things up.'

Florence Ames took off her old shoes and left them on the step. 'We are coming on,' she said.

'I am making us coffee. How good of you to do all that work – and it is such hard work! And how long it would have taken me alone!'

Florence Ames smiled.

'I am so glad you are here,' Dorothea said, wanting to laugh or cry, 'I am so glad, you cannot imagine!'

'And I am glad to be here,' Florence Ames said, 'so we must enjoy ourselves.'

'Oh, I am, I am,' said Dorothea pouring the coffee, 'Indeed I am!'

'It is his mother,' Mrs Ames was saying later, dropping a blob of cream on to a warm scone, 'she is seventy-four. That is a lot for one man, alone, being responsible in that way.'

'And he has never married?'

'Never.'

Dorothea paused, cup in hand, thinking of Hallam, sun-tanned from his hours in the garden deckchair, reading, reading. 'How sad that is,' she said. 'Even sadder than for a woman. Men are not so resourceful, they do not know how to be friends and companions to themselves.'

'He is not a *clever* man,' her friend said and Dorothea recalled that she had said it before, anxiously, determined that Dorothea should understand but, nevertheless, accept. 'He is not – well, he is perhaps not the man you would expect. Not . . .'

'You forget,' Dorothea said gently, 'you forget that I have seen him.'

'Oh, *seen* him, yes, but . . .'

'And I remember him very well, I remember him still. I could not get over the kindness of it, his attention. Another man would have gone away, would have pretended we were not there, would have stood looking up at the wall-plaques and the windows until we had gone safely away. But he stood there in a pew, with the flowers. I do remember him so well.'

Dorothea had told Florence Ames the story of Gaily in the church twice before, and neither of them was yet tired of it, Dorothea because it pleased her friend so to hear it, and Florence because it pleased her that the man had been somehow vindicated, turned out to be as good as she had thought, and a friend. She remembered Isabel Lavender at the tea. 'He wore *boots*,' she had said.

'I was afraid you might not think him the right friend for me,' said Mrs Ames.

'And would you have been influenced by my opinion?'

'Oh, no!'

'Any friend is the right friend. I am happy for you. One needs friends, one needs to *be* a friend.'

'He is a good man,' Florence Ames said, 'and excellent company. He has made me look at the world again, made me see things I had never seen before, and see familiar things in a new light. Things you would perhaps be amused by.'

'No.'

'Can you understand?'

Dorothea nodded. How right for one another they must be,

how happy together, each with his gift for presenting the world anew. How glad I am for them! For as a girl, she herself had been taken through the world, as through a series of doors, by her young husband, each door opening on to fresh joys and colours and perspectives, and she had exclaimed in delight, followed him, learned, and even afterwards, when the final door had shut, she could retrace her steps, spend a longer and longer time in each place, as in a series of gardens, and gratefully. All this her friend Florence Ames was now to have.

On the lawn, the cat Hastings lay stretched out like a rabbit pelt, his fur ruffled by the breeze, and feigned sleep.

'If he digs up any more plants,' Mrs Ames said, smiling, 'I shall be very angry.'

But even Dorothea did not mind. She went to answer the ringing telephone.

'Dorothea,' the voice said, the words running together indistinctly. 'Dorothea, you will have to come, now, at once. You must come Dorothea. I am ill, I cannot go on.'

Dorothea Shottery held the receiver a little away from her ear, startled and trying to identify the voice.

'Please!'

And she recognized Alida Thorne.

'Whatever is the matter, my dear Alida, whatever is wrong at five o'clock in the afternoon?'

'I am ill, very ill. Nobody can do anything, Doctor Sparrow does not answer, he refuses to listen, he gave me no reassurance, but I know, I know that I am seriously ill and there is no one here except my mother, and who is to look after her, Dorothea? I cannot, I can no longer do it. I am so afraid.'

Dorothea gathered her wits, calm and reassuring even to herself in a crisis.

'Now do not upset yourself, Alida, do not worry at all. Of course I will come and of course something can be done. I will bring my friend Florence Ames, she has been a nurse – perhaps you remember her? We will come at once, do not worry at all.'

Alida Thorne wiped away the tears with the back of her soft hands, only wanting to be taken to bed, like a child, and soothed, to have someone decide and make arrangements, tell her that all would be well, she should have her way. She sat on the hard hall-stool beside the telephone, safe in the semi-darkness and waited for Dorothea and her friend Florence Ames who was a nurse, someone who would recognize her condition instantly, who would be on hand should emergency treatment be required, who was trained and capable. Upstairs, her mother slept or woke or dreamed. Alida did not know. 'It is not my fault,' she whimpered in the dark of the hall, 'indeed it is not my fault, and nobody can blame me, nobody can raise their voice to me, for it is not my fault.'

'I would like to go away from here. I would like that very much.'

Eleanor Thorne half-sat up in the great bed, astonished at the freshness, the absolute appeal of her idea.

'I would like to go away from here.'

It was in the nature of a revelation but like all revelations, she thought, it has been just below the surface of my mind, lingering unrecognized, waiting, and now I see it and it is a familiar friend. For what do I have, what can I miss, from here? She looked around the room and lifted her head to see, beyond the window, the tops of spruce-trees and the slope of Tantamount Hill. Well, yes, I have that, I would perhaps miss that, so largely and happily does it figure in my dreams.

Age and this way of life seemed to have crept upon her unaware, she had not questioned any of it, scarcely looked back. And now, she thought, how is it that my world has shrunk to this one room, which is, in truth, rather a nice room, exceptionally light and airy and quiet but nevertheless a room, one room, instead of acres and miles and countries, of a world. How is it? I would like to be away from here, I am not too old for new surroundings, not so old that I feel dread and insecurity in the prospect of a change. I am eager for new faces, for a life elsewhere. The answer seemed to her quite plain. Alida did not need her, Alida could surely manage, surely was not afraid to be left alone?

I should like to live in a community, Eleanor Thorne decided,

I should like to taste the fruits of life in a small home, a retirement home, an old people's house, whatever it might be called. She smiled to herself, at a vision of new friends and television programmes, of various people having tea on a lawn, sharing parcels and visitors and family photographs, being alone when they chose to be alone.

There is no need for me to live and die in this little world with my only view a view out of the same window, at the same spruce-trees, the view from my bed.

But perhaps she could say nothing, for Alida would not like it, there would be financial considerations. 'You don't think,' Alida always said, 'you do not know how much we spend, simply to keep alive, you have no idea how much things cost. You do not think.'

This time, Eleanor Thorne decided, I must think, I may not be selfish. For what would my daughter do alone, a single woman of sixty-two, without relatives of her own age, without children, without memories? She has been so strange, a sullen, lumpy girl, given to peering in the mirror and walking despondently in and out of empty rooms, scorning experiences and emotions. A strange daughter, and a woman I have never known. I am to blame. I can say nothing, not yet.

She turned restlessly on to her side, and back again. When had life become all bed, all pillows and sheets and lying down? She did not remember. 'I would like to go away. Oh, I would very much like to go away. I am a selfish old woman.'

Voices sounded on the stairs and came nearer.

'Do not let anyone in, I cannot see anyone,' Alida Thorne said, turning on Dorothea. For visitors would stare at her, ask her questions, would talk and expect a reply, and Alida knew that she could say nothing, could not cope with any demands.

'But it is Doctor Sparrow. You wanted to see him and here he is. Everything is going to be all right, you will be looked after, Alida.'

'Now then, Miss Thorne,' he said, brisk of voice, weighing

down the end of the narrow bed so that Alida, if she moved her left leg, could feel the pressure of his body.

'Mrs Shottery has explained,' she said, looking away across the room, 'I can tell you no more.'

'You were in pain?'

'I collapsed.'

'You were unconscious?'

'I was weak, I could not get my breath, I was dizzy and my limbs were shaking, I have explained it all to you before now. They found me sitting in the hall, I had to be helped upstairs to bed.'

But she could see the misunderstanding, the impatience, like a shadow across his face. He does not believe me, she thought, and I can tell no one, there are no words to convey the fear, the blank fear. Instruments can lie, after all, heart disease can remain undetected. For only that morning, she had read in the paper a case of a man, and not an old man, who had dropped dead in the street of some heart complaint. That had not been spotted and the coroner had pointed out how all the instruments in the world could not have detected it. The man had had a full medical check-up only a month before.

'I am going to give you a sedative, Miss Thorne, and some tablets.'

'Tablets for my heart?'

'Mild tranquillizers.'

'I do not need those drugs, I am not insane. Tranquillizers are for the control of manic patients.'

'Nonsense.'

The locks snapped shut on his case. He is going, Alida thought in despair, and no more is to be done, no examination is to be made, tranquillizers are the only treatment I am to have ... 'a full medical check-up only one month before.'

'Have a rest today, take things easy tomorrow, that's all. You'll be fit. Don't worry.'

'Doctor ...'

'Miss Thorne?'

'My mother ...'

'Yes, I'll have a look at her while I'm here, cheer her up a bit.'

'No, it . . .'

'Good afternoon, Miss Thorne . . .'

The door shut on the hopeless, silent room and Alida turned on to her side. '. . . only one month before . . .' People forget these things, she thought, they do not bear them in mind, doctors work to routine, finding only what they expect to find, they glimpse these cases in a newspaper and then pass on, they are hide-bound, they do not remember. Only I remember and nothing can be done.

'Now I have made you some tea,' Dorothea said, coming into the room. Alida did not move. 'And you are to swallow your tablet with it – what a gaily-coloured tablet, such a bright orange! Everything will be all right, I am going to cook something light for your meal – an omelette perhaps? Do you like omelettes? Eleanor has said she would like an omelette.'

Alida Thorne took her tea-cup and felt better now that someone was taking charge, running the immediate affairs of the house.

'I am tired,' she said.

'Yes, dear.'

'That is a symptom . . .'

'Oh, but when you have taken your tablet and had a good rest, you will be perfectly all right, has Doctor Sparrow not told you? But then, they are such busy men, they rush away. Yes, there is nothing wrong with you, nothing that a rest cannot cure. There, is that not good news? A weight off your mind.'

Alida turned her face away, her thoughts bitter.

'Then what are we to do for the best?' Dorothea asked her friend. They sat in the cold front room, not daring to light a fire in the strange house.

'She is quite adamant,' Florence Ames said, 'nothing will satisfy her, she says she will get no rest until it has been arranged.'

'Doctor Sparrow does not agree.'

'And yet, he does not experience the situation full-time, he has only one view of it. Because she has worked herself up into a pitiful state of fear and tension, this does not mean that her suffering is not real. Indeed it is some small proof that it *is* real. It is all very well for doctors.'

'I saw this coming,' Dorothea said. 'Several weeks ago the first hint was given. Her mind was made up long before today. It has made me very sad. Eleanor Thorne has long been my friend. Her only sin is age.' And what sin is that, she thought, for I am old and Alida is old, everyone grows old, so why must Eleanor Thorne be punished? But I must think of Alida, too, and of her suffering. It cannot have been easy, all these years, and who am I to criticize, to look askance, I who have been lucky, who have only myself to please, whose time is free.

'So that is what you think?' she said aloud.

'I do not see that anything else will do, not for the moment. The situation is too far gone. This is what she wants and so perhaps it is what she needs. We can only carry out her wishes, we can only try.'

'You are so sensible, you have always seen things in a clearer light.'

Florence Ames shook her head. 'It does not make me happy. I have seen too much of this.'

The two women thought, but did not speak, of Florence Ames' disabled father, lately dead.

'I have her name and telephone number here,' Dorothea said. 'Perhaps I should ring, as they are both asleep.'

'It may only be a temporary measure. That is perhaps all it can be.'

Dorothea sat for a moment longer, remembering Alida, her tears, her loss of all control. She will not like me to refer to this time when she is better, Dorothea thought, she will avoid my company and we will only wish one another the most formal good morning. That is how it has been in the past, we have never been friends, and perhaps it has been altogether my fault. Alida Thorne is a lonely woman, but it is easy enough to make an effort, to understand and accept and perhaps I have not tried. Well, I will try now. I will think of her welfare.

She rose from the stiff armchair. 'Her name is Miss Cress,' she told Florence Ames, 'I have it written here.'

Dorothea left the room.

Chapter Ten

'I WISH you would not do it,' said Isabel Lavender, descending the stairs. Her sister jumped back from the letter-cage.

'You are like a child on a birthday. Who do you expect will write letters to you?'

Kathleen Lavender stared at the three envelopes, two white, one brown, one long, two small.

'Well?'

'I am sorry, Isabel.'

'The letters will be for me, they are always for me. I would prefer you to let me take them in.'

'Very well, Isabel.'

'How acquiescent you have become!'

Isabel Lavender paused, her left hand hovering above the letter-cage. 'Well?' she asked again, waiting for her sister to go. Kathleen turned away.

'Yes. I will get on with the dining-room.'

'It is only because you want to pry, to discover who writes to me, that you come out in this way every morning.'

'No. I am not at all interested, Isabel.'

'Then why have you developed your powers of hearing so acutely that you are able to detect the click of the gate and the snap of the letter-box, even above the roaring of that vacuum cleaner?'

'I heard nothing at all, it was purely accidental. I came out into the hall and . . .'

'Why?'

'Why?'

'Why did you come out into the hall?'

'For . . . oh, I cannot remember now, Isabel.'

Kathleen Lavender turned away from her sister's glance of triumph. But it is true, she told herself, alone in the dining-room, I cannot remember why I went out into the hall but there was a reason. My mind is wandering, as Isabel has said, I forget things. Did I forget things before now? Yes, she knew that she had. Their mother had been forever running after her with a pencil box or an exercise book or a threepenny piece for church collection, and the maid had turned up a lost doll, a coin, a glove in every corner. 'Wool-gathering again,' their father had said, rubbing his hand roughly through her dry curls. 'Day-dreaming Kathleen Opal Lavender.' Yes, and Isabel must know, must surely remember it, Isabel who had such a well-developed, care-ful, private system for the storing, ordering, labelling, ar-rangement and organization of things, whose books were in a certain line, so that she could tell you at once, and without ever having to get up, what sat next to what and where Lewis and Short or Cassell's French-English would be found, were she to consent to your borrowing them because you had lost your own.

That is why, Kathleen told herself, she took such a pleasure in packing up the parcels. The parcels. I am not a prying woman, I have never really been interested in the affairs of others, I would never examine the contents of their drawers and cup-boards and bathroom cabinets, as Isabel did, wherever we went to stay. She is mistaken in accusing me of that. Nevertheless, I cannot help wondering about the parcels, for that is something so out of the ordinary, and about the things which are now missing. Kathleen had not dared to mention those things, must pretend that she had not noticed their absence. A small clock had gone from the sitting-room, and a watch in a slightly mild-ewed case. A set of leather-bound novels by Thackeray and the Works of William Shakespeare in red morocco had gone, too, leaving obvious gaping holes on the shelves.

What had gone from the attic she could only guess, for she did not remember half the things they stored there. But a short fur jacket that had belonged to Faith, one which fitted Kathleen and which she had looked forward to wearing the following winter, that had gone from its polythene bag in Faith's wardrobe. Isabel had locked the door to Faith's old room, and taken the keys off somewhere. She would not open it, even for cleaning.

Well, all those things had gone in the parcels, parcels that Kathleen had been obliged to carry down to the post office in five separate journeys, parcels that were heavy and had cost altogether two pounds four shillings to send. Isabel had not offered to refund that money.

Kathleen Lavender saw herself, for a moment, standing vacantly in the middle of the dining-room, the vacuum cleaner at her feet. But I will not be ordered this way and that, she said, I will do the work in my own time, as I choose, for my sister has no right to treat me like a maid, to give orders and expect me to run her errands. All this Kathleen Lavender told herself, knowing that it would never be voiced aloud, but even the thoughts were some small comfort. She switched on the vacuum cleaner.

I shall have to go out, Isabel Lavender decided, sitting in the armchair in her bedroom, behind a locked door and holding the three opened letters in her hand. I do not wish to see people, to have to talk and explain, to be stared at and wondered about, to become the object of scorn, for they are all foolish. But once again, a sacrifice is necessary, and there is no one else to make it. I shall have to leave this house for the first time in many weeks. My sister can never understand what I am prepared to do for her, for our welfare.

The letters had made her angry, though at first she had simply not been able to believe them. Only one contained a cheque, that from Regis, the bookseller in Maidenhead, and the cheque was for one tenth of the sum she had confidently expected. The other two letters were simply refusals, statements, that regrettably, parcels would be returned, no value, no possible demand ... The clock belonged to my grandfather, Isabel thought, it was made not later than the year 1850 by a craftsman, but such things are clearly no longer appreciated, nothing has value, it is all gimcracks and gewgaws. The dealers and auctioneers are clearly dishonest men, for did not the newspapers contain, almost daily, stories of this or that forgotten family possession, found in an attic or lumber room or trunk, and fetching colossal sums? It is only the American buyers who are now attracted by genuine *objets d'art*, they are the only ones who understand their true worth and what kind of reflection is that upon us? Perhaps, Isabel decided, it is the wrong time of the year and I must wait until July or August, when they arrive as tourists. Meanwhile, we have a cheque for five pounds, and no reply from the furriers. I shall have to go out. I may go to see Alida Thorne. Yes, for she has money and an acquisitive nature. I have things to offer her that she cannot help but want.

Isabel Lavender opened her bedroom door and shouted above the noise of the vacuum cleaner. Four times she shouted, before the house went suddenly silent.

'It is extraordinary,' she said, when her sister appeared, 'very, how your ears are attuned to the noise of the letter-box and not to my voice. But I can quite understand how the one is so much more interesting.'

'What do you want, Isabel?'

Isabel Lavender raised her eyebrows. 'Well, is it not coffee time?' she asked.

'I might have known,' Ma said. 'Oh, yes. That's about typical, that is.'

Ma had taken to knitting again, long grey pullovers and slip-overs and socks. It was socks today, the four fine needles shooting in and out like shuttles, click-click-click.

'Nothing surprises me any longer about you. It does not.'

Ma was an expert knitter, a knitter by feel not by sight of pattern, a measurer by holding up, by arm-length, not by inches and tapes. So she could knit and watch the television, knit and read, she had no need to follow the needles. Gaily knew that. Only it still managed to give her an excuse not to look at him.

'I just thought I'd tell you,' he said, 'that's all. In good time, so you know what's going on. You can't complain I don't tell you things.'

'Forty-five, forty-six . . .'

'Can you?'

'I'm counting, aren't I? Forty-nine, fif . . .'

'You're always game, aren't you? You don't give in.'

'You don't want socks then?' Ma said, laying down her knitting.

'What's that to do with it?'

'You can't do it, not to fit. Haven't you learned by now, when I'm counting, I'm . . .'

'. . . counting. All right.'

'Well?'

'You've finished counting, then?'

'It looks like it, doesn't it?'

'So I can talk now?'

'You'll talk if you want to talk. Nothing I can do.'

'I like you to know what's going on. Not that you believe it.'

'At your age.'

'I'm fifty-four.'

'I suppose I didn't know that either?'

'Jody Beach – you remember Jody Beach, don't you? I told you about him. He was sixty-eight. He got married.'

'You've said nothing about getting married. It's all coming out, isn't it?'

'No, it's not, and I'm not. I was only giving you an example. Jody Beach . . .'

'. . . got married at sixty-eight years old. Well, he should be ashamed of himself, he ought to have better things to think about.'

'Why?'

'Stands to reason – a man of his age.'

'I don't see that, myself.'

'Well, you wouldn't, would you?'

'And nobody's said anything about getting married. I just thought I'd tell you.'

'Only good friends, are you?'

'It's nothing for you to snigger at.'

Gaily watched Ma's face. He couldn't tell, not really, what

she was thinking. Only sometimes he could. She presented him with barrier after barrier of enigmatic remarks, as now. She had said nothing, nothing at all to reveal to him how she took the idea of Florence Ames, whether she cared or did not care. He wondered if she knew herself.

'Maybe I'll bring her to see you,' Gaily said.

'Oh, yes.'

'You'd like that.'

'How do you know what I'd like?'

'You would.'

The needles shuttered in and out faster, glinting in a single bar of sunlight.

'She was a nurse at one time,' he said.

'Oh, yes?'

'You'd have plenty to talk about.'

'Such as?'

Gaily turned back to his book. Anyway, he'd tried hadn't he, and what more was there? His book was fascinating, it gave innumerable hints, told him a dozen short cuts, helped with clear diagrams for various well-known difficulties. *A Complete Illustrated Guide to Card, Balsa and Matchstick Models*. It had cost him twenty-five shillings, but worth it because of not being able to keep it out of the library long. There was always a demand.

'So it's Sunday,' Ma said.

'That's it.' Gaily did not look up. Two can play, he thought.

'You won't be back here till all hours.'

'Not very late.'

'Have to mind what you're doing, won't you?'

'Very likely.'

'Be getting a car, I suppose, before we know where we are. To take your lady-friend out. They all have cars these days.'

'Public Transport's good enough for me. It should be.'

'You could afford a car.'

'I daresay.'

'I could get out more if there was a car.'

'Nothing to stop you from getting out now.'

'Oh no, nothing at all! Heaving myself on and off buses, sitting in smelly trains.'

Gaily looked up instinctively. That had to be answered, after all. 'Trains these days,' he said slowly, 'do not smell. It's years since you went on a train, you haven't any idea. Trains aren't what they were, there's been a revolution in trains.'

'You wouldn't be trying to sell me a ticket?'

In spite of himself, Gaily grinned. She still had an edge, Ma, you could only hand it to her.

'Elsie's off on a coach trip,' Ma said, 'just booked up, she says. Tour of Scotland, seven days.'

'Well, why don't you go on that? I'll give you the money to go on that. You'd enjoy yourself.'

'Stuck in a stuffy bus.'

'And that's something else you don't know, there's been a revolution in buses as well. Luxury coaches they are now, with air-conditioning and reclining seats and a toilet even, comfortable as they can be. You want to go?'

'You what? With the "Evergreens", with a gaggle of old fogies? Catch me!' Ma put a spare needle in her mouth and began to count the rows down, but she spat out 'Evergreens!' again, between her teeth.

Gaily sat back with his book. You couldn't blame her, not about the 'Evergreens'. No.

Kathleen Lavender, hat and coat still on, flung open the siting-room door.

'They have taken away Eleanor Thorne,' she said.

Her sister did not look up from the list of figures.

'Did you hear me, Isabel? I passed the house on my way from Tibbetts, I saw the ambulance, a navy-blue one. I did not stand staring but I could not help but see. Dorothea was there and the person she used to bring as a partner for Faith's bridge games when I could not play. I cannot remember her name. They don't seem to have been much together in recent months, I thought perhaps the friendship had petered out. Apparently not, though, for there she was. I wish I could remember her name. Perhaps you can. Well – they have taken Eleanor Thorne.'

She stood, panting a little.

Isabel Lavender glanced up in disgust. 'And of what possible interest is it to us?'

Her sister did not reply, confused by the question, and the anxiety that had been aroused by those few moments, during which two men had helped old Eleanor Thorne down the front path and into a waiting ambulance. Of Alida there had been no sign.

'Or rather,' Isabel said, 'of what interest is it to *me*, since clearly you are enthralled by the news? Your eyes are pro-truding with excitement, at such an appearance, you have the air of a gold-digger. I cannot bear this obscene, grubbing curi-osity about the affairs of others, it has never failed to repel me. Is it not quite plain, even to you, that Eleanor Thorne became senile long ago, and even plainer that Alida wished to be rid of her? She is going to some home, that is all, nothing could be less remarkable. And yet there you stand, gloating, without even the self-command necessary to remove your outer clothes and leave the shopping basket behind before rushing in here.'

But when her sister had trailed dejectedly from the room, Isabel Lavender laid down her pen. So they had taken Eleanor Thorne away. So Alida had not been there. To be deprived of freedom and of choice was the final fear, and Eleanor Thorne had been carted away like a splitting and discarded mattress beside someone's dustbin.

Isabel became suddenly aware of her own vulnerability and of the need for preventive action. Arrangements would some-how have to be made, for Kathleen, unstable, light-headed and suggestible as she was, might some day take outside advice and consign *her* to an institution. Such a move was by no means beyond her.

I am neither very old nor at all senile, Isabel Lavender thought, but I do have a sister who is selfish and easily led, and in this world, none of us are safe from the navy-blue ambu-lance.

Kathleen Lavender sat on the end of her bed and wept a few tears of fear and uncertainty and regret. I am not going out of my mind, she thought, and if, at the moment, the outside world does not recognize me for what I am, my sister knows she has only to speak a word here and there, to take a decision, and who will listen to me?

And where have they taken Eleanor Thorne? Madness had a smell, as Kathleen Lavender had watched the very old body move down the garden path. I should do something now, because perhaps it was for want of normal company that Eleanor Thorne lay until her mind turned the corner into madness and final decay, I should go out, I should not allow myself to brood, to carry out my sister's peculiar whims and defer to the judgements she passes upon me. I should visit Alida, who is now also alone, and Dorothea, for she has her friend whose name I cannot remember, and that is yet another person for me to talk to, make friends with. I should not run home and stay here in fear, for my sister cannot harm me.

The sight of Eleanor Thorne had been disturbing, unreal, something that should not have been allowed to happen. Kathleen had run home, and she now understood that it was, on this occasion, for reassurance, as though, by conveying the news to her sister, she would convey by implication something of her own anxiety, and receive comfort in Isabel's own concern. It had been altogether too much to expect.

'You wouldn't have a hand-drill, I don't suppose?' Gaily asked.

Dorothea Shottery shook her head. She was most anxious to supply the right tools and be of all possible help. But a drill, no.

'Large screwdriver, then.'

'Oh, yes, I have several screwdrivers. I shall bring the cardboard box with everything in it, and you shall sort out exactly what you need.'

'Now *see* how well you are getting on together,' said Florence Ames, when Dorothea had gone, 'I am so pleased. I do so enjoy introducing one friend to another.'

Gaily nodded. It was strange, his feeling of contentment, sitting here in this garden, empty coffee cups in front of them on the white table. You couldn't have expected it, he had been doubtful about this day from the beginning. It was not his sort of place, this friend Mrs Shottery not his kind of person. Or so he had thought at first, hearing her voice, looking round the well-furnished rooms, the shelves full of old china figures, in her polished house. She was some years older than Florence Ames, too, and older than him.

But it hadn't been like that. The sun had shone so that, after their lemon meringue pie, they had come out here, where the long-haired cat danced about the lawn, and Gaily had noticed the back-gate swinging off its hinges.

'I could mend that for you,' he had said, hating anything broken or untidy only for want of a firm nail. He was shocked when she told him that the gardener came three times a week and did not offer to mend it.

'You have had plenty to talk about,' said Mrs Ames, sitting back in her canvas chair, her eyes closed. Gaily watched her. Delicate lines, like tracings, rayed out at each corner of her eyes. They seemed to him beautiful, showing up the texture of her skin. Noticing things like that, about Florence Ames, had become usual, something to look forward to almost. He never knew, from one meeting to the next, what he might discover in her and it astonished him.

'I like to learn,' he said now, 'you can always learn things.'

Mrs Shottery's husband had collected everything, and china figures in particular. He had, she said, been unable to pass any shop in any town, any market-stall or window, for he might find a Nelson, a Gladiator, Henry Irving, a Shepherd boy with dog, twins, Dick Turpin. The named ones were apparently the most interesting and valuable, and he could see their charm, the fresh colours and glazes. Her house was full of curious objects, hidden away in corners. In a glass case were some early scientific instruments, clocks and watches, and on the walls plates and dishes in blue and white, vermilion, and gold.

'It was all my husband,' she told him, 'he knew about them, he bought them all. I only read a little in the books he gave me, picked up what I could. But I love them, I would be lost without them. I suppose the house must seem full of clutter.'

But it was not clutter, for everything had its place, Gaily could see that, all was arranged and polished and separate. He felt a plan behind it. He would have liked to talk to her more about her husband, but he couldn't really bring himself, not yet, to ask any more questions. He scarcely knew her after all.

'He'd have been an interesting man,' he said to Florence Ames.

'I didn't know him. They were only married a very few years. She had been widowed some time when we met.'

Gaily nodded, and, bending forward, clicked his fingers at the cat. It rolled over and over several times, preening its paws.

'Oh, Hastings is spoiled,' said Dorothea Shottery, returning to the garden, 'but you are honoured. He can be so funny with strangers, even bite them. Now here you are, a boxful of tools. I'm sure they are in a mess and perhaps you will not find the right thing, after all.'

'I can make do. You learn how to make do, it's surprising.'

'You don't have to begin working, doing my jobs and setting my house to rights. This is your holiday, too.'

'I like to see a job done.'

'Then thank you.'

Gaily selected the tools and took them off down the path to the back-gate. The cat Hastings followed at his heels.

'Oh, that is very kind!' Dorothea said, settling back and picking up her crochet work. 'This is an enjoyable day!'

Florence Ames smiled. Down at the gate, Gaily had taken off his jacket and rolled up his shirt sleeves. His head was bent. What long arms, Florence Ames thought in surprise. I have never seen such long arms.

'And so Alida did not come,' Dorothea said. 'But perhaps after all, they would have had little to say to one another.'

'I think I am not surprised.'

'It worries me. But then, I have never found her an easy person. I have always known that she did not care to have me as a friend.'

'She was glad of you when she needed help.'

'Oh, but that is natural you know and she was very upset. We are all glad of whatever help we can beg, in that case. But I do not like to think of her, shutting herself away, unwell.'

'There is nothing really wrong with her, Dorothea, you understand that? Doctor Sparrow is clearly a sensible man. Once she has had a good rest, her world will put on a fresh complexion.'

'I hope so. I would so like to see Alida lead a fuller life, less anxious and restrained. I would so like to see her make some new friends.'

'She may do so, she has to work out her own salvation now. You cannot do that for her, cannot alter her frame of mind. She has her respite and she must use it. I am sorry if I sound harsh.'

'You could not be harsh.' Dorothea smiled.

'I do feel for her. It is not that I am heartless. But perhaps I have not your generosity. And I am not proud of that.'

Dorothea shook her head. I cannot allow myself to be praised, for that is not a virtue, she thought. I am not generous. If the truth were known, it is only because I have for so long been lonely that I welcome demands for help. It is only that I feel I may make a new friend and be rewarded with company. That is not selflessness or goodness. No. I have, after all, my own interests at heart and I must recognize this. Dorothea sighed shortly. Well, that is the way I am. But I would not have Alida need friends or be lonely in any way, however difficult a person she may be. I would so like her to find some relief.

At the bottom of the garden, Gaily bent to lift the gate back on to its newly-placed hinges, and the cat forestalled him, leaping on to the top bar, tail waving in his face. Gaily shook his head and, watching them, Florence Ames laughed with delight.

Why, Alida thought, in the middle of stripping bare the great bed, why I can go away on a holiday! She sat down. She had forgotten about holidays in recent years, merely snatching an odd day or two in London for shopping. If anyone can be said to deserve a holiday, she told herself firmly, then I am the one. I have worked, I have exhausted myself day in day out, for years, and nobody has ever considered my age or health, it never entered my mother's head that I might welcome a break, new surroundings, a chance to be waited on.

Well, she is comfortably settled in now, being very well looked after, and in a wholly suitable atmosphere. She is back in the house that she is always remembering and talking endlessly about, she has her precious Miss Cress. And I can go away on a holiday at last.

It was a comfort that the money was solidly there, presenting no problems and solving many. Alida began to think about where she might go, as she piled sheets and blankets on to the floor. A very comfortable small hotel it must be, with home cooking and a choice of breakfasts, with armchairs and small tables in the lounge, morning tea at whatever time one chose, and a good bedside lamp. There were numerous hotels of this kind, she must make inquiries, send for brochures. That would be something to look forward to, the arrival of brochures. Blattern should not pass by the gate again without delivering any letters.

Groups or pairs of ladies, often sisters or cousins, ran hotels of the kind she required and they understood the necessity for quietness and a late-night pot of tea, for Egyptian cotton sheets and a hot water bottle and plenty of cushions, for sufficient pastries at the tea table and permission to have one's own wireless set in the bedroom. Yes, she would go into the country rather than to a seaside resort, for they were full of old, retired, ill-tempered people and had she not had her full share of that? And they were the hunting grounds, too, of unscrupulous proprietresses and café-owners.

A small market town, a place by the river, a Suffolk village or a Spa, one of these would suit her, though it must not be too quiet, too isolated. Alida had need of company, a variety of faces, after the years of being shut up alone with her mother.

And what is more, she decided, in order to go away I must have suitable new clothes. Oh, there are all manner of things I need, it is so long since I went shopping. A trip to London for the day, or even two days, staying overnight in some good hotel, that is what I shall have.

Alida Thorne glanced round. She needed someone to talk to about it all, needed a sharer of secrets, an ear to listen to her plans and, above all, someone to agree that she was on the right course, that both shopping expedition and holiday were what she stood in urgent need of. She walked slowly downstairs and sat in her own armchair beside the sitting-room window. The house was very quiet.

Now, if she had gone to lunch with Dorothea Shottery after all, there would have been three people to talk to. Perhaps she had been foolish to remain here, eating a poached egg and spinach off a tray. But no, for Dorothea might ask if she felt well enough to go away, might start prying into her affairs. And Dorothea talked so, about nothing at all, spinning her phrases out and forever trying to win attention and applause. It is the occupational disease of widowhood, Alida had long ago decided, they are none of them self-sufficient, they have been cushioned for so long they cannot keep silent or rely upon themselves.

Besides, I do not wish Dorothea's friend to know of my arrangements. It is better not to extend what was, after all, an accidental and purely professional relationship. Nor do I wish to meet the man from the funeral. By no means.

The man from the funeral. Alida had been shocked, seeing him with Florence Ames walking from the bus stop towards Dorothea's house. You could not always tell, of course, and today he looked smart enough in a navy-blue suit and highly polished black shoes, his hair well flattened and combed down. But he was the same, odd man, who had hung about at the church in boots at Faith Lavender's funeral. Alida felt that it was quite unseemly, in a woman of Florence Ames' age, to bring a man-friend openly through the place, to flaunt such a curious person.

No, she had done the right thing in ignoring the invitation to luncheon. But she thought that she would have been glad of someone to talk about her new plans with, all the same.

And at that moment, up the front path came Isabel Lavender, dressed in black.

*

'You can do it with golden syrup tins,' Gaily said, 'easier than with coconuts. I mean, they're easier to get hold of.'

'Are you sure? I've inquired into the question of coconuts, and they can be bought wholesale.'

'Yes and you have to pay for them, don't you? Well, treacle tins people just save and give you. They give you all the prizes, too, tins of things you see and for every tin you knock down, you win a tin of something. Or maybe you have to knock down two or three tins to win a prize – yes, that'd be best. You'd start running out of prizes unless – too many people would be winning them.'

'You are clearly a man with a wide experience of garden fêtes, Mr Gaily!' said the Reverend George Jocelyn Bottingley. 'What a pity you are here only for the day – I could pick your brains very profitably.'

'It's only what anyone knows, really, you couldn't say I'd had exactly *wide* experience. No. I ran a fête, two years at a trot, some time back now, though, it was. I organized it for a boys' club. That's all, that's only how I come to know about the treacle tins.'

'But,' said Dorothea Shottery, 'but surely, it wouldn't be possible to get enough empty treacle tins between now and the day. It takes such a long time to use up a tin, you probably wouldn't realize. I think we should have started asking people a year ago.'

Gaily nodded his head. It was right, and he was sorry about it, because he'd have liked to think his idea had helped them, been taken up so that he could feel part of the activity. It was a long time since he'd organized anything like a fête. He used to enjoy himself.

And then it came to him, and he had to wait, fidgeting his hands while the rector talked on. Florence Ames glanced across at him.

'I know,' Gaily said at last. They looked at him and he began to explain about his models.

'I've done the Tower of London, and Nelson's Column – that was hard, very hard, because of the balance, you see – and I'm thinking of doing Westminster Abbey. Now *that* will be hard, that needs a good deal of thought and it'll take a long time. I'm saving that up for winter.'

'Amazing,' said the Reverend Mr Bottingley. 'Yes, indeed!'

'What I thought – well, if you're agreeable, if it'd be of help – between now and August, I could make a model of St Paul's Cathedral. And I'd keep a very careful record and it'd be on display. The day of the fête, people would have to guess the number of matchsticks in it altogether.'

'Like raisins in a cake,' said Dorothea.

'Or peas in a jar,' said Mrs Ames.

'And they'd win . . .?' said the Reverend Mr Bottingley.

'The model of course,' said Dorothea, 'what a splendid idea! Now aren't we so lucky to have you here, Mr Gaily, and all full of ideas!'

'Of course,' Gaily said, 'I'd need a good photograph to work from.'

'Oh, you shall have that.'

'And mind you, a lot of people might not want to win the model. I mean, they take up space and so on, they need dusting. A lot of people might not have any taste for such a thing.'

But they all exclaimed that, oh yes, of course, anyone would be pleased, and especially a model of St Paul's Cathedral, as was suggested, anyone would be quite delighted to win that, indeed they would, and Gaily blushed with pleasure. He would bring Ma to the fête, that's what he'd do. She'd been going on about the outings, never getting away, hadn't she? Well then, he'd give her an outing, he'd bring her here and she could enjoy herself, have a tea, go home by train or bus, whichever she chose.

In the end, he found himself being asked to advise about the hiring of marquees, and the erection of stalls, the choosing of sites for swings and the marking out of an area for the donkey ride. He would come down for the week-end before and see to the final arrangements, of various things. The Reverend George Jocelyn Bottingley was extremely grateful, for a man like Gaily was what they needed. The village was too peopled by women, fit only for the baking of cakes and arranging tombola stalls.

It was odd really, Gaily decided, on the way home, odd how easy it had been, how he'd seemed to fit there without too much trouble, and settle down into a way of talking, and acting without any strain. You wouldn't have expected it at all. He'd worried, often enough, that he hadn't got the measure of Mrs Ames, that their friendship would one day founder on a simple misunderstanding. She didn't say much, you couldn't tell. But he liked her friend, too, Mrs Shottery, even to thinking he knew what Florence Ames meant about her being a good woman. She took you for granted, as though she'd always known you, that was really what it was.

And it was funny how he had looked at them all, during that funeral, and thought about them afterwards, but they had all been just strangers, not people he was ever likely to meet, or even see again. Here he had been, though, sitting in that garden, eating her food, offering to give a hand at their garden fête, and it all seemed to come easily enough. Thanks to Ma really, he thought, and grinned, thanks to her fall and not being able to manage the washing herself. Otherwise, he'd never have met Florence Ames.

Yes, he'd bring Ma to the fête, by way of introducing her to the new life. Gaily settled back in the bus seat.

'I am sorry, I simply do not understand, I cannot follow what you are saying at all,' Alida Thorne said. 'Is this some kind of game or elaborate joke? What is it that you are trying to tell me? Have I understood correctly? That your sister, Faith, left a large sum of money, which belonged to the three of you, to a hospital, that the money would have supported Kathleen and yourself in the years to come? That you are now almost penniless? But surely, in that case, your solicitor can invalidate the will? If the money can clearly be proven to belong to you all, and to be your only means of support, it cannot be let out of the family, casually, at the whim of one member. I assure you of that. There is nothing you can tell me about solicitors and the ways of the law with regard to legacies, Isabel. You are sure to be given every help by your firm.'

Isabel Lavender, hands resting on black handbag, black handbag on black gloves, looked over Alida's head and out of the sitting-room window, an expression of disdain on her face. She had been here for twenty minutes, during which time Alida Thorne had backtracked and made difficulties, pretended not to understand. It was a considerable strain.

'The solicitor can be of no help,' she said at length, 'he has refused, he has passed judgement and there can be no appeal.'

'Well, I simply cannot believe that, for it is not for him to say. You must change your solicitor. If what you have told me is true . . .'

'Are you accusing me of telling lies?'

'. . . if you have not confused matters . . .'

'Or of madness? I am clear in my mind, I am an honest woman.'

'I have no doubt.'

'You can be of no help to us, then? You are turning your back, I see.'

Alida stared at her. So she had not misunderstood, she had not misheard.

'You are asking me for money,' she said, shocked.

'Yes. Or failing the gift of a sum in cash, I am asking you to make it a business transaction, to buy what you clearly must need and what we can no longer afford to keep. I am asking you to take up the privilege. I have asked no one else, I have given you the first opportunity of owning these things.'

'Why, you sound like a salesman!'

'Is it surprising? We can never know, any of us, to what level we may be reduced. You do not know, Alida.'

'But I do not wish to buy anything from you! I have no use for second-hand books and unfashionable clothes and bits of ornament. I am quite astonished that you should suggest such a thing. Are there not shops or agencies to which you can send off parcels? Are there no longer any second-hand dealers in the town?'

'They are dishonest. They will give me next to nothing for valuable objects. It is out of women in distressed circumstances that such people line their pockets, and run their motor cars.'

That Alida Thorne could believe, but she was not prepared to agree with Isabel Lavender at this moment, with a woman whose behaviour had become disturbing in the extreme. It could not be true, surely it could not, that the Misses Lavender were destitute. No. Alida thought of her own capital with some alarm. It was not so very much, after all, she might easily live another twenty years or more, and money was not endlessly elastic. There could be no question of a gift to the Lavenders.

'How is Kathleen?' she asked, to give herself some time and in an effort to restore the conversation to a level on which she could cope. 'I have seen so little of anyone recently, with my illness, and before that with the twenty-four-hour tie of my mother. I am to go away shortly, on a convalescent holiday.'

Perhaps now, Isabel would listen to her in a normal manner, help mark the newspaper columns with hotel advertisements.

'*We* cannot look forward to holidays,' Isabel said.

'Well, I am sorry for it but there is nothing I can do. Only give you the name of a good solicitor.'

'I have no need of such a thing.'

'This is a legal matter, it cannot be dealt with by friends and laymen.'

'You are not prepared to help us,' Isabel Lavender said again, but in a cold, flat, accusatory tone, without any note of pity or pleading. Alida wished the woman away.

'I have been very ill,' she said, 'I have a heart condition. You must excuse me now, Isabel, it is time for my rest.'

'And what am I to do when there are hospital bills to find payment for?'

'Hospital bills?'

'My sister is becoming mentally ill. It has shown itself all at once, she cannot remain at home for very much longer.'

'Kathleen? When did she become ill? She seemed to me quite normal the last time we met.'

'And when was that?'

Several weeks ago, Alida realized, and so, perhaps it was true and Isabel Lavender was living under a double strain, of fear of a demented sister, and of poverty. Alida could understand her state of mind. It is very near to all of us, she thought, we are none of us free from the threat.

'I will write you a cheque,' she said abruptly, 'but that must be all. I am not a wealthy woman, Isabel, and my own mother's hospital bills are draining my income. But I will give you money, and without strings. I am not an unfeeling woman. But you must understand that, after this, I can do no more. There are state agencies to help you, you must apply to them.'

When the cheque, for fifty pounds, had been written, Alida Thorne felt better. I have discharged my duty, she thought, I cannot be troubled by my conscience in that respect. We can never know when these afflictions will strike us on our own doorsteps. Fifty pounds is a good sum, however, she should have no need to beg any more.

'I advise you to see your solicitor,' she said, folding the cheque into an envelope, as a mark of privacy. 'Something may yet be done.'

'All the responsibility devolves upon me. My sister cannot be trusted with any but the simplest of tasks.'

'I am sorry,' Alida said.

But Isabel Lavender walked out of the door, the envelope in her handbag, without a further word, of acknowledgement or thanks. Alida watched her black figure, stiff as a crow, from the window. That is the last time I shall put myself at a loss or disadvantage for her, she decided, unable as she was to thank me. And, if she has a sister who is going out of her mind, I have had a mother eighty-nine years old and senile, I cannot be said to deserve any further burdens nor to have failed in carrying out my duty.

She turned from the window, back into the room that still smelled faintly of Isabel Lavender's black coat and black feathered hat. And a sudden lightness of heart took her. There were no longer any cries from upstairs. That is all over, Alida Thorne said, that is past.

Chapter Eleven

MRS CLEMENCY spat a grape pip neatly into her hand.

'Go on,' she said.

The windows were open wide on to the garden, and beyond them was Tantamount Hill. In the garden, a man wearing fawn overalls bent in the planting of lobelia, row upon row. Eleanor Thorne watched him with delight.

'The gardens now are just as good as ever they were,' she said, 'just as good. I would never have expected it. One prepares oneself for change, for other people's carelessness or business. But the gardens have been lovingly tended, and soon there will be rhododendrons. Those have always been the pride of The Gantry.'

'You've forgotten,' said Mrs Clemency. Eleanor Thorne looked up. Just the two of them in a very large room. Mrs Clemency had Parkinson's Disease and shook. Eleanor already felt responsible, the one to do the looking after and the thinking.

'What have I forgotten?' she asked, her eyes still on the gardener, for it was so pleasant to talk through the afternoon, to have a companion and to give company. Mrs Clemency had no family living, and she had mentioned her loneliness obliquely.

'You shall not be lonely now,' Eleanor had said firmly, 'you will never be lonely so long as I live to help it.'

And now, she was peeling another grape and it was painful to watch how slowly, but Mrs Clemency would accept no help. 'I do what I can,' she had said, at the very beginning.

'I remember,' Eleanor Thorne said, 'I was telling you about the Mundays.'

'Of course you were, I wondered when you were going to get back to it.'

'Yes but back to where? Where was I?'

'Helena Munday, mother of the daughters you knew, your contemporaries – Helena Munday had just become engaged.'

'That was it! Yes, of course. I was only told of all this years later.'

'I can't see that that matters.'

'Why, no. But you must not accept my story as gospel, you know it is only a retelling, in parts.'

'It's a story,' said Mrs Clemency equably, 'that's the point.'

'Well then – Helena Munday became engaged to Digby Kean. And one month after her engagement she came of age. I told you they were in the brewery business? Yes, well her father bought her this house The Gantry – just like that! "You need a house," he said to her, "an establishment, and here is a suitable house, not two miles from your present home. If you like it, you shall have it." '

'Imagine!' Mrs Clemency's hand was, for one second, stilled on the counterpane.

'Yes, to be handed such a house, as a twenty-first birthday gift, and all furnished and equipped and staffed, too. Yes.'

'I feel privileged,' said Mrs Clemency, 'to belong to such a house. Oh, I am so glad to know a little of its history.'

'We think alike,' said Eleanor Thorne happily, 'the same things matter to us.'

'So it was a family home.'

'They had five daughters, all born here. Each daughter was married from here. And Helena Munday died here. Her husband died at sea. The eldest daughter, Ellen Kean, who became Ellen Frilsham, inherited the house.'

'And where is she now?'

'Ellen? Oh, goodness, Ellen is dead, they are all dead, Mrs Clemency. Yes, Ellen married a man I could never have liked under any circumstances, a self-indulgent man years older than herself. She was such a silly girl. Once, when we were no more than eighteen, she told me she was ugly, that nobody could ever find her attractive, nobody would want to marry her, she would live and die a spinster. Girls have such silly fancies, but nothing could have been as silly as Ellen Kean thinking herself unattractive. She was a beautiful girl, bonny and gay and with such thick, beautiful hair, the colour of chestnuts. But she married Lester Frilsham because he was the first man who asked her and she supposed that he would be the last. She was most unhappy. They had no children and Ellen died when – oh, she cannot have been more than twenty-five or -six, I forget. Yes, Ellen died and in just no time at all her husband remarried. They left for America. It was Lester Frilsham who sold The Gantry – we were so sad. And after that another family came, the Tomlinsons, they lived here for many years. We tried to welcome them, befriend them, you know, but they were curious people, they would have none of us. And then the house was sold again, for a school, as I remember, but a school that never came to anything.'

'And then?'

'Do you know, it is so odd, I remember every detail of so many years ago, the colour of curtains, the position of every ornament in the rooms, and yet there is such a blank in my memory for the times near at hand. I do not remember at all. How foolish you will think me!'

'Oh no,' said Mrs Clemency. 'Oh, no. We are all that way, aren't we? I am that way, I forget my own name. I can quite understand.'

Eleanor Thorne nodded. No, it did not matter, for they were all 'that way' and they accepted it. You had to reach old age to accept. She watched the gardener outside bend and rise as the long earth-bed was filled up with plants. On the lawn, under a flat-branched cedar, lay a cat. She had noticed the cat several times. A cat, quite at home, made The Gantry into almost a family house again.

It is a great good fortune, Eleanor Thorne said to herself, that I have had all my wishes granted and without their ever having been spoken aloud. I have returned to this house, of which I have for so long been fond, which has always played a part in my life. And I am in a community with at least one constant friend, and near to Miss Cress who is so kind and patient, so ready to talk and to listen. I am no longer lonely in that poky room. For I was lonely, I see that now, and the room *was* poky, all walls and bed. And it is all because Alida was so thoughtful, so sensitive to my unspoken wishes. I have misunderstood Alida too many times in the past. That is one penalty that growing old inflicts on others. But Alida brought me here, it is all thanks to her.

In the other bed, Mrs Clemency had gone to sleep, bunch of grapes on the newspaper resting below her knees, and in sleep she shook, so that the fruit and the newspaper rustled. I am so fortunate, Eleanor thought, looking at her, I have been pulled up short and made to realize how fortunate I am.

She turned back to watch the gardener at work in the afternoon sun.

Alida Thorne walked along the path beside the railway. That morning she had read a long and serious article in a national magazine on the cause and cure of heart disease.

'The patient must take gentle and regular exercise,' it had stated. 'Preferably he should go for a daily walk, of about half an hour's duration, and always on level ground, never up hills. A country walk, or at least a walk over short turf is far more beneficial than a tramp over hard city pavements.'

And so, on a heavy May afternoon, Alida Thorne had taken the advice and walked almost a mile already, across the fields that ran beside the railway.

Since nobody else cares, she decided, I must care for myself, I must institute a healthy régime, in the matter of diet and medicines and exercise. Doctor Sparrow may not be concerned, he may toss his head with all the false confidence of a mistaken diagnosis. He does not know. But I know, I am the only one who knows the situation fully. Well, I will care for myself.

She paused for breath. The air was dry and close and her silk dress clung to her back in patches, with the heat and effort. Perhaps it had been foolish, and not the best time to exert herself, with the air so still. In the sky over Haverstock the clouds lay, livid and bruised with what was clearly an approaching thunderstorm that she had not noticed on leaving the house. Nobody walked here, only the children sometimes played after school. Now, the children were in school, it was three o'clock.

I am alone, for a mile and perhaps more, Alida thought, quite alone. If I were to have a heart attack here, there would be nobody to attend to me, nobody to come to my aid, I should scream and cry and lose consciousness alone, on a field path. I should die, of that there can be no question. How foolish to walk just here, when there are other, better populated parts of the village. I have learned my lesson and I must return home at once.

Alida Thorne turned round, her back to the silent railway line and the leaden metal, dark in the afternoon heat. Beyond her lay the field, quite deserted, with a path crossing it diagonally and a gate at the far end, out on to the road.

Her legs lost all power, they turned to water and to air. Above her, the sky was wide as the world, stretching away, and Alida felt herself alone, a tiny figure, crouching in terror beside the bank. For she could never cross the field, she could not expose herself to that sky, launch out across the middle of that great green space. Beside the bank and close to the hawthorn tree, it was safe, dark at least, a little enclosed. The field stretched on for ever.

Oh God, I cannot cross the field, I cannot move, Alida thought, there is nobody to accompany me, to hold my arm, the sky is high, and huge and I cannot cross the field. Then I must stay here, completely alone, hot and unwell and at the mercy of the gathering storm. And which is the more dangerous, to cross the open field and be the only focus for so many miles, or to linger here beneath a tree, the very worst place in a thunderstorm? If I were not struck by lightning, I should have a heart attack, my heart could not stand up to such nervous strain. And if I were not to have an attack, I should be at the very least soaked through to the skin and those with heart conditions are highly susceptible to other illnesses, to pneumonia and pleurisy, that is well known.

Then the only alternative is to go now, to walk across the

field and quickly, as one would pull a plaster from a wound, before there is time to think, before the storm and the rain. I am a sensible woman, I am surely able to make the right decision, to see which course of action involves the least risk. Very well then, I will take my decision. I will go.

She took a few short steps away from the shelter of the hawthorn tree. And stopped. Oh God, oh God, she thought, I cannot cross that field, what is happening to me? Of what am I afraid? Why am I now breathing in gulps and why is my heart squeezing in that way, why must I stay here? For if I were to step out across the open space of field, where there are no walls to touch, no door-handles to hold on to, no people to call for, if I were to do that I should fall flat on my face, I should have to feel the earth beneath my fingers for safety, I should quickly die. Oh God, I cannot cross the field.

Alida Thorne began to cry quietly. And from the dark sky, raindrops and the first peal of thunder.

'Now, here is a thunderstorm coming,' said Eleanor Thorne, waking up, 'and it will rain on the newly-planted lobelias. How splendid! I always feel they get off to a good start, if they have rain on their first day.'

But when she glanced over to Mrs Clemency for a reply, she saw her companion still asleep, trembling gently beneath the newspaper.

'Oh, I am so sorry,' said Eleanor and turned back to the window in time to enjoy a spectacular flash of vivid green lightning. A thunderstorm was always something to make the most of.

Mrs Clemency awoke, pulling herself up as best she could in the bed. 'What is it? What did you ask me, Mrs Thorne? Oh, a thunderstorm! I was dreaming of the lightning, isn't that odd?'

'But you did not dream, for here it is!'

'Oh, it is better than a film show, don't you think? That has always been my opinion – better than a film show. And people think one so odd.'

'I do not think you odd,' said Eleanor Thorne, smiling as the thunder burst jubilantly overhead. 'And how many tastes we share, how compatible we are, Mrs Clemency!'

Mrs Clemency smiled and nodded, as she nodded all her days.

Isabel Lavender, too, sat at her bedroom window, though scarcely aware of the storm and the peal of hail upon the conservatory roof.

She thought of Eastbourne, when she had been eight years old, and Faith had been eleven. Their father believed in Eastbourne as the universal panacea, it was at Eastbourne that they spent the whole of each July and it was there that Isabel had first encountered her elder sister's deceit over the matter of money. That, she now realized, had been a portent for the future, if only she had paid sufficient attention.

They had not been allowed to spend every afternoon on the beach because for some reason Theodore Lavender considered it unsuitable. His daughters should not be spoiled, he said. The family rented a large house – always the same house – with staff, for the month, and on those non-beach afternoons, Faith, Isabel and the very young Kathleen played in the garden. It was on a Wednesday, Isabel now recalled, most certainly on a Wednesday, that Faith had abandoned their game of Grand Hotels – at which they wished they could have stayed – and sneaked away. For several minutes, perhaps five minutes, Isabel had not noticed – because she was in the middle of ordering the De Luxe dinner with wine from the waiter (Kathleen, who was pulled up on to the lawn in her pram). It had been hot, very hot, and they had all been wearing their blue Liberty prints with matching petticoats.

Straight-backed in her bedroom chair, Isabel Lavender heard the thunder, saw the lightning and remembered a Wednesday at Eastbourne with anger. Of course, it was typical of Faith, to leave her with the baby, to *trap* her – because they were both 'trusted' with Kathleen and forbidden to leave her alone for a moment. Kathleen had always been a petted child. But the very second Isabel discovered the betrayal, she *had* left her, left her to look for Faith.

Faith was behind the wide curve of rhododendron bushes that divided the top of the garden from the bottom, a shrubbed and wooded and altogether more interesting end. She had been in the act of bending over to set a large stone back into place beside a clump of London Pride.

'What are you doing?' Isabel had asked, in her sharp voice. Faith had straightened up quickly and her face had flushed. 'Nothing,' she had said, 'nothing to do with you. You go away.'

But Isabel had known and they had fought, fought violently, scratched and screamed until Isabel had won and had kicked the stone triumphantly away, to reveal a shilling piece, bright against the soil.

'You said you had lost it, you told our father you had it stolen on the beach – you told a *lie*,' Isabel said, and her sister had stood, square, flushed and unable to reply because her words always tumbled over one another, somehow, and caught her out.

'I shall tell them. You had the shilling all the time, you were hiding it. You're a sneak, a liar and a sneak.'

And it had been the ability in her sister to hide money quietly, to make a point of running her own life and decide for herself, deliberately excluding her, that had infuriated Isabel.

That was the first time, she told herself, that was the beginning, and I should have known, I should have learned my lesson. I had a sister who could not be trusted on the question of money. She became financially secretive at the age of eight. Oh, I should have been amply warned then!

Having recollected the incident in detail, a considerable feat of memory, Isabel was tired and yet refreshed, too, because there was a clear line of behaviour which could be grasped. She had always needed to see things clearly, just so.

Only now did she become fully aware of the storm, in full spate over Haverstock. Her sister had gone out. Well, was that not typical of her? The woman could no longer connect two pieces of reasoning – a storm is coming, it would be best to remain indoors for another hour. A deranged mind could hardly be expected to cope with such an everyday matter.

Isabel Lavender sat on in her chair, watching the deluge. After a time she drifted off into a half-sleep. The hall clock struck three-thirty, and did not waken her, nor did the single thunderclap directly overhead nor, at first, did the banging, banging, banging, banging ...

'Kathleen,' she said eventually, and with some sharpness, 'what is she doing? Are we to suffer this noise through the quiet hours of the afternoon? Can she no longer bear to dwell in silence, with her own thoughts, as I can? Bang, bang, bang.'

Isabel Lavender opened her eyes on a windowpane thick with raindrops, and then she heard the banging again, not the rolling of the thunder but the incessant, hysterical banging upon the front door of the house. Not only does my sister go out in the middle of a thunderstorm, she thought, disregarding all signs and warnings, but she forgets her key, she returns to hammer imperiously on the door and I must get up, my afternoon's sleep having been broken, and walk down two flights of stairs and across a long hall, to let her in. If I were asleep still, and could not hear, if she were obliged to spend ten or fifteen minutes in the conservatory, it would be a lesson to her. Yes, that is what she must do.

But the banging went on without pause, grew even worse, and Isabel knew that, of course, as one was never unkind to children, animals and the very frail, so one was never deliberately unkind to the mentally ill. They could not help themselves. Her sister was mentally ill.

Isabel Lavender rose from the bedroom chair. 'Now,' she said briskly, with the slightly raised, emphatic tone she had taken to Kathleen recently, 'now perhaps you will admit to a condition of forgetfulness?'

She spoke the words as she opened the front door and came face to face with Alida Thorne.

'The nearest house,' Alida had promised herself, in her short, desperate journey through the storm, 'the nearest house,' and she had spoken the words to Isabel, sweating and terrified by the harshness of her own breathing, by the lightning and rain, while skirting the edge of the open field she dared not cross. Seeing the black and white timbering and green gate of the nearest house, the house of the Lavenders, she had burst into tears of relief and fear and it was in tears, her face blotched and creased and old with them, and with rain, that she waited and hammered upon the front door for minutes, hours, an unbearable time, and it was in tears and sobs of terror that Isabel, straight-backed in a chocolate-coloured afternoon frock, found her.

'The nearest house,' Alida Thorne said, the words coming out in rasps on the tide of hard breaths, the beats of her heart. 'You will not believe me, Isabel, you can never believe how glad I am that yours is the nearest house!'

Isabel Lavender frowned. 'My sister is not at home,' she said.

Alida stared.

'I can only wonder at you both. I thought you a sensible woman, at least, Alida, but you also took no heed of the clear warnings, you wandered out in the middle of a violent storm. You amaze me. And my sister is out.'

She held the door to her, a little more closely.

'But I hardly knew . . . you were the nearest house . . . I am ill, I almost died, I hardly . . . you were the *nearest house*, do you not understand, Isabel?'

Alida saw the figure of Isabel Lavender in the doorway and the dark hall beyond quiver and recede, and she took in her breath sharply, held it. 'I am ill,' she said, wondering that she should need to say it, that Isabel was not going to let her in because of the incident over the items for sale, that ludicrous, shameful incident. But no, Isabel could not do that, for they were old, if not close friends, and there was the matter of the fifty pounds, Isabel could not leave her on the doorstep in the pouring rain.

'My sister is not at home,' she said for the third time, 'I was taking my afternoon rest, the knocking disturbed me.'

'The knocking . . .?'

'And I assumed that Kathleen had once again forgotten her key. She forgets everyday objects, times, the essentials of life, she

138

is undoubtedly deranged, and I am totally responsible for her. Even now, in the middle of a storm, I have no idea where she is. I am sorry for that, Alida, but one hardly expects callers in the early hours of a weekday afternoon, during a thunderstorm.'

'But I did not "call", is that not abundantly clear? It should be, from my appearance. I am not visiting your sister for afternoon tea. Do I care who is or is not at home, terrified and soaked to the skin as I am?'

But Isabel stood, sharp-faced, stiff, and Alida would surely have collapsed, not from the anticipated heart-attack but from cold and fright. Only that, from behind her, quick footsteps came up the path and Kathleen Lavender's voice.

'What is it?' she called, out of breath and anxious, glancing from one woman to the other, on the doorstep. 'Now, whatever is the matter? Isabel, what are you thinking of, that you have kept Alida outside in all this rain? Alida, you are drenched, soaked to the skin, where have you been? I am wet in just the short step from the post office . . .' She stopped and looked with alarm at the two faces, that of Alida Thorne, flushed and crumpled with fear, and of her sister, powdered and severe. And then Isabel turned away, walked across the hall and up the stairs, dismissing them both without a word.

Chapter Twelve

IN 1948 Mrs Braceby, widow of the old Rector of Haverstock, had died, and Eleanor Thorne was at her bedside.

'It is no place for you,' Alida had said, home from her school for the Christmas holidays, 'you are not a young woman and you are not a nurse. You are seventy years old. A sick room is not the place for you. Why can Mrs Braceby not be cared for adequately in hospital?'

But Eleanor Thorne, not at all burdened by her seventy years, had given her company and affection and aid, day and night, until her death.

'She was glad to have me with her,' she had said afterwards, 'she was glad of another person. One cannot leave people to die alone.'

'She would not have been alone in a good hospital, and you would not have worn yourself out.'

'A hospital!'

'Had she no family at all? Surely there must be cousins, nephews and nieces? Well, they will come soon enough now that she is dead, they will come for the reading of the will.'

But nobody came, there was nobody but Eleanor Thorne and old Doctor Tinsley to hear the short, sad will, leaving what few hundred pounds there were to the church. Alida remembered that her mother had cried for a moment or two, in this same, cold front sitting-room of theirs, into which the sunlight rarely came.

'Mrs Braceby is at rest,' Alida had said awkwardly, turning her back on her mother's tears.

'Oh, yes, it is all right now. Everything is all very well. I am not thinking of her now.'

'She was a very old lady. She could not have been happy, living there alone.'

'No,' Eleanor Thorne had said, 'that is what I am afraid of. For she had nobody, no family, scarcely any friends, not because people did not love her but because they did not know her, she had outlived them all. It is her past that I am so distressed to think of.'

'You did what you could.'

'Perhaps.'

'You saw to it that she did not die alone,' Alida had said, and walked from the room to end a conversation that alarmed and disturbed her. She had always been a firm, sensible woman, always seen the great events of life for what they were.

But Eleanor, tearless now, had stood anxiously at the window looking out on to Haverstock Green, not comforted.

'She was glad to have me with her,' Alida remembered her saying, 'she was glad of another person.'

Alida began to walk about the house, from the cold front sitting-room, down the hall into kitchen, dining-room, scullery and larder, and then through bathroom and boxroom and the bedrooms one by one. Except her mother's room, with the great bed laid bare. Into that room she did not go.

Her own creams and lotions and scents, her cushions and the velvet spaniel with jewelled eyes holding her nightdress, her wardrobe with the silk and tweed and woollens, the matching hand-made belts and petit-point brushes, each one she touched for comfort. But none of them comforted her. Perhaps, she thought, now that my mother has settled in, I could slip on my coat and walk up to The Gantry, I could pay her an evening visit?

But how foolish, for had she not almost died of anxiety and shock today, might she not have contracted a serious chill in the rain? Moreover, the storm had not freshened the air and beyond the windows of her bedroom, the sky hung in pleats and folds of mushroom cloud, yellow-tinged. There was no wind, no coolness after the rain. How could she think of going out, of crossing the green and taking the open, empty lane towards The Gantry alone? To go out would be simple folly. Her mother would not wish her to make the journey in such poor health, to take another risk for the sake of a few minutes' conversation. It was not as though there was anything to say.

But it is not that, she thought, sitting down on the edge of her soft bed, hands folded in her lap, it is that I am afraid of meeting my mother's eyes, of seeing blame and her unhappiness, of the accusations that an old woman, wandering in her mind, might make, accusations of selfishness, and my lack of caring. Heaven knows I have cared, I have spent myself tirelessly for years, but she is not to understand that, she is senile, these things cannot be explained or boasted about, I can expect no gratitude. All she will remember is that I had to put her into a home and that I have not been able to visit her. Nothing else. That is why I cannot go to The Gantry, not yet. Not yet.

Alida Thorne sighed. And suddenly, glancing up, was overcome with fear that the ceiling might fall in on top of her, not to crush her but to leave a great roof rent, exposing her room, her possessions, and herself, to the wide and thunderous evening sky.

In a fever of apprehension, she took each stair down to the hall and safety, for here below it could not happen.

Instead, as though she had set it off by putting her foot on the last stair, the front door bell rang. Alida shrank back towards the wall, lifted her hand to her heart. If I am very quiet, she thought, if I do not move, they will go away, they will realize that I am not available, and go away and I shall not be disturbed. For another person would come inside and peer at her face, see her emotions and detect her thoughts, speculate upon her secrets, might even offer help and advice. Questions would be asked, too, and Alida resented questions, never asked them of anyone herself.

It had been hard enough, humiliating enough, with Isabel Lavender on the doorstep, and then with Kathleen, facing her across the table and the teapot. Kathleen had been flustered, chatting and drying her hair, offering a towel to Alida, confiding at length about her sister, and watching. But if she did not go out, she would not have to face other people and their prying, she would be quite independent, no help would be required except of a purely professional kind. For she had always counted it as a sign of weakness to become dependent upon others, friends or strangers, had throughout her life been careful not to slip into a position of physical or emotional helplessness. Until now, when there had been first Dorothea and her friend, who had seen her distress, entering the house, taking over, drawing their conclusions. And then the Lavenders, both of them suspicious of one another, and extending their suspicions to the world outside. Today had been one of humiliations, the lowering of standards. And now the doorbell again, in the silent hall, and the caller would not understand, would not leave her in peace and go away.

Dorothea Shottery waited fretfully on the doorstep, aware of Alida's shadow, after her progress down the stairs, wondering what might be wrong. If she were ill and could not call out, how could the door be broken down, ought she to *try* and break it down? Yet Alida would hardly be standing there, were she too ill even to raise her voice.

Then the time was inconvenient, she was about to take a bath or, quite simply, she did not care to see Dorothea. One must not assume that one's company was always welcome. What, then, should she do for the best? She could not simply leave her friend alone, ill. Dorothea turned away, and then back again, fidgeting with her gloves, aware of Alida's coldness, even hostility, since those few sick-room days, and understanding it, too, not liking to encroach. They had never really been friends. It was scarcely a vital errand, there were plenty of other people interested. Only that she had wanted to make the gesture, draw Alida out a little, now that Eleanor was gone, and so happy and settled too, which must be a relief and comfort to her daughter. This was no time for retreat, for the loss of friends.

One last time, Dorothea pressed the doorbell.

Perhaps it is about my mother, Alida thought. She has been taken suddenly ill, she has already died, they have come for me and I cannot refuse. I am to go there, probably during yet

143

another thunderstorm, and sit the night through among the moans and rattling breaths of the old, the sick, the insane. This is my duty. Well, at least they will see now that I was right, that I could not have coped with a dying woman, they will offer me some sympathy after all. Miss Cress will at last be forced to admit the rightness of my decision.

Thinking this, preparing herself, Alida moved out of the shadows and opened the front door.

In the end, Dorothea sat down, though only on the very edge of the chair, for Alida had not invited her to sit, but stood, hands clasped, rigid, just inside the door. It was very awkward. Alida's unspoken resentment lay between them, and anyone else, entering this cold sitting-room, would have sensed an atmosphere. But I am here, Dorothea said, and I will persevere.

The subject of the coffee morning had just been broached, but Alida Thorne had not commented, and her pulpy face held no hint of an expression to guide Dorothea. It was all very hard.

'Now, would you like to help?' Dorothea began. 'Please do not feel that I am pressing you, do not agree to give me a hand against your inclinations. But you are so good at that sort of thing.'

'At what sort of thing?'

'Why, at making people feel at home, at being a hostess, at entertaining.'

'I did not think so.'

Nor did Dorothea. But she could not tell the truth, give the real reason for her request, could not say, I am asking you to help me at my coffee morning, because I feel you are lonely and afraid and weighed down by your own conscience, I feel you need to get out of this lonely house and forget yourself, make an effort to think of others, live *normally*. Yes, that was the word, but it could not be uttered, none of it could be uttered.

'You always look so smart,' Dorothea went on, 'you would enhance any gathering of this kind, people would be so impressed, it would give *me* confidence. For, after all, I have done nothing like this before.'

'But they are all neighbours, they already know me. It is

not as though you wish to make some kind of impression upon strangers. You are surely presentable and courteous enough for any gathering?'

'I have not your *style*,' said Dorothea.

Alida Thorne straightened her back. 'Well,' she said. And at last sat down, opposite Dorothea.

'Yesterday, I called to see Eleanor,' Dorothea began to say, but seeing Alida's face, did not continue. Anger was there, and shame and guilt, but starched over by an expression that said, do not pry, do not ask for a communication on that subject, do not expect me to speak of my mother, this is forbidden ground.

And so, the slight headway that she had made was again lost, and Dorothea looked at her own arthritic hands during the silence. Eleanor Thorne had been happy, companioned by the nice Mrs Clemency in the sunlit room. Her attention and concentration had not lapsed during the afternoon, her eyes had been alert, wholly aware of the present, and they had all laughed together and eaten the fruit and sultana buns Dorothea had brought. That was the sadness of it, that Eleanor was so settled, so very much happier, but her daughter was nevertheless eaten up with guilt.

'Alida is not a strong person, she does not care for the company of the old and infirm,' Eleanor Thorne had said. 'That is why she keeps in touch with me by letter. What would she find to say or do here, with a couple of old women chattering? She is not like you, Dorothea, but we cannot blame her at all for that.'

An excuse, an excuse, because Alida had only once been to visit her, only once, though she lived hard by. But, seeing Eleanor so happy, Dorothea had smiled with relief and slept peacefully through the night for the first time in many months. It was not Eleanor who needed attention and company and care now, it was Alida, who sat staring at her own reflection in the doors of the china cabinet.

'I am going to divide the money,' Dorothea said at last. Alida's eyes were pale upon her.

'The proceeds of the coffee morning,' Dorothea explained.

Alida made her feel a fool. She heard her own voice pressing on, forced and bright.

'Now you can give me your opinion. I thought it could be divided between the NSPCC . . .' she looked up inquiringly, but Alida only stared, blank-faced, '. . . and the Mental Health Trust.'

Dorothea stopped. A thin smile moved over Alida Thorne's mouth. 'Isabel Lavender,' she said in a precise tone, 'is deranged. She has become mentally ill. We shall be drinking our coffee in aid of her.'

Chapter Thirteen

'WILL you come on holiday with me?' Gaily asked at last, 'for a week?' He twitched his feet, as she did not at once reply. 'The company,' he went on, explaining what he had thought about for perhaps a month, or even longer. 'We get on so well. Like today, for instance.'

Today. Tuesday, his movable day-off. Florence Ames turned to look back, from their comfortable bench beneath the box hedge, to the house, Pencote Manor, high-Elizabethan married with an eighteenth-century east wing.

'I should like that,' she said, 'that would be very nice.'

'The holiday?'

'Yes, the holiday.'

Gaily nodded three or four times. Before him now was the pleasure of filling in newspaper forms, receiving sun-coloured brochures through the letter-box, eliminating, relishing deciding with her. And he would send for information about places he could not possibly choose, too, to add to the glamour of it – Malta and Kashmir and wild-game hunting holidays in Africa, as well as the resorts, Brighton and Eastbourne and Clacton and Scarborough, the coach tours and the country retreats. Because she had agreed, he could parcel all of this and store it away for later, get on with the enjoyment of today. Gaily was glad that he had spoken.

'I like it here,' he said, 'I like it where they leave things alone. That's how it should be. Not have entertainments and zoos and so forth, to distract you.'

'Oh yes! And I like coming on days like this, when it's quiet.'

For they had seen perhaps a dozen other visitors, with their National Trust cards, and otherwise only gardeners moving about the lawns, and custodians reading newspapers in the house.

'It's a good place,' said Gaily, 'I'd have liked a house of that kind.'

'Queen Elizabeth I gave it to him. For services rendered in the Spanish War. To Sir Thomas Furton.'

'Later First Baron Furton of Pencote.'

They had studied the catalogue yesterday and decided to come. They spent every free day of his travelling round the countryside. 'There are so many things we ought to see, we should take every opportunity. That's what they're here for,' Florence Ames had said, and so they visited Stately Homes and Castles and Museums, a deer park, a Spa, a Roman Bath and two Norman churches, cathedrals and gardens and galleries. And later, at home with Ma, Gaily read about the places, what he called his background work, read history and horticulture and biography and art appreciation.

'All this reading,' Ma said, 'all books and the radio all of a sudden. I don't see it.'

'How about me being a Sir?' Gaily said now, looking at Mrs Ames, smiling. Fifty yards away, a pair of swans floated between green banks, and that stream led, a few miles further on, into the River Avon, Shakespeare's river. In Hubert Gaily's mind, history was a series of coloured pictures, lit up at random by some association. Shakespeare's river. Francis Drake and the bowls. Ruffs and farthingales. The Royal Exchange. Or the Battle of Culloden fought in a swirling mist. Flora MacDonald on the shore – though he knew that was a myth, like much of the rest. He knew, but he found the pictures entertaining.

'Elizabethan times,' he said reflectively.

Florence Ames frowned at him. 'More people are happier now,' she said, 'don't be sentimental about it.'

Gaily was alarmed, sometimes, by the way she picked up not the content but the mood of his thoughts. He flexed his fingers one after another.

'Sir Hubert Gaily,' she laughed at him.

'Well, it's a good name, you need a good name for a title. Makes it ring.'

'Perhaps she had that in mind all along. Your mother.'

Gaily did not reply. A tall couple walked past them, Americans with buff-coloured mackintoshes and buff-coloured faces. They nodded pleasantly, having seen Gaily and Florence Ames in the Portrait Gallery. There was a doll room, too, and what Gaily had most admired, a clock gallery, with row upon row of assorted timepieces. For his money, Pencote Manor was the best place they had visited, packed with interesting objects.

'But what will she do?' Mrs Ames was saying. At that moment, the sun shifted behind a cloud, and they rose, so as not to get cold.

'Your mother,' she went on, 'if we go away.'

But Gaily had planned this, too, only waited for the courage to mention it.

'I'd like her to go somewhere as well. On a holiday. I can pay for her easily, for a week in a nice hotel.'

Florence Ames had taken his arm as they walked towards the rose gardens, and now he saw that her face was anxious.

'It'd do her the world of good,' he said, 'it's what she needs.'

'But is it what she *wants*? On her own somewhere? Do you really think she would enjoy herself?'

Gaily faltered, not wanting this misgiving of his to be touched upon.

'You don't know Ma,' he said stubbornly.

'No.'

They turned their faces to catch the full scent from rose bush and tree.

'But I know that I shouldn't like it. If it were me, I'm sure I should prefer to stay at home.'

And he knew that, in truth, Ma would, too. She would never go away.

'Could we take her with us?' Florence Ames ventured.

'No, we could not. I'll not do that. I've spent time enough and holidays enough with her in the past.'

He stopped. Ahead of them, the American couple were photographing an Ena Harkness.

'It's you I want to take,' Gaily said, 'it's you.'

149

She touched his arm. 'But we must do something for her,' she said, 'think of something. The right thing.'

They walked on slowly in the sunshine.

'I am not blind,' said Isabel Lavender, 'nor even poor sighted. That is the handwriting of Alida Thorne.'

Kathleen Lavender stood, her left hand shielding the letter against her breast. Lately her sister had taken to opening the post, even stealing it away to her own room. Anything addressed to Kathleen, if she could manage to get hold of it, she slipped on to the hall-stand, later, and the marks where the envelopes had been steamed or peeled apart and put together again were always visible.

'And why should a woman who lives not a quarter of a mile away write a letter to you? What has she to say that could not be said face to face? Why will she not come to the house? What secret is there between you?'

'No secret at all. I do not have secrets.'

'That is an untruth.'

Kathleen Lavender wondered herself why Alida Thorne, whose Italianate handwriting this unmistakably was, should be sending her a letter. The fact alarmed her a little, especially after that last, panic-stricken visit during the storm, when Isabel had so nearly shut the door in Alida's face.

Instinctively, Kathleen felt that the letter must be kept from her sister, though she could not have given a clear reason. And Isabel, in her turn, sensed secrets, a conspiracy.

'Let me see the envelope again,' she said, holding out her hand.

'No. I shall open it later. I must go and make up the laundry.' Kathleen Lavender backed away down the passage, still clutching the envelope close to her.

'Why do you not open it?'

'Oh, Isabel, I will open it later, why do you go on and on about it? I am busy, I must make up the *laundry*.'

It was eight o'clock in the morning. Diagonal black and white floor tiles separated the sisters, Isabel Lavender wearing a black dress, for she always wore black now, and her sister aproned and alarmed.

'Birds of a feather,' Isabel said.

Kathleen hesitated at the kitchen door but her sister said no more as she crossed the hall and began to mount the stairs, back to her own room, back behind the permanently locked door. But, just outside of it, she stopped, and her voice came to Kathleen, down the well of the stairs.

'She too is demented,' Isabel said, 'Alida Thorne. You are in excellent company.'

Kathleen shook her head, as she always did now, an unconscious action to clear away these remarks of her sister, about madness and ill-health. Otherwise, they stuck like burrs in her mind, all the day, and irritated her with their unfairness.

In the kitchen, her left hand went to the laundry book and her right to the radio knob, but like a reflex came her sister's voice. Kathleen Lavender opened the glass-paned door once again.

'And I ask you not to play the wireless,' the voice said, before the key turned again in the lock upstairs.

Kathleen sighed and sat down to the listing of towels, bath sheets, flannelette, pillow-cases, cotton, unaccompanied by the Gold and Silver Waltz, which she had requested three weeks before, on a postcard to the BBC, and which they might even now be playing for her. She stared at the dial of the dead radio, and thought of her own name and address being spoken into silence. Years ago, she had asked for a record to be played, and had listened, to the amusement of her mother and sisters, day after day, through the earphones, with growing disappointment. And now, she had plucked up courage to ask again, it seemed such a harmless thing, but Isabel, as though she knew, had forbidden the playing of the radio, the music could be heard easily upstairs, she said, and disturbed her. Besides, it was a sign of weakness. 'Something is surely lacking in your personality, that you need incessant accompaniment to your activities.' That was three weeks ago. 'But you were never resourceful,' she went on, 'as a child, you could not play alone, you could not exist without pestering Faith and myself.'

Perhaps that had been true, but only because she had been the third child and the baby, and grew used to fond companionship. Nobody had ever taught her to fall back upon herself, it had not been necessary. But it was not true now, she only liked a little music and the charm of learning unexpected facts from strange people over the air.

Table napkins, linen. Four. But perhaps they would not play her record this morning, either, for not many people now could wish to be entertained by the Gold and Silver Waltz.

On the table before her lay Alida Thorne's blue manilla envelope. Kathleen Lavender did not open it.

'Oh, I do not think that was right,' said Dorothea Shottery, her heart sinking at the news. 'You may be quite mistaken, after all, it was only an impression. But to have written a letter . . .'

'I know madness when I see it,' said Alida Thorne firmly, 'and I saw it in Isabel Lavender.'

Dorothea was beside herself with agitation, but sitting on a telephone chair in the hall, with Hastings the cat cramped on her knees, she could not think clearly what to say or do.

'Kathleen Lavender has always been an irresolute woman. She clearly has no idea about what must be done. So I have simply written to her. Someone must take the initiative and the responsibility. The woman is not fit to be in the outside world. She is a danger to herself. You have not seen her, Dorothea, you cannot know.'

Dorothea wondered sadly, why Alida must always be putting people away.

'You can back me up,' she was saying now, and the note of firmness in her voice also sounded like a note of enjoyment. It was a long time since she had seemed so well and vigorous and assured. Dorothea supposed that at least must be a good sign.

'Oh, I do not think I should interfere. I do not see that it has anything to do with me.'

'And yet you are holding a coffee morning, in aid of mental

health, you are setting yourself up as a woman with a sense of social duty.'

Dorothea had not thought to set herself up as anything. 'No,' she began, 'it is not like that, I . . .'

'Send her an invitation. Send it addressed to Isabel.'

'An invitation?'

'To the coffee morning. And state clearly the nature of the cause for which it is being held, underline the words.'

'But that would be unforgivably tactless and unkind. I could not possibly do that, Alida, what has come over you? If you are right, how could that be of any use?'

'It would be a hint, a direct intimation. Kathleen Lavender has always been irresolute, even my letter may well not prompt her.'

'I will not do such a thing.'

'Very well.'

'And neither will you,' Dorothea Shottery ordered, astonished at her own tone of voice. 'I must ask you not to mention it, Alida. You do not realize what distress you may cause.'

'Mental illness is not a sin, there is no shame attached to it, in this day and age. You will do no good by concealing the truth.'

'And you will do harm by cruelly acting upon suspicion and rumour.'

Dorothea put down the telephone and sat on the chair, stroking and stroking the cat nervously, and shaking with anger and distress, because she had not been able to say, clearly and concisely, what needed to be said to Alida Thorne – who herself, Dorothea reflected, had recently behaved in a hysterical and unbalanced manner. No, she had been ill, physically ill, and under strain because of her mother, so that reflection was quite unfair. The cat Hastings shifted heavily on her lap. But it was true, of course, about Isabel. Dorothea had known it ever since the episode of the jewellery, only not allowed herself to admit it in so many words, and to shrug now and disclaim all knowledge and responsibility was surely wrong, because they were friends, after all, someone should care.

No, said Dorothea, standing up stiffly and looking back into the resentful face of the awakened cat, no, but Alida must not be allowed to take these actions, that is by no means the way.

Cruel to be kind, Alida Thorne had often said, in similar contexts, I believe in being cruel to be kind. Perhaps she was right. But Dorothea, going to open a tin of salmon for her cat, did not believe it.

Kathleen Lavender could not believe her eyes.

I was most alarmed [the letter read] to see how Isabel behaved when I last visited you. For some time, I could not at all make out her manner, and wondered if I had done something, albeit unconsciously, to offend her. But of course I have not. I know precisely how it is, living in close proximity to a relative with whom all is not well, and so I can understand that you have tried to gloss over the symptoms. An outsider though not, of course, a stranger, is more fortunate. I must tell you that to me it is evident that Isabel is unwell – in a word, mentally unbalanced. It cannot be otherwise, given her manner towards me.

Now, something must be done, it is quite wrong for you to continue in this way. Your sister needs treatment of a kind which cannot be got from Doctor Sparrow – in whom I have no confidence whatsoever. Nevertheless, he is the first person to approach, and quickly. He must be told.

I am sure you will appreciate that I am better able to write to you because of my experience recently, and because of my health, than to pay you a visit. A further encounter with your sister, in her present frame of mind, could be most upsetting.

Kathleen Lavender's hand shook gently. And then, she jumped up, her face suffused with alarm, and turned the key of her bedroom door. Isabel must not see the letter, and she would *want* to see it, would search for it when Kathleen was out, would ask and ask about it. What was to be said? Secrets, secrets, yes, now there were secrets and Kathleen was uneasy, did not want anything to do with them.

Now, she thought, let me sit down, for I must think about this carefully. Isabel tells me I am going out of my mind with age, or some illness, and I have wondered, but only because she confuses me and because, if someone insists and insists, doubt is bound to follow. But I am well, I am sane, I am altogether myself. For self-inquiry follows hard upon doubt, and by that means the truth is attained.

But I have, in my turn, wondered about *her*, and suppressed such disloyalty. Yet it is true. She buried the jewellery in the garden, and parcelled up books and clothes and ornaments for sale, she wears black constantly, and locks herself away, she will not eat fish, and in the night she walks about the house trying doors and windows, she will not have me talk to her, she cannot bear noise or visitors or new recipes, she is afraid of letters and of the barking of dogs. And now that Alida Thorne has brought it into the open, I can see a pattern and recognize the truth. My sister needs help.

For a moment, too, she thought how tactless and interfering, how rude and unkind and malicious of Alida to write this letter. A gloating and impertinent letter. It insinuates, Kathleen said, that I am too stupid and ignorant to understand the true situation. How dare Alida!

She sat, turning the sheet of paper over and over in her hands, astonished at her own anger, and then growing calm. For the truth was unpleasant and the truth was that she had been afraid of Isabel, had let matters ride, hoping. That had been wrong and cowardly. She deserved such a letter, she was justly reprimanded. Something must be done.

'What are you doing? Why have you locked yourself away?'

Like the heroine in a Victorian romance, Kathleen stuffed Alida Thorne's letter down the front of her dress, between corset and skin, and opened the door to her sister.

'She has taken to locking herself away, in her room alone. And that cannot be a good thing.'

'I see. But you say she appears to be physically well.'

'She has never been sick in her life.'

'That is no reason why . . .'

'I know she is quite well, Doctor Sparrow. It is not her body, it is her *mind*. As I have said.'

'And you could not get your sister to come to me of her own accord? Has she some fear of consulting me?'

'Oh, I have not asked her. I felt that it was best to do all this unbeknown to her.'

'Why was that, exactly?'

Isabel Lavender stared at him. 'My sister is mentally unbalanced,' she said, rather loudly, as though this were sufficient explanation for all things.

Doctor Sparrow, hair thinning, leaned back and tapped his pencil. She wore black still, for the other sister, months dead. But nothing in this village was surprising to him now, so many of them behaved oddly. Women, ageing, peculiar.

'If what you say is true . . .'

He met her gaze without faltering. 'I shall of course wish to see your sister, Miss Lavender.'

'Naturally. I understand that she cannot be taken without an examination. You will find . . .'

'Taken? Taken where?'

Isabel Lavender sighed. But it was Doctor Sparrow who went on. 'Your sister may or may not require some kind of treatment. That will be for me to decide. But unless she is severely ill, nobody is going to take her anywhere. No, do not interrupt me for a moment. Not into a hospital or home or asylum, or wherever else you wish her to be confined at your own whim. It is convenient to come here and expect me to relieve you of a troublesome relative. You would perhaps be surprised how often it happens, how many people would sign away their mothers and fathers, grandparents, children – their sisters and their cousins and their aunts, indeed.'

Isabel Lavender did not smile.

'You will not succeed, not in my surgery. If you send your sister to me – and I am sure she can be persuaded – or, in the event of a serious disturbance, you telephone for a visit, I will treat her with pleasure. And these days, most symptoms can be controlled with ease, you should have no trouble of any kind with her. Is she depressed at all?'

'I would not know the workings of her mind.'

Isabel Lavender stood.

'Oh forgive me, I thought that you did,' said Doctor Sparrow.

'We are at liberty to change our doctor. I am at liberty to obtain specialist advice.'

'Indeed – the former is your privilege. And if you are prepared to pay for it, so is the latter.'

Doctor Sparrow smiled – a sweet-faced smile, and watched the thin woman until she put her hand to the door-knob. Then, he asked, 'And *you* are perfectly well, in every respect, Miss Lavender?'

She halted and then inclined her head. Doctor Sparrow came round the table briskly, wishing her good morning. 'And,' he said, even taking her through the surgery to the street door, and seeing her courteously through that, 'and do not forget that many people lock their own doors. It is a convenient indication of the desire for privacy. Good morning to you.'

It was many weeks since Isabel had gone out. Kathleen Lavender did not know where and did not wish to know, she was only delighted. Twice, she had walked upstairs and down, all round the house, like touching wood, for fear she imagined it, and her sister still lurked upstairs behind the locked door.

But she did not, and now Kathleen returned to the kitchen, the one part of the house into which Isabel never came, the territory she could feel as her own, and comforting. She turned on the knob of the wireless set and, as though by magic, came the notes of the Gold and Silver Waltz, though it could not be playing for her, it was not a request programme. Kathleen Lavender took a small step forward and to the side, and then, because the kitchen was large, and she was suddenly happy, she began to dance gently, singing in time.

At the end of the dancing, she remembered Alida Thorne's letter, and burned it, while she had an opportunity, but what it said could not be destroyed or forgotten. Isabel was unbalanced, needed treatment, needed, even, to be put away. Thinking of life without Isabel, of the doors and windows of this house all open, and visitors to lunch and tea, of card parties, shopping expeditions, music on the wireless at all possible times, Kathleen Lavender's heart rose. She had never wanted to go away, had always loved home and family and everyday occupations, the baking and brushing and gardening. She did not wish to go away anywhere now, only to have freedom of coming and going, and no fear or shame, to have what meals she chose and any amount of music.

They had finished the Gold and Silver Waltz and launched into a Scottish medley, Bonny Dundee, Ye Banks and Braes, The Road to the Isles. She turned the volume up and began to dance again.

Chapter Fourteen

'Good afternoon,' she said. 'My name is Florence Ames.'

Ma Gaily pulled another yard of knitting wool up from the ball in her apron pocket.

'I'm a friend – a friend of your son's . . .'

'I know,' Ma said. 'So you'd better come in, hadn't you?'

In the back parlour, the cat leaped without hesitation on to Mrs Ames' knee, turned about twice and curled up into sleep. Ma was impressed.

'You're honoured,' she said. 'He knows people, that one.'

Florence Ames looked about her, and then at the row of photographs on the mantelpiece, and it was all as he had described and as she expected. She recognized them, from what he had said, the two girls, Alice and May, Eric, the dead little brother, and Gaily himself, with a scrubbed schoolboy face.

'Yes,' said Ma, 'that one's him.' She was still standing knitting from the wool in her pocket. 'I'll make us a pot of tea,' she said, 'when I've done this row.'

Florence Ames liked her, and would like the tea. 'You seemed to know who I was,' she said later, sitting with her coat and hat off, the cat still settled on her knee.

'I know him. He mentioned it once though never again. Besides, it's not before time, is it?'

'That I came here?'

'No,' Ma said, 'that he found someone.'

Florence Ames looked up, startled. This was not as she had heard the situation, not as she had imagined it.

'They've been a let-down to me,' Ma said, 'my children. There's my sister now, married and surrounded with them, grandchildren and sons and daughters-in-law, and all their families, never at a loss. They've been a let-down.'

'I have a boy.'

'And?'

'I hardly see him. Perhaps he is a disappointment, too.'

'It's the way,' said Ma.

'But you have *this* son. You've always had his company.'

'Two girls off abroad as fast as their legs would take them. And one dead, the youngest boy. You hadn't inoculations in those days, you expected to bury one or two.'

'You have had his company,' Florence Ames persisted.

Ma shrugged. 'Forever under your feet, though,' she said, 'he grew too big from the start, too big for chairs and too tall for the doorways. Forever knocking things over.'

'I hadn't noticed that.'

'Have another cup.'

'Yes, thank you.'

In the hall, a clock chimed the half hour. 'And what,' asked Ma, smiling to herself, 'do you *call* him?'

Florence Ames drank her tea, acknowledging the canny way this other woman had of putting her finger on point after point. Because they had talked and thought and even joked about it, and how hard it had been from the very beginning, this business of names. Neither of them had easy ones, names you could use, still less pair together, they were names to be looked at, on paper, that was all. To start with, they had carefully *avoided* them altogether, called one another nothing at all, and then she had started to experiment, saying Hubert, or Bert, or plain Gaily, but in the end had decided to make do with Hugh as the least improbable. But he still called her nothing, and though her second Christian name was Ann, and she would have liked him to use that, make it his name for her, for some reason she had not brought herself to ask him.

'Hugh,' she said now, 'but perhaps you don't like that.'

'*I'm* not bothered, it's not to do with me. Call him how you like.'

Ma got up heavily, stuck the knitting needles through the ball and set it aside. 'You'd better stay for your tea, then,' she said, 'I'll do a pie.' Florence Ames knew that there was no possible way she could refuse, and she did not really want to refuse on her own account, only thought of Gaily and what he might say. He did not know that she had decided to come.

'You can talk to me in the kitchen, you know,' said Ma, 'unless you'd rather not.'

Florence Ames set down the cat and followed her.

But he did not mind, after all, he was only surprised to see her there, setting the tea table for Ma and talking about late chrysanthemums. It was all right, too, he could see that, Ma was enjoying herself.

'The cat went to her,' she said, 'straight away, up on her knees and right as ninepence.'

'It's only called cat,' Gaily told Florence Ames, 'we've never given it a proper name, it answers to cat.'

She smiled at him, and he saw how happy she was to be there, how he should have brought her long before.

'There's letters for you,' Ma said, slicing open the pie, 'two letters.'

He went to the mantelshelf, and in the mirror Ma's eyes met his.

'One,' she said conversationally, 'has got "Come to Sunny Scarborough, Watering Place of the North", stamped on it.'

Florence Ames did not look up.

'Oh, yes,' said Gaily, 'so it has.' He sat down to his pie.

'You're close,' Ma scraped out the last flakes of pastry on to his plate. 'Always were.'

'It's a long time,' said Florence Ames, 'since I tasted pie like this. A very long time.'

Ma nodded, and in the kitchen, the cat scraped round his dish of gravy with an abrasive tongue.

'So you're going on holiday,' Ma said in the end, 'you're going off to a resort, with your free week.'

But she looked at Florence Ames, not at him.

'Now ...' Gaily began.

'Oh, *I've* nothing to say. You do as you please.'

'The point is, we want you to have a holiday, too. We thought you could go off somewhere and have a good rest.'

'I never needed a rest in my life yet.'

'Change,' Gaily said patiently, 'change of air, change of face.'

'Where are you thinking of packing me off to?'

'Not packing you off anywhere, giving you a holiday. It's what everybody should have, you ought to be grateful.'

'I ought?'

'You'd be waited on, there'd be no housework. Think of that.'

'The dust'd settle in here, wouldn't it, waiting till I got back. It's always twice as hard after you've been away from a place.'

'You've not . . .' Gaily's voice rose, 'you've not been away, not for years, how can you recall what happens?'

'I'm not stopping *you*, you go where you fancy – do you good. I shall have you from under my feet, I can have a good turn-out.' She looked at Florence Ames. 'He hoards,' she said confidentially, 'clutters his room. With those models.'

'We want you to enjoy yourself as well,' Gaily said again doggedly. 'You ought to be grateful. I've given it a lot of thought.'

'Thank you very much.'

Florence Ames, unaware that the balance of good humour was not yet destroyed between them, said anxiously, 'When you've finished St Paul's, for the fête, you could do a model of Pencote Manor.'

'I'd thought of it.' He took his pipe from the bookcase corner. One pipe a day, that was all, after tea. It settled your stomach.

'And I'll do the pots. You can sit down.' Florence Ames noticed herself falling into the other woman's way of talking. You didn't add decorative words, unnecessary politenesses, nor hesitate over a sentence, wasting your breath.

'Thank you very much.' Ma Gaily took the cat on to her knee, and settled for the evening, her plump fingers moving over the four needles.

'Scarborough's a nice place,' she said, 'the air's bracing. You'd enjoy yourself there.'

And Gaily, taking advantage of the good humour, mentioned the garden fête.

'I've been asked to give a hand, advise about the tents and setting up stalls and so forth . . .'

'You'll enjoy that,' Ma said, 'king-pin.'

'I know about fêtes. I can save them trouble and expense. There's nothing you can't tell me about fêtes.'

'You will come,' said Florence Ames, through the kitchen doorway. 'There's a very good bus service and you'd have a real day out. I have a friend in the village.'

'You don't let the grass grow,' said Ma, through the needle in her mouth.

'You took me to a fête,' Gaily said, lying back behind the puffballs of pipe-smoke. 'When I was a lad.'

Ma raised her eyebrows. He felt suitably mocked.

'Next Saturday,' Florence Ames came in, hands blotched red from the dishwater. 'That's all arranged.'

'Maybe,' said Ma, 'I haven't a summer coat.'

Gaily looked across at Mrs Ames, but saw that she knew how to deal with this, as with all things as long as Ma didn't wear her down, too, as long as the liking remained. Because Ma was happy enough just now, a pie had been baked, the clearing away and washing up of dishes had been relinquished to another, as never before.

'Besides,' she was now saying, casting off at high speed, in the swing of the conversation, 'it generally rains for garden fêtes. That's the way of them. You're better off at home.'

'We'll see anyway,' said Florence Ames, holding out her hands for the new skein of wool. Gaily wanted to laugh about it all, and almost did laugh, having to bend down and pick the cat up instead, as a cover. There was nothing, nothing at all to worry about.

'Now!' someone said.

Eleanor Thorne took her hands away from her eyes, very slowly, for she had a lifelong fear of being startled.

'Oh!' she said, but the word only came out on a breath, without sound. 'Oh.'

'You didn't guess, you see, you didn't guess at all!' said Mrs Clemency, shaking harder, with the delight of giving such a surprise and of having held on to her secret. And behind, and to all sides of her, the others sat and stood and nodded and smiled and murmured.

The cake was square and of two tiers, like a small wedding cake, with white columns between, and around the edges ribbons and trellis of pale blue icing, interlaced with roses at each knot. Around the top were the candles, ninety of them, flickering and glowing white and gold in the long drawing-room.

'Come,' said Miss Cress, smiling and holding out her left hand, 'come and cut your cake, Mrs Thorne.'

'Yes, oh yes! That is what you must do now!' At her side, Mrs Clemency almost danced for joy. 'You must cut it, just like a bride! And you didn't guess, I didn't let slip a word.'

'Cut it,' they said, 'cut it, cut the cake.'

Eleanor Thorne looked around her, dazed and dazzled by the candles and by their faces, the faces of her new friends. 'Oh,' she said, 'it is too much! For someone who is ninety years old, it is far too much!'

They all laughed, then, and murmured, and because she would not disappoint them, she advanced and cut her cake, firmly and without help, and then stood back triumphant, while they sang to her and smiled and called out their greetings.

Nor, thought Eleanor, shall I weep. I do not believe in embarrassing others, in making a sentimental scene. I am happy and content and they shall enjoy my ninetieth birthday, there is to be no weeping.

'Thank you,' she said to them, 'oh, thank you, thank you!' and wanted to say more, say, I am happy here, I have not been so happy as this for years, you are all my friends and I am at home in this house. Instead, she pressed the hand of Miss Cress, and they broke into little groups for tea, chinking plates and murmuring and moving chairs, and she went among them slowly, answering questions about her cards and inviting them up to see her gifts, thanking, thanking.

Beside her came Mrs Clemency, rolling the wheels of her chair, most anxious to be seen as her friend.

'And tonight, my daughter will come,' Eleanor said to the deaf Miss Bunce.

'Alida. She will come for an hour.'

'She has had four visitors, you know, four visitors already, one after another,' Mrs Clemency told them all. 'Imagine!'

'Oh, it has been a day,' Eleanor Thorne sat down abruptly on a chair. 'It has been a day! I am ninety years old.'

'I will tell her,' said Miss Cress, 'of course.'

'It is the rain, that and having been unwell, and now with the beginning of a cold. I would not want to give it to her, and to have it spread all about the house. Colds spread like a forest fire among the old, I do know that.'

'It is most kind of you to be so concerned, Miss Thorne.'

'That,' said Alida, 'is the way I was brought up. To care about others, to think of others.'

The Matron said nothing, only stared at a wild-life calendar on the wall of her office.

'In any case, by tonight, I am sure my mother will be tired.'

'She has had a most happy day, thank you,' said Miss Cress, 'with four visitors and gifts and cards. The lunch she chose herself – all our birthday residents choose their own lunch, and now she is eating her birthday cake.'

'Someone has sent my mother a cake?'

'We always have one baked and iced for anyone with a special birthday. Ninety is a special birthday, you will agree. It is a large cake, that everyone here can share.'

'And will that . . .' Alida Thorne changed her tone of voice, '. . . the cake, that is, will that be paid for out . . .'

'Oh, do not worry about the payment, do not alarm yourself at all, Miss Thorne. I would not have you troubled on that account. That is taken care of by a bequest which one of our patients made some years ago, specifically, it was to provide for a Christmas cake each year, and for these specially baked birthday cakes for particular patients. Particularly old, that is, or particularly lonely and in need of such an attention. Good evening to you, Miss Thorne.'

But Miss Cress was not really angry. On the calendar, two young giraffes plucked at overhanging branches. Miss Cress stared at them, afraid, as she so often became afraid, sitting here, that she might weep.

Chapter Fifteen

'The sun is shining, the day is going to be fine!'

The Reverend George Jocelyn Bottingley sat up in bed, stretched, accepted the cup of tea from his wife. 'But it is early,' he said doubtfully, 'you don't think it may cloud over?'

'There is a mist, a heat haze over Tantamount Hill,' she said.

'Ah!'

'It is our garden fête, and therefore it will be fine!'

He believed her, as he lay back on two pillows to look out of the window at the blue square of sky. It was seven-fifteen. A satisfactory beginning to the day.

Gaily's alarm had sounded at seven o'clock, as though it were a working day, and the sunshaft between the curtains struck on his completed model of St Paul's Cathedral, and illuminated the dome, cut carefully from a child's ball.

'Seventeen thousand, four hundred and thirty-eight,' Gaily said contentedly to himself. 'Seventeen thousand, four hundred and thirty-eight.' Though he would not forget the number of matchsticks, which only he knew and which was not to be written down at all. The guesses would be sorted and eliminated by him and Florence Ames, to whom he would tell the correct number in the course of the afternoon.

In the kitchen below, Ma dropped a saucepan on the floor, in case he had overslept the alarm.

'I heard,' Gaily said to himself, 'I heard,' and got out to let the cat into his room. It knew better than to paw at his models.

And across the town, Florence Ames was already up and sitting at her breakfast, a flutter of excitement playing inside her stomach. She laughed at herself.

Haverstock was awake and talking of the sunshine, and Dorothea Shottery clapped for joy as she saw the heat haze above her lawn. Only Isabel Lavender slept on, unconcerned with garden fêtes, despising the common enthusiasm. In the kitchen, her sister baked, in secret, the final batch of the promised cakes, and opened the garden door while she did so, to enjoy the August morning.

'What a day!' said Florence Ames, looking out at field upon field of corn, through the windows of the train. 'What a perfect day!'

Beside her, Ma Gaily, pinched into her best blue suit and formal in a hat, said nothing.

'You'll be too hot,' Gaily had told her, 'you'll be scorched.'

'I've been caught outdoors before. There's time for the temperature to drop yet. Drop right down. Anything can happen.'

'In August . . .?'

But Ma knew her seasons and wore the blue suit. August, she said, was a treacherous month, that was well known.

'It'll not be my fault if the marquees have come down,' Gaily said, satisfied with the previous day's work, when he had headed a team of men manoeuvring this and that to a careful plan. 'No.'

Florence Ames touched his hand. 'At least there hasn't been a wind,' she said.

'I hope it's not going to be crowded. I can't stand a crowd in a tent,' Ma said.

'There's plenty of things going on outside of them. Besides, we want a crowd, a crowd'll bring in some money. That's what we're hoping for.'

'Oh,' said Ma, glancing out of the window at a petrol station, 'we are, are we?'

Dorothea laid out fifty-two jars of lemon curd and stood back to admire them, thick and glistering in the sunlight. 'There,' she said, 'that is everything arranged and now we are ready.'

'I'll have a jar of that,' Ma said, 'before it goes.'

She had a bag, huge and made of brown leather-cloth. She intended to buy what was wholesome and value for money and ignore what was not.

'Never buy tinned stuff,' she told Dorothea Shottery, 'at a fête. They mark it up when it's for charity, you pay through the nose. I don't see the sense.'

'But don't people like something for their money rather than just giving?' She twitched at the white cloth covering the trestle.

'People only give away to fêtes and jumble sales what they've had stuck at the back of their cupboards, things they're glad to be rid of. That's all. They've maybe been there for years.'

She picked up a dented tin. 'Whole guavas in heavy syrup,' she read aloud. 'You see? Somebody's once bought those and then not fancied them because they don't really know what they are. Bought them cheap because the tin was dented. That's why those are here.'

'Oh, dear!' said Dorothea. She had been proud of her stall. But Ma Gaily nodded to the jars of jam and curd and pickle, to the baskets of fruit and eggs. 'That's what people want,' she said confidentially, 'that's what'll go, you see. The home-mades. Don't worry about that.'

Dorothea, for three years past holder of the provisions stall, knew that she was right.

Behind them, Gaily stood, surveying the field like a general, enjoying the sight of the flags flying, and the hurdy-gurdy music. 'That's all right,' he said.

'It looks very well.' Florence Ames smiled at him. 'You should have a pair of binoculars.'

He was not too proud of the correctly erected marquees, the well-positioned donkey run, the awnings and the overall look of the thing, to laugh at himself.

'We are ready,' said the Reverend George Jocelyn Bottingley, clapping his hands, 'the sun is shining and the gates can be opened. We are quite ready.'

'That's it,' said Ma, poking at a melon for its softness, 'let them all come.'

Slowly, the children's roundabouts began to turn, flashing

gold and green, red and blue, and the horses danced up and down, up and down, to the music, and in the sunshine, the gates were opened, everybody came.

'It is most kind of you, Doctor Sparrow, most kind. You cannot think how very grateful we are and what a treat this is!'

'Oh, I'm sure I can!' And Doctor Sparrow smiled in the driving mirror at Mrs Clemency, who sat and shook among rugs, on her way to the garden fête.

'But it is only for a short time, now, I am not allowing you to be exhausted. Ladies of ninety years old!' For Eleanor Thorne sat beside him, in her best purple coat, still dazed by the concatenation of excitements.

'We are going to spend money, you know,' said deaf Miss Bunce, in the back next to Mrs Clemency. 'Oh yes, we shall pay our way.'

'Everyone,' said Doctor Sparrow, drawing up at the gates, 'is to enjoy themselves.'

It is that wireless, said Isabel Lavender, getting to her feet, it is that loud music again, in spite of what I have said, and I will not have it.

But when she unlocked the door and called out sharply, there was no answer, the music did not stop and when she went downstairs, it was to find the house empty.

Yet I am hearing music, brass band music and an organ, quite clearly, she said, and her own voice echoed in the quiet hall. My ears must need attention.

One by one, she inserted her finger into each ear and pulled it out again sharply, hearing a little pop and a cracking noise, and then turned her head this way and that and swallowed hard. The music went on.

'Are you sure?' asked John Fitzsimmons, 'I mean – it's hard – it's not easy, you know.' It was difficult to know how to put it. Ma Gaily glared at him, holding out her sixpenny piece, but did not answer.

'Well, all right, who am I to say?' And he glanced around for support.

'Here,' she said, giving her bags to Florence Ames, and stepped back. Quite a crowd, onlookers and cheerers, were around the three-balls-for-sixpence booth.

'Just be careful,' Gaily said, but Florence Ames frowned, knowing that it was all right, and he stood, silent again.

'Right! Now then!' shouted John Fitzsimmons, from the greengrocers, and looked embarrassed. But the little wooden balls went home, one, two, three, cans clattered down, to the surprise and applause of the crowd.

'That is just typical,' said Gaily, 'just typical, that is.' He watched Ma collect a polystyrene bowl full of hyacinth bulbs planted ready for the autumn flowering. 'That'll save a chore,' she said, taking her bags from Florence Ames, 'I've no need to think about bulbs for Christmas.' She caught sight of Gaily's expression. 'You needn't look,' she said, 'I've sent down more of those than you've had hot dinners. I know what I'm doing at a garden fête. And she turned away. 'I'm going for my tea,' she said.

Alida Thorne stared and stared. The man was here again, the man who had worn boots and hung about at Faith Lavender's funeral. She watched him across the tea-tent, handing a plate of fancy cakes to a fat woman, unsuitably dressed in navy-blue wool, and to Florence Ames, the friend of Dorothea. Alida did not wish to be seen by Florence Ames. There had been the recent episodes, after she had suffered her attack and now, better forgotten, for if she made her way through the hot crowd, Mrs Ames, who had once been a nurse, might refer to the incident in too loud a voice. Besides, she would not wish to be introduced to the man, they could have nothing whatsoever in common to talk about.

Clutching handbag and tea-cup and, ridiculously, a coconut, Alida Thorne turned away. And, after one shock, received another. Beside the urns and the rows of white utility cups and saucers, sat her own mother, on a straight-backed chair. She was talking to Mrs Clemency with the senile tremor, who shared her room, and to the Rector of Haverstock. Alida Thorne felt faint, her mother, of ninety years old and demented, had no right to be here, Miss Cress must truly be an irresponsible and careless woman. And not a word had been said, no permission had been asked or granted. So, it is for this that I pay two-thirds of my income, Alida thought, for my mother to risk her health and senses in a crowded tea-tent on a broiling hot August day. Not for proper care and good food and a private room. And when she is taken ill in the night, I shall be sent for in the confusion. I shall suffer the anxiety and stress. Oh, it is too bad! Alida was beside herself with irritation, and with the heat, wishing that she had not worn a close-fitting hat. But there was nothing to be done, and her disapproval could not be expressed, because she could not move. The marquee had filled up, voices chattered and cups chinked upon saucers, and the space between Alida and her mother was quite blocked. Nor could she see the matron, and wondered who might be in charge of the two old women.

There was a smell, too, a hot, thick smell of canvas and trampled grass, women's powder and brewing tea. The entrance, an oblong of sky and fresh air, was very far away. A line of sweat broke out through the skin on Alida Thorne's forehead. I cannot get out, she thought, I cannot breathe, it is happening to me again. The voices about her swayed and rose like waves of the sea and, in her left hand, the cake plate trembled.

Isabel Lavender did not intend to walk through the gates. She had remembered the garden fête and tracked down the source of the music. Now, there was only a complaint to be made to the authorities about brass bands and fairground organs and the wild shriekings of uncontrollable children. The letter would mention the disturbance of the peace, ratepayers and the rights of the elderly. But she had to come and see the situation, to gather what facts were available about the noise. She began to walk away, and then saw her sister, several yards beyond the fence, handing something in a white paper bag to a woman in green. Isabel Lavender returned, and made her way through the gates, brushing aside the boy who importuned her for ticket money. She did not expect to see a member of her own family selling behind some stall. Under her feet, she felt the grass trampled and hot.

'This is a fine example to set the community!' she said to her sister, and am I to have no tea today?'

Kathleen Lavender swung round, her mouth pursed in the act of counting change.

'I am to sit at home, alone in the house, and there is to be no tea, because you are standing in the sun selling *cakes* to all comers.'

'Oh, now Isabel, I have told . . .'

'And cakes . . .' Isabel Lavender went on, 'from our own kitchen.' She pointed to a vermicelli-scattered chocolate sandwich, priced at three shillings and sixpence. 'Is that, or is that not, the cake I saw being decorated by you yesterday evening?'

'Of course it is,' said Kathleen Lavender angry but uneasy, too, because of the curious onlookers and the approach of the Reverend Mr Bottingley. 'Of course, I have told you about the cakes, I told you weeks ago. I clearly recall the day, it was . . .'

'You did not say that we, out of our own larder and pockets, were to provide the ingredients, you did not mention the fact that you were to stand behind a counter and *sell*. You simply mentioned that there was to be a stall, and that you were to be in charge.'

'But what else did you imagine I could mean by that?'

'Our money, such as we have, has been spent on the buying of butter and flour and eggs and chocolate, to stock this stall. I do not recollect that you ever asked my opinion on the matter.'

'We have not provided *all* the cakes, of course we have not. And please lower your voice, Isabel, you will be overheard.'

'I fully intend,' said her sister, removing her gloves, 'to be overheard. Anyone may witness what I am about to do.'

And she picked up the vermicelli chocolate cake, looking about her on the stall, for a suitable paper bag.

'Miss Lavender, Miss Isabel Lavender, how very . . .' The Reverend George Jocelyn Bottingley was red and sweating and cordial in his tight collar, his hand outstretched in greeting. Isabel Lavender ignored the hand and, behind the trestles, her sister was flushed and trembling with shame and rage.

'And you are buying a cake!' said the Rector, 'how very kind of you! Not content with . . .'

'I am buying nothing,' Isabel Lavender emptied a dozen iced buns into another bag, shaking off her sister's restraining hand. 'And what else is there?' she asked, 'from our own larder? Tell me, I would be grateful to know. Especially since there is to be no tea.'

Kathleen Lavender burst into tears.

'Seventeen thousand four hundred,' said Mrs Clemency firmly, 'and one.' Gaily did not flicker, did not so much as glance at Florence Ames, only set down the number that was Mrs Clemency's guess, and took the sixpence.

'It is a very nice model,' Eleanor Thorne said, 'it is some time since I saw St Paul's Cathedral, but this looks most accurate and beautifully done.'

'That is St Paul's Cathedral,' said the deaf Miss Bunce.

'Yes, dear, we know. It has a label, do you see?'

But Miss Bunce, smiling, had moved on.

'Whoever made that,' said Mrs Clemency, her face suffused with sudden mirth, 'whoever made that would have to have a steady hand. It would never do . . .' she took Eleanor Thorne's arm and rocked a little with laughter, 'never do, as a hobby for *me*!' And because of her own delighted laughter, everyone about the stall smiled, too, and did not feel ashamed.

'Excuse me,' said Eleanor Thorne to Florence Ames, 'you seem to be the lady in charge, though I am afraid we have never met. But who made this beautiful model? From where has it come?'

Gaily busied himself with the papers on which the guesses were recorded, the flesh just below his ears rising red.

'Now,' said Doctor Sparrow, joining their group, 'another quarter of an hour, ladies. I am obeying Miss Cress, you see, to the letter, and besides, I have a surgery to go to. Another quarter of an hour.'And he, too, looked down at the model of St Paul's Cathedral. 'Four thousand and eighty,' he said, handing over his sixpence, and looking satisfied. 'Four thousand and eighty and not a matchstick more.'

Gaily, expressionless, wrote down the number. 'Doctor Sparrow,' he repeated.

'Doctor Sparrow,' a voice called, over the hurdy-gurdy and the knocking of balls against tins and coconuts. 'Doctor Sparrow has gone? Someone is ill, someone has collapsed in the tea-tent.'

Gaily lifted his head and looked at Florence Ames, sharing a thought.

'You needn't take on,' said Ma, coming up to them, 'I'm here, I'm going to make myself useful.' She gave her bags to Gaily to set behind the stall.

'You should know better,' she told him, over her shoulder, 'than to think of me passing out. I thrive on heat.'

Florence Ames began to laugh, looking at the list of guesses over Gaily's shoulder.

'Right,' Ma said, going round behind the trestles of the provisions stall. 'You can go for your tea.'

Dorothea went, gratefully. It was very hot indeed.

'Roll up,' said Ma, quietly, experimentally, and then nodded, her eye turned away from her son, and Florence Ames. 'Roll up, come along, buy your groceries, buy your eggs, four bob a dozen, beautiful brown eggs! Everything home-made, roll up, come along then, roll up.'

They began to do so.

Doctor Sparrow was very patient. He had escorted Alida Thorne from the tea-tent, shooed away the crowd of helpers and eavesdroppers, and now, she was sitting in his car, being driven to her home. He had been careful, too, to avoid any encounter between mother and daughter.

'I shall go to bed,' Alida said, 'straight to bed.'

'Oh, unless you feel really ill, I shouldn't think that necessary. Put your feet up for half an hour, you'll be right as rain.'

She could not bring herself to reply. The man was careless and ignorant. Had she not just collapsed, might she not have suffered a heart attack, however mild?

'You did not appear to lose consciousness at all, though it was much too hot in that marquee. Many less hardy souls would have fainted away.'

'But I have never been able to withstand extremes of temperature.'

Doctor Sparrow lowered the window of the car a little further, full of consideration.

'Claustrophobia,' he said, 'is a very common affliction. Distressing but controllable. It tends to get better spontaneously, given time.'

Alida flushed with anger. 'There is nothing wrong with my nerves, Doctor Sparrow, I do not suffer in that way. My nerves are quite in order.'

'Oh, I am sure they are! Very few people do suffer from what are so often known as nerves. It is a popular misnomer.'

Alida did not care to ask for what it was a misnomer, and did not welcome Doctor Sparrow's medical chat. For the rest of the short journey they were silent, and half-way round the green they passed Isabel Lavender, marching towards her own house, her hands full of white paper bags. Alida Thorne saw her face, for a second, in passing, the skin tight and the mouth working, before she averted her own to avoid recognition.

'You will be perfectly all right,' said Doctor Sparrow, opening the car door and giving her his hand. 'Have a short rest, and then open all the windows and find yourself something to do. You are quite well now.'

Alida barely managed to thank him for his trouble.

'Don't forget we've a train to catch,' Gaily said, watching Ma accept a second glass of sherry. But he was content, his own glass of beer in his hand, to sit in the last of the sun, on Dorothea Shottery's lawn, and never to catch a train.

'I do not know what I would have done without you,' Dorothea said, 'what any of us would have done, without the Gailys. I have made such a profit as I never dreamed of, never *dreamed* . . . and sold everything.'

'Even,' said Ma, 'a tin of Whole Guavas.'

'The Rector was delighted, quite delighted, he told me so. Things have never gone so smoothly and successfully before.'

The cat Hastings stalked out of the shrubbery and began to smell his way around Ma Gaily's skirt, and in a flurry of violet and old rose, the sun dropped out of sight.

'You enjoyed yourself, then,' said Gaily, 'didn't you?'

'Cats,' said Ma, bending forward, 'know those that like them.'

'The train,' Florence Ames got up slowly, 'really we must not miss the train.'

'No,' said Ma, 'not with free tickets, we must not.'

And, in the meadow, a team of boy scouts walked in line, up and down, picking up the last of the litter and dropping it straight into paper sacks.

'Do you think we could have someone to fix up a little light,' asked Mrs Clemency thoughtfully, 'so that we could switch it on at night? It would shine through the windows, it would complete the picture.'

'We will ask,' said Eleanor Thorne, tired beyond belief, 'tomorrow, Mrs Clemency, tomorrow.'

But for another hour, Mrs Clemency did not sleep. The model of St Paul's Cathedral stood beside her on a small table, especially provided by Miss Cress. Every now and then, she stretched out a shaking hand, to touch the roof of it happily.

'Such a display,' said Isabel Lavender, picking up her cup of malted milk. 'Such a ludicrous display in a woman of your age. I was deeply ashamed.'

'Display? You are the one to talk to me of displays?' Kathleen Lavender had overcome her tears and embarrassment and confusion, and for once in her life she allowed anger and resentment to break through. Her day had been blackened and spoiled, there was no pleasure left, living with this bitter and demented sister.

'I shall wish you good night,' said Isabel.

But, as she closed the door, Kathleen turned the knob of the wireless and there came the voices of a girls' choir. She waited. The door opened again. She said, 'And please, do not tell me again about the wireless. It is mine and the volume is low, it cannot possibly disturb you. Please do not make yourself disagreeable over the matter, let us have a little peace. Harmony and peace.'

Her heart was pounding from fright, and the effort of putting her shoulder against such a wall. But Isabel said nothing. Isabel turned away and went out of the room and up the stairs, saying nothing.

'Now, you will come to stay with me – that is all settled,' said Dorothea Shottery, seeing them on to the last train. 'These two good people shall take themselves off to the seaside and you will come to stay with me. I will not take no for an answer.'

Ma Gaily said nothing, nothing at all, while the train raced through the dark countryside. Gaily put his hand over that of Florence Ames. But walking down the street, towards Maxstone Villas, Ma said, 'I know a lady when I meet one. You can't tell me anything about *that*.' He knew that she would go.

The Reverend George Jocelyn Bottingley paused, looking out of his bedroom window at the deserted meadow.

'You see, it did not rain,' said his wife, 'did I not tell you?'

'Yes. You did.'

'I enjoyed myself,' Mary Bottingley switched off the light. 'It has been a most happy day.'

In her bedroom, Alida Thorne lay awake, her arms rigid by her sides. She had made up her mind about it, and there was no other way. But all the same, she could not sleep.

Chapter Sixteen

ETHEL MACVICCARS, her teaching colleague who now lived in Cheltenham, took longer to reply to the letter than Alida thought either necessary or polite. Eleven days, and during that time Alida slept badly, ate little and saw as few of her neighbours as possible. She wished that it had not been necessary to ask the help of a third party. But Ethel Macviccars was discreet and respectable, and moreover, lived some distance away. It was four and a half years since they had met.

The name of the specialist [she wrote at last] is Dr Combridge. He is a most thorough and efficient man, and I am sure, will be glad to see you. He is expensive, but that will presumably not trouble you?

I was alarmed to hear of your illness, Alida. You must take care – but not too much care. My mother is able to live virtually a normal life since her attack. She does splendidly. So do not worry. In this day and age, a heart condition is often almost a minor complaint.

Alida Thorne was not grateful for the medical advice. People, she thought, could be very foolish. Even a woman like Ethel Macviccars. But she had always been a slightly hysterical schoolteacher, given to creating classroom dramas and having favourites among the girls, making herself look foolish. She was several years older than Alida but had only recently retired.

The letter to Doctor Combridge was answered by return of post. An appointment was given for the following week. Alida felt satisfied, even in better health, as a result. On the day that she received the letter, she visited her mother in The Gantry, for half an hour, taking a bunch of dahlias from the garden. The fête was not mentioned.

Early on the Thursday morning, she took the train to London, being careful to talk to no one in Haverstock of her journey, and relieved that she met no one she knew, at the station. She carried a small, Black Watch tartan overnight case, and was to stay in a quiet hotel off Piccadilly.

It is time I had a holiday and some enjoyment, she told herself, and the shops of London will be packed full of the first autumn goods, shoes, coats and hats in the newest colours, and I shall spend a long afternoon in the perfumery department of Harrods, where one may sit down at the counters.

London was hot and the trees of St James's Park had not the faintest tinge of autumn, the grass was of the brightest green. Alida was happy and startled to discover that she was able to cross the park quite freely, walk half a mile under the open blue sky, without fear or alarm. The ducks moved about in the sunshine. I am well, she thought, it is London and a holiday free from associations and the women of Haverstock, this is what I needed. Perhaps, after all, I do not need to consult a specialist.

But she kept her appointment for the following day, intending to pay for consolation that would last her through the winter.

'I see, yes, I see, yes,' Doctor Combridge said, and only that, over and over again, in answer to her list of symptoms, the careful description of her attacks. He was polite, attentive, no more. He did not embroider his questions. And, 'I see, yes, I see, yes,' he said, when she replied.

His surgery was like a Wedgwood bowl, blue with white and a moulded ceiling. This, Alida told herself, is what I pay for, and rightly so, for these bronze chrysanthemums perfectly arranged, for a leather armchair in which I may sit, for a Harley Street address on the notepaper. All this and the skill of a specialist besides, and how much more pleasant and discreet, how much more civilized this is, than an afternoon spent in Doctor Sparrow's shoddy room, Doctor Sparrow, who tumbles everything, prescription pads, pens, hypodermic syringes, drug samples, into a leather briefcase.

The nurse who helped her undress and dress again, in a separate centrally-heated room, smelled of clean hands and did not look at Alida, only assisted.

'Now,' said Doctor Combridge, folding his hands together on the rosewood desk. 'Now, Miss Thorne,' when she was quite ready and seated again, and a cup of tea had been brought to her on a small tray – for this, too, she was happy to pay.

'There is nothing whatsoever wrong with your heart, Miss Thorne. It is a perfectly sound, healthy heart, a splendid heart for a woman of your age. Nor is there anything else organically wrong, your digestive and nervous systems are perfect, you are fit and well. But you are not happy. You are physically well but you do not *feel* so. Well, that is by no means unusual. So I would like you – that is, if you would care – to see a colleague of mine, a Doctor Finch. He will be able to help you now, a great deal more than I can, to a feeling of health and fitness. Would you try that?'

'Doctor Finch?'

'Yes, he is a psychiatric specialist. A very good man – I recommend him to you most warmly.' And he held up his hand. 'Now, do not fear that you are out of your mind, Miss Thorne, or that I suspect such a thing, or that you will be obliged to lie on a couch and relate your dreams and childhood fantasies. No, no, nothing of that kind. Doctor Finch, a doctor of the mind and the nervous system, is not an analyst. And he will be of help to you, I am sure.'

And why not, Alida thought, for *who is there to know?* Nobody – only this stranger and myself. Very well, I shall consult this Doctor Finch, this other man with the name of a bird. I shall spare nothing, neither pain nor money, in the quest for health. Her own determination surprised her.

'Then perhaps,' she said, 'you would be so kind as to make me an appointment?'

Isabel Lavender woke up. A line of light ran under her bedroom door. It was three o'clock. How extraordinary it is, she said, that my sister cannot even get up to go to the bathroom without waking me, and she does not listen, let alone believe me, when I say that, afterwards, I cannot get back to sleep. I must lie here, staring at the dark ceiling, until it is morning.

With old age and her illness has come this inconsiderateness. Not that she was ever a thoughtful or caring woman. No. She was the youngest, the baby, and spoiled, she did not have to care for other people, they cared for her. But I must speak to her again about this. It is a bad habit which she must break, wandering about the house in the night. She must not drink anything during the evening, that will solve the problem. And now I shall not sleep.

The line of light did not go out under her door, and after several muffled sounds from the bathroom, the house was quite silent. But Isabel Lavender slept until morning. And in the morning, she found that the light was still on.

Once again, Dorothea did not know what to do for the best, whether to go or continue knocking, or begin to peer through one of the windows. But it happened this time that she did not have to decide, for the gate clicked shut behind Doctor Sparrow.

'Oh,' said Dorothea, 'I knew, I knew that she was ill, I knew something must be wrong. And now there is no reply, Doctor Sparrow, and I was really alarmed. But how foolish of me, she is in bed ill, and cannot answer the door – that is why you are here.'

'No, Mrs Shottery. As far as I know Miss Thorne is not ill, not in bed. This is only a routine call and to have a word about her mother. I am not coming to a patient. But surely you do not need to be alarmed? Could she not simply be out, shopping or visiting?'

Dorothea, knowing that Alida had not left the house during the past two weeks, was uncertain how to reply, or how much Doctor Sparrow himself knew. But then she remembered the reason for her own presence. 'There has been no light,' she said, 'no light in the house for two evenings. And the windows are shut, all the windows.'

'Then she has gone away.'

Doctor Sparrow seemed neither alarmed nor very interested. 'I must be on my way, Mrs Shottery. And are you quite well?'

'Oh, I am well, thank you, I am always well, Doctor Sparrow. But Alida . . .'

'Why are you so anxious, Mrs Shottery?'

'Alida . . .' she hesitated, and then said only, 'I do not think that she would go away. Not at present and without a word.'

'But I think we must assume that she has done so. There is nothing else for it.'

'No,' said Dorothea, walking unhappily down the path. 'No, probably you are right.'

Doctor Sparrow waved as he drove off, and Dorothea looked back at the shuttered house and was still anxious, and worried, too, that he had thought her merely inquisitive and interfering.

Well, she said, perhaps that is what I am, after all, and he will simply have to know, for I cannot help myself.

In the London consulting room of Doctor Finch, Alida Thorne began to talk. Doctor Finch wore spectacles and had thick white hair. Alida thought him a very handsome man. She talked and Doctor Finch leaned back and looked at the ceiling and listened.

Kathleen Lavender lay awkwardly on the bathroom floor, her left leg pulled up beneath her.

'Get up,' Isabel said, 'you will do no good lying there.' And she stepped across to open the window wide. Her sister breathed but did not stir. After several minutes, watching the breeze lift the curtains and push them to and fro, Isabel Lavender returned to her own room and locked the door.

'I do not know what to suggest about your cat,' Dorothea Shottery wrote to Ma Gaily. 'Of course, he is most welcome to come here with you, except that I do not know how Hastings would take it. He has always been the master here, and it is his territory. Have you nobody who could come in daily and feed and let him out? He would then be able to stay in his own surroundings, and be perfectly content. Failing that, the veterinary surgeon in this village will board animals, and they are most carefully looked after. Would you not change your mind about that? It is not at all the same thing as putting him into some strange and perhaps unauthorized kennel. You could go and see him, then. But do not think of putting off your visit because of this. I am sure we can get round the problem, and I am so looking forward to your coming.'

When she walked to the corner of the road to post this letter, Dorothea passed Alida Thorne's house again, and saw a parcel on the doorstep. Blattern the postman delivered parcels usually about eleven o'clock and it was now four-thirty. So Alida *was* away? Dorothea hoped so, not liking the thought of her friend lying in the house, ill and unable to call for help. You heard so many stories about milk bottles left on doorsteps for days and weeks on end. Dorothea walked back to the gate. There were no milk bottles at all, full or empty. She felt considerably relieved.

Doctor Finch lowered his head and looked at Alida. Encouraged, she talked on.

They had still been living in London, Isabel knew, in the tall, narrow house in Portman Square. Kathleen must have been about eight or nine years old, and as aware as ever of her position as the youngest child, perhaps even more aware now, with the growing realization that, in all probability, no more babies would come to usurp her.

In the afternoon, they had been playing, in the walled garden, mostly on the swing, which belonged to all of them, had been a joint Christmas present from their father. But Kathleen spent the most time on it, always finding someone, mother, the cook or Carlotta, to push her backwards and forwards, and she was home earlier in the afternoons, too, so the arrangement was not at all a fair one. So this day, Faith and Isabel had taken over the swing and would not allow her more than one short turn. Kathleen had sulked and shouted and screamed, but then, seeing that none of this would succeed, had quietly disappeared. They had got on with their game.

184

Kathleen did not appear to tea, and Isabel was sent in search of her. And found her, lying in the playroom, by the hearth, very still. She had not answered, her eyebrows had not flickered in response to her sister's voice or touch.

'Kathleen is ill, Kathleen is dead!' Isabel had shouted, and ran on to the landing, not wanting to be alone in the playroom with what might be a corpse.

'Kathleen is dead, Kathleen is dead. Oh please come, please! Kathleen is dead!'

She had been unable to stop screaming after a time, and Carlotta had slapped her legs twice, very hard. Kathleen had not, of course, been dead, nor ill, nor even asleep. Only a fine actress.

Isabel Lavender nodded. Downstairs in the hall, the clock struck five.

There was nothing more to be said. Doctor Finch knew, now, everything that had happened to her, all she had felt. Alida Thorne sat, and it was as though all her troubles had simply got up and walked across the desk to the other side.

'Well, thank you,' he said at last, smiling, 'thank you for explaining everything so fully. I have a clear picture of your symptoms, very clear.'

There was a small silence. Doctor Finch's surgery was lit by a fluorescent light and the carpet was darkest navy-blue. Alida felt quite at home. And then he began to talk, quietly and with charm, detail by detail and step by step he laid bare her illness, explained what had been so puzzling, related this to that and paused, to ask, if she understood, if this 'sounded right'. Alida was enthralled, her attention completely held by this man with the spectacles and the thick white hair. She listened.

Isabel Lavender stood over her sister and looked down. Kathleen's lips were faintly blue.

'You have brought this upon yourself,' Isabel said, 'and now there is to be sickness in the house and I am to look after both of us without any help. Will you not make some kind of effort?'

185

Beyond the open window, it was raining softly. Unnerved suddenly by the silent bathroom, the motionless figure in the empty house, Isabel went quickly downstairs to the telephone.

'Please come at once,' she said to Doctor Sparrow, 'my sister has just now collapsed, she is on the bathroom floor and I cannot move her. Do not delay, she may even be dead.'

'I'm not at all sure,' Ma Gaily said, letting her chip basket drop rhythmically against the side of the pan to loosen all the fat, 'not at all sure.'

Gaily read the letter over again, and removed his spectacles. 'It's very helpful,' he said. 'A very kind letter indeed.'

'He can't stay here, that's plain.'

'I've asked you, what about her next door?'

'You think I'd trust my cat to her? She'd forget the first day off, she would, he'd be roaming the streets.'

'Well then, take it with you and put it in this place that Mrs Shottery suggests. If she recommends it . . . and you'll be able to go and see him.'

'Oh yes, I suppose they have visiting hours, like a hospital!'

Gaily split open each of his chips to let the steam out. 'It's very remarkable,' he said, 'how you've got so attached to that cat all of a sudden. I can't say I'd noticed it before.'

'You're accusing me of cruelty to animals now, are you?'

Gaily shot her a look.

'Well,' she said, forking open the pickled onion jar, 'I'm sure it's very kind of her, and you obviously want to get me out of the house while you're gallivanting in Scarborough, though why I cannot imagine. But I'm not sure at all, not at all.'

'It's because,' Gaily said patiently, and for the hundredth time, 'we want you to enjoy yourself as well.'

The cat scraped at the underside of the door, and he got up to let it in. It glanced at him, sideways, and malevolently.

'You're only making excuses,' Gaily said, 'and you know it.'

'Come on puss – puss, puss! Come and have some fish. Come on then, pussy, pussy!'

Ma passed down some of the flaked cod on a spare saucer,

avoiding Gaily's eyes. The cat sniffed at the unexpected food suspiciously, before beginning to eat.

Alida Thorne came out of Doctor Finch's surgery with a light heart. London glittered in the sun, and people looked down at her from the tops of red buses. When she looked back, it was without any kind of anxiety. She was well, she had everything clear in her mind, and the fact that there were thousands and thousands of women like her, and considerably worse, was comforting above all. There only remained a complete and relaxed enjoyment of the following two days, before she returned to Haverstock. As a beginning, she walked into an agency to inquire about the availability of theatre tickets for that evening.

'Something gay,' she told the smart young man behind the counter, 'something light and gay. A musical, I think, don't you?'

'This is not the time to stand about arguing, Miss Lavender. Let it be sufficient to say that I do not believe you. You are very much to blame for not calling me before, your sister is extremely ill – *extremely* ill.'

Isabel Lavender, unbending in her black dress with tucks down the bodice, watched the tail lights of the ambulance disappear around the green.

'I am going to the hospital,' Doctor Sparrow said, 'if you would care to put on your coat, I will take you there at once.'

At the gate people were hovering, walking dogs unnecessarily, or posting letters, curious. This, she supposed, was only the beginning, there would now be a stream of unwelcome callers.

'Miss Lavender?'

She turned from the window. 'I do not intend to come to the hospital,' she said, 'I have enough to do now in this house, and of what possible use would I be?'

'I beg your pardon. It seemed likely that you would want to be with your sister, who may easily die, Miss Lavender, who may well be dead upon arrival at the hospital.'

It was not the kind of thing that Doctor Sparrow usually said.

Isabel Lavender shook her head. 'You do not know my sister, Doctor Sparrow. Kathleen will not die, that I do know.'

Doctor Sparrow walked from the room and from the house, not trusting himself to say more.

Chapter Seventeen

'OH, I did enjoy that!' said Florence Ames. 'I can't remember when I last enjoyed a meal so much.'

She took Gaily's arm in the dark street. He nodded. 'You can rely on it,' he said, 'that's the thing. I like to know a place where you can rely on the food and the service and everything, whenever you choose to go.'

'Thank you for taking me.'

She always thanked him, after their days or evenings out, never seemed to take anything at all for granted. It was one of the things he had first noticed and admired.

'Well, we had to celebrate somehow. It's only right. Especially since it was such a surprise – you could call it a shock, almost.'

He paused to look at a painting of the sea, standing on a chair in the furnisher's window. 'Now I'd like that,' he told her. They played the window-shopping game often, choosing houses full of furniture and fittings, and then clothes and cars, electrical goods and gramophone records and gardening equipment. They had selected, Gaily once said, enough between them to stock Pencote Manor all over again.

'Why not buy it,' she said, and seriously. 'Put it on the wall of your room. You could afford it.'

'No, I've got to save, just the same.'

'What, every penny?'

'Well – I'll see. It won't mean a lot extra, you know. Not a huge rise, or anything.'

'You don't seem to have done much saving tonight, then,' she said.

'That's different.'

'It's the position that counts, isn't it, not the money?' For he was now Superintendent clerk, head, that was, of the whole booking department at the railway station.

'I shan't spend as much time on the counter, now,' he said thoughtfully. 'I suppose I shall miss that. I'll be in the back more, organizing and so on.'

'*Administrating!*' she said, laughing.

Gaily wanted to stop, then, and ask her to marry him. But he could not, there was too much to think about and sort out, too many problems. He hoped she knew that he meant to say it, however, that it was what he wanted in the end. She seemed to catch most of what he thought.

'Now, don't come on the bus with me,' she said, 'it's very late indeed, and you've to be up in the morning. You save yourself some trouble for once.'

But Gaily walked her firmly past the green bus shelters. 'You're not getting any buses tonight,' he said, 'I told you, we're celebrating. I'm putting you in a taxi, that's what I'm going to do. And you needn't start on, I am and that's that.'

He walked towards the rank of dark cars in the middle of the road.

'Oh, you are so kind and good!' said Florence Ames. 'You are much too good to me.'

Gaily held open the car door for her.

He was pleased with the evening, all the same, pleased with his promotion, about which he thought while walking home. A promotion he had long ago given up hoping for. He was pleased with his supper and with Florence Ames. It surprised him, at times, his pleasure in her, though he could not have put a name to it. But the previous week, he had read of a woman, crushed to death by a car that had pinned her against a wall. She had been walking to the shops, doing nothing, carefree, and it had killed her. When Gaily had thought of that, or something as bad, happening to Florence Ames, his stomach had knotted up and he had been unable to finish his meal.

Only a policeman was in sight along the street, and most of the lights were already out in Maxstone Villas, the people being early workers and early bedders. Well, he would buy a better house than this, detached perhaps, not a terrace, when he could marry her. For he knew she would marry him, he felt sure of it, and he was happy.

The moment he opened the door, even before he switched on the hall light, he saw Ma. She had fallen heavily backwards down the stairs, on to her right leg. Gaily bent down. 'What were you doing? However long have you been here? What were you doing with yourself?'

Ma shook her head and her skin was grey. 'I never thought I'd be this glad to see you,' she said, 'I never did.'

Gaily ran out of the house and down towards the telephone kiosk. He wished he had brought Florence Ames back for a cup of tea, as he so often did, wished she was with him now, knowing what to do. The box was a quarter of a mile down the straight road, and when he reached it, he could not get his breath to speak, for several minutes.

Dorothea could not pretend that she had not seen the ambulance. Their houses almost faced one another across the green, and she had been in the front garden, tying back the Michaelmas daisies. Now, I will not go knocking on the door, and making inquiries and proffering help, she told herself that evening, as she worried about Kathleen Lavender. For Isabel is so peculiar now, she will resent me, and will not allow me to help her as I would like, to do shopping or a little cooking. She is not, these days, the kind of person you can treat normally, in that way. She shifted the cat Hastings gently off her bag of tapestry wools and put on her spectacles.

But it worried her, all through the quiet evening. Isabel had never learned to cook and clean, had concerned herself as little as possible with domestic affairs, even when Faith was alive. The garden had been her only province. And so, she would be very helpless without her sister. I should invite her for a meal, Dorothea decided, that is my plain duty. Otherwise, she will live on tea and bread and butter and bought cakes, like so many old people living alone. Though she knew that, in all probability,

Isabel Lavender would not come to her if invited, for it had been weeks since Dorothea had seen her outside the house.

'Oh, what shall I do?' she asked despairingly of the cat Hastings, 'what shall I do for the best?' Hastings blinked topaz eyes.

And there would be nobody, apart from Isabel herself, to visit Kathleen in hospital, and that too was a plain duty, her friend could not be left there day after day, without sight of a friendly face. Dorothea could rest no longer, she would ask for the name of the hospital, and if Isabel would not give it to her, then Doctor Sparrow surely would. Also, she would invite her for a meal, although prepared for a curt refusal. Dorothea laid down her tapestry and switched off the standard lamp. The cat ran behind her to the door.

The small hospital room seemed very white and bright to Doctor Sparrow, as he stood looking down at Kathleen Lavender, who did not stir or speak, but who breathed still, and whose eyes opened from time to time. She was almost totally paralysed. Once, her eyes had rested on his face and perhaps held recognition, he could not be sure.

The room was very silent. But her colour was better, the charts and the electrical machines that traced each beat of her heart, each breath in and out, were even a little hopeful. Miss Lavender was not yet dead, and therefore she might survive altogether. The thin hospital curtains moved slightly, in a puff of wind. Doctor Sparrow made a gesture with his hand, and walked from the room.

On the floor above the paralysed Kathleen Lavender, Ma Gaily watched her own foot being hoisted into the air above her bed.

'That's clever,' she said appreciatively, 'that's a very clever contraption.' The pulley stopped and locked itself together.

'How long have I to stay like this, then, staring at my own feet?'

'Quite some time, Mrs Gaily, quite some time.'

The doctor was young, and Indian. Ma hadn't been very sure about him, until he gave her an injection so gently that she scarcely felt the needle, and until she saw how good his teeth were, strong and white. She had long known that you could judge a man by his teeth.

'I'll go mad like this,' she told him now, 'I will.'

'You won't. How does it feel now?'

'Peculiar,' said Ma.

'Painful?'

'No. Peculiar.'

Though it was painful, still, the pain reached its hands right the way up her back, but not as it had done the previous night, not nearly as bad as that, and so you couldn't complain.

Ma turned, and surveyed the woman in the bed on her left, before speaking. She had been watching her covertly, liking to take her time before offering to get to know a person. In the bed on her right, the woman with the permed hair had already chatted and chatted and proffered unasked-for information. Ma didn't like that. She was bursting herself to talk now, that was plain.

'Now that is a nice young man,' said Ma, to the patient on her left, turning her head right round, 'that doctor. Very courteous, I thought.' The woman put down her magazine, nodding. 'Yes,' she said, 'I prefer them, personally. I think they take a lot more care than some of ours. They've had to work harder, do you see, to get where they are. I'm Mrs Golightly.' Ma settled herself back on the pillows happily.

The light in Isabel Lavender's room remained on all evening, and for three nights in succession. No other part of the house was illuminated, and Isabel did not answer the doorbell or the telephone, though she was there, and apparently well, for Dorothea had caught a glimpse of her once or twice, in the window. It meant that she had not been to visit her sister at all.

On the third day, Dorothea could bear it no longer. She telephoned to Doctor Sparrow who was, he said, most relieved that someone wanted to visit Miss Lavender.

'Her sister will not answer the door to me,' Dorothea told him, 'although I do know that she is there.'

'Yes,' he said, 'I know about that. Something may have to be done.'

Dorothea could not bring herself to inquire further but was happy that the matter was in his hands, and she only promised to visit Kathleen Lavender that day, twelve miles away in the Hospital of the Cross.

'That is a cruel and thoughtless thing to say,' Florence Ames told him. 'I would never have expected it of you.'

Gaily stirred his tea round and round, flinching from her disapproval which he had never before experienced and did not wish to feel now. It made him panicky and irritable.

Mrs Ames cut him a slice of the cake she had baked only an hour before, and it fell and crumbled, soft and brown, off the knife and on to his plate.

'All the same,' he said, because somehow he could not apologize, nor take back what he had said. Florence Ames shook her head.

'I'm sure you could not have meant it.'

What he had said was only that it was funny, wasn't it, how Ma had managed to fall and break her leg just the week before they were due to go away on the holiday she had never wanted them to have. Because it *was*, and after his first alarm, when he had known she was to be all right, that had been the thought in his head. Resentment, he supposed. All his life, she had done this sort of thing to him.

'I know she couldn't help it, I know it was an accident. Of course I do. All I said was, it was funny how she managed it. Typical really.' He knew what he should have done, not try to justify himself. Florence Ames refilled his tea-cup and was silent.

'It won't make any difference,' Gaily went on, 'if we do go. There's no reason why we should spoil our holiday. It's not as if she was on any danger list, she's full of it, in there, with more people to talk to and queen it over than she's ever had. We can still go.'

He caught himself doing what Ma did, avoiding her eyes.

'You could go away for a week? When she wouldn't have a visitor?' she asked. 'You could do that?'

Gaily bit into his cake.

'Is that the sort of person you are?'

'Well, what difference will it make to her, you tell me that? With a whole ward full of people? What does she want to see *me* for? Do you think she does?'

'You know she does.'

Gaily did, and knew that he knew.

'All right,' he said, in the end. 'All right then.'

'There isn't any need to cancel it altogether. Only delay it until she's better. You can easily change your week's holiday, can't you, now that you're in charge?'

He hadn't thought of that, either, only wanted to go away now, on the holiday to which he had looked forward, and for which he had planned, so long and carefully.

'Yes,' she said, 'you see?'

Gaily grinned. 'You and her,' he said. 'You do well together.'

Surely it was Dorothea's face? The other had been Doctor Sparrow, but this, with the unmistakable blue eyes, was Dorothea Shottery, though why she should be looking down on her in this way, smiling a little, anxious, Kathleen Lavender could not tell. Behind her, was only a wall, very white, but blurred too, for she had not her glasses on, and so there might be anything there and she would not know it.

Dorothea, she wanted to say, Dorothea, to show that she recognized and was glad to see her, but although her eyes saw and her brain told her to say the name, it was as though her mouth and throat had forgotten how to move in the way that formed words. Indeed, she was not at all sure where her mouth and throat might be, for there was no sensation. It occurred to her that she might be very ill.

'Kathleen,' said Dorothea gently. 'Can you see me now? Do you know who it is? Can you hear me?'

And it *was* Dorothea, though her eyes would still not focus for more than a second or two, but she heard perfectly and all of a sudden, after only hearing a muffled and rushing noise in her ears. If only she could reply, or move her arm, something. She could not feel her body at all, it was as though, below her eyes and head, nothing existed, she had left her body some-where else, like luggage on a seat. It was difficult to know what had happened, for she remembered nothing at all, and her thoughts were very confused and unreliable and sometimes they were not thoughts at all, only a series of flashing pictures across the screen of her brain.

I am so glad you have come, she wanted to tell Dorothea, I am so happy to see you. But she could only look, for a second at a time, at her friend's face, before her eyes closed themselves again.

'There's to be no more argument,' said Ma. 'I'm ill and it'll set me back if you argue with me. You,' she told Florence Ames, 'ought to know that, having been a nurse. So there's an end.'

Gaily did not know what to think, whether to believe her or not. It was Florence Ames who had talked and begun to argue.

'You're going,' Ma said. 'I shan't mind losing sight of your face for a day or so.'

'And what about visiting times?' he said, 'when the chairs by everybody else's bed are full and yours will be empty. What then?'

'Oh, you'll have me in tears!'

'Well, if we go . . .'

'You'll go.'

'*If* we do,' he said, 'you'll not go on and on afterwards, about how you were left alone. That's to be understood.'

'As if I would.'

'You would if you felt like it.'

'Is your leg giving you pain?' asked Florence Ames, anxious to put an end to the bickering before anything unforgivable was said. She knew both of them much better now, and yet had not grown used to their way together. Ma looked at her own foot, sticking up in the air on the end of the pulley.

'Damn nuisance,' she said, for a reply.

'But does it *hurt*?' Gaily asked.

'Yes,' she said, 'since you want to know, it does. It hurts.'

Then, he did not know what else to say, and looked round the ward, instead, at various women in bedjackets and dressing gowns and cardigans, being visited, while Florence Ames talked to Ma about the routine of the hospital, and the woman two beds down whose wound would not heal. The thought of their holiday in Scarborough, to be taken after all, filled him with satisfaction and goodwill.

They met Dorothea by the glass exit doors into the courtyard. When they had told one another of their reasons for visiting the Hospital of the Cross, got over their surprise, there was a mutual sense of relief. Dorothea had found it a strain, bearing the burden of visiting Kathleen Lavender and knowing about Isabel, virtually alone, but now her two friends would listen and advise her. And she, of course, would visit Mrs Gaily, the very next day, because Kathleen would not miss five or ten minutes. Moreover, when they were away on their holiday, she would go regularly, each afternoon, they were not to worry at all about his mother having an empty chair beside her bed.

They went out into the hospital courtyard, talking together, and then on to Maxstone Villas, where Florence Ames insisted upon cooking them all supper.

In her ward, Ma Gaily entertained those within a radius of six beds on either side with the story of her escape from a bombed and burning house, on hands and knees and in night-clothes, in September 1941.

And, on the floor below, Kathleen Lavender lay awake, looking at moving patches of light on the ceiling, knowing at last where she was and remembering a little of what had happened. She wondered why Isabel had not been to see her but she did not very much care.

Chapter Eighteen

'THERE you are,' said Alida Thorne. 'Good morning, Dorothea, I have come to discuss the arrangements.'

Dorothea, who had not quite finished dressing, stood at the front door, trying to fasten the topmost hook of her dress, and wondered whether her clock was very slow.

'Arrangements?' she said. Alida Thorne looked very smart, in what was surely a new, raspberry-pink coat, and a hat of some sleek fur.

'What *is* the time? I did not think it was yet a quarter to nine.'

'It is not,' said Alida. 'But it is always best to discuss these things early. One's brain is fresh, and all the details present themselves.'

Dorothea did not feel at all that her brain was fresh.

'It is a cold morning,' Alida said.

'Oh, I am so sorry! What am I thinking of? Come in, of course. I am afraid I have not yet had my breakfast, will you join me?'

'I breakfasted at seven,' said Alida. Dorothea felt old and tired and slovenly and guilty. 'But you will have a cup of coffee?' she asked.

Alida settled herself in the rocking chair. 'That would be very nice,' and she smiled at Dorothea, who could not recall that she had ever done so, with such warmth, before.

'Is something the matter?' Alida's eyes did not leave her face.

'Why no. No, of course – I am only half asleep, that is all, you know how it is in the mornings?'

'Yes. Though I have always been an early riser, I am at my best before ten. I find the new day so full of promise.'

Dorothea Shottery stared and became conscious of herself,

staring as she stood in the middle of the kitchen, still fastening the hook of her dress. Alida stood up. 'You had much better let me do that.' She reached out her plump hand towards Dorothea's neck. 'And to put the coffee on, since you are clearly in need of some further quiet moments, to gather yourself together.'

Dorothea sat down, the hook efficiently fastened. She needed to do so indeed. This was a new, an astonishing and even an alarming Alida Thorne. One woman had gone away, without a word, and a few days later another woman, the same and yet not the same, had appeared, behaving as Alida was now behaving. Dorothea shook her head. Though it was something of a relief, too. She perceived that when she had time to get used to it all, to sit quietly and sort out the whole question, she would welcome the change. At least she would know where she was with the new Alida, there would be no mysterious illness, and unspoken atmosphere of guilt. Or it seemed not. But perhaps she was jumping to conclusions and this was all merely the effect of a crisp early morning and a short holiday.

Alida set down the blue-flowered coffee pot, together with a plate of hot toast and butter and marmalade. Dorothea was ashamed. I am not senile, nor an invalid, she thought, nobody should have to prepare breakfast for me.

She said, 'You mentioned some arrangements, Alida?'

'Yes. Or have you prepared everything? Oh, come, Dorothea, you cannot still be drugged with sleep. Not unless you are taking barbiturate tablets and, if so, that is a bad habit which must be cured at once. They are inclined to leave one in this drugged state for most of the day. Besides being otherwise undesirable. Let us have some fresh air, let us open a window.' And she did actually rise and open both the kitchen window and the back door. The cat Hastings came running in from the garden. 'He will want his food,' Dorothea said.

'Then he will have to want and wait. The *coffee morning*, Dorothea!'

With her anxiety, first over Isabel Lavender locked away alone in that house, and then the visiting of the speechless Kathleen, and of Mrs Gaily, Dorothea had postponed her plans for the charity coffee morning, until things should be less confused and tiring. And she had not thought that very many people were interested in the idea, it had been only she herself who felt the stirrings of concern that she should be doing more, taking positive action, for the ill, the deprived and the under-privileged. It was so easy to think general, sympathetic thoughts, to care as one cleaned the windows, or pruned the roses, to send a cheque in answer to an appeal. For some time, Dorothea had known that this was by no means enough, and it was towards people like herself, with time and a comfortable amount of money, that others rightly looked.

'Do not say,' Alida laid down her coffee-cup for a second, with an air of wide-eyed surprise, 'do not say that you have abandoned – or even worse, forgotten – the idea?'

'Oh, no! No, not at all, Alida.' And she began to tell her of Kathleen Lavender, and the hospital visiting.

'Well, I am sorry for that,' Alida said. 'Illness must be so distressing. I am thankful that I have always been a healthy woman, perhaps unnaturally so. But Kathleen Lavender has never looked well, she does not care for herself properly, and neither of them have ever taken sufficient exercise or the proper foods.'

'And then there is Isabel, I am so concerned about Isabel. Her sister is, after all, being looked after, nobody could be receiving more care and attention. But Isabel, locking herself away . . .'

'Oh, she has always been of an unstable temperament,' Alida Thorne said. 'I should not be at all surprised to hear that the Lavender family had a history of mental illness. It is all a question of heredity – true mental illness, that is, as against temporary anxiety. It is a question, largely, of chemical changes in the body and brain.'

'It is?'

'In cases like that, oh yes. Yes, that is why my old mother, you see, is as she is. With extreme age, the composition of the cells changes – decay sets in slowly and the mind is gradually

200

affected. That is why she wanders and refers back to her past so very much.'

'Oh, but you cannot say that *now*! Eleanor is happy and content and quite aware of everything going on about her. She does not wander, she is not at all senile, or disturbed in her mind, Alida.'

'Charity, and kindliness do not necessitate the telling of untruths. My mother is ninety years old, the situation must not be glossed over.'

'She is in possession of all her faculties,' Dorothea interrupted. She stood up and began to prepare meat for Hastings, beginning to feel more in command of herself, and determined to hear none of this, from Alida Thorne of all people.

'Surely it would be possible for you to hold the coffee morning,' Alida went on, 'it would do you good to take you out of yourself, Dorothea. It would make a change from all this hospital visiting.'

'I do not think I could manage on my own. I should need some help.'

'And is that not why I have come? What can you be thinking of? Did I not offer my help some time ago?'

'Oh,' said Dorothea, bending down with the dish of chopped meat, 'did you? Thank you so much.'

'Whatever else,' asked Alida blandly, 'were you expecting?'

Later in the day, Alida Thorne sat in the office of Miss Cress, who was saying, as she half-turned towards her, 'Of course, you have not seen her recently. Though I understand that when one is ill ...'

'Ill?'

'Yes, one does not feel like visiting others, the old or the sick or those in some way distressed.'

'You have been ill, Miss Cress? Oh, I am so ...'

'I was referring to your own illness, Miss Thorne.'

'My illness? But I have not been ill. You are mixing me up with someone else, you are quite mistaken, Miss Cress. I am never ill. I have always been a most healthy woman.'

There was a silence. Alida did not move her eyes from the Matron's face. But then her own face opened out into an expression of sudden understanding. 'Of course,' she said. 'You will mean the day of my mother's ninetieth birthday, I had the beginnings of a cold, and did not wish to spread it all about the home. Oh, but that did not come to anything, you see, did not develop. I simply went to bed, and the following morning, the symptoms had subsided. It has always been like that with me, I am able to fight off any germs with the greatest of ease.'

'Well, I am glad to hear of that, although it was not your cold to which I was referring.'

'Then you are mistaken entirely. I have not been ill, Miss Cress.'

'I beg your pardon.'

'We all become confused at times.' Alida Thorne inclined her head graciously, in the glossy fur hat.

'You would like to see your mother?'

'I would like to talk about her with you. I have formed what seems to me an excellent plan. I hope you will agree to it.'

Miss Cress did not speak.

'There is no question of my mother returning to live with me,' Alida said. 'It would be wrong for her and I certainly could not make myself responsible in that way again. I realize how foolish it was of me to have tried to go on so long before. One should admit defeat and sacrifice one's sensitivity, Miss Cress. I have learned that that is important. Yes, her return is out of the question.'

Miss Cress did not speak.

'But everyone needs a change of scene, an alteration in routine and surroundings from time to time, do you not agree? I myself have just taken a long-overdue holiday and feel completely refreshed. Perhaps my mother would feel the benefit of a week – no longer – but a week, at home. It would be in the nature of a holiday. I should be so happy to have her back for that time.'

'That is very generous of you, Miss Thorne.'

Alida opened her bag and took out a lace handkerchief.

'Then it is arranged,' she said, 'and I think the beginning of next week, if that is satisfactory. Just for seven days.'

Miss Cress did not speak. Let her go, she thought, and then refuse to have her back, say that the bed has been urgently taken, for that will awaken the elegant Miss Thorne to her responsibilities.

But she knew she could not do so. Mrs Thorne was happy here, had put on weight and was taking an interest in everything and everyone about her, was living as she had not lived for years in the great bed in that lonely bedroom. Vindictiveness would not do, would only harm Mrs Thorne, who was so loved by everyone in The Gantry, nor would it teach the daughter any kind of a lesson. That was not the way to behave. So the plan, the motive behind which Miss Cress was at a loss to understand, must be accepted. It would create the appearance of harmony, and might it not be for the best?

Miss Cress rose. 'Perhaps,' she said, 'you would like to ask your mother herself about this? It would be as well to know what she thinks of the plan.'

'How could she be other than delighted? To come home, to stay with me?'

'Oh, but we cannot arrange matters so summarily, over her head. That would not be right.'

Alida Thorne stood and smiled, with some indulgence, at the Matron. 'I am her daughter,' she said, 'I know her mind. But I will come this evening and ask her, as you suggest. I am afraid I cannot stay just now, there is a great deal to be done on return from a holiday. But this evening, Miss Cress.'

The Matron opened her office door. 'That will be something to look forward to,' she said.

'You can have oysters,' said Gaily, pointing to the chalked label. 'Oysters. Three for 2s. 6d. That's something I've never eaten in my life, oysters, never fancied them – all slippery. Besides, what's the point of eating something you don't even *chew*. It just slides down your throat, doesn't it? No chance for the taste buds to get at it at all.'

'I don't know,' said Florence Ames, laughing at him, 'I've never had oysters either.'

Scarborough was beautiful, Scarborough was a magnificent success at the end of the season and not so crowded, very rugged and open and hard of landscape. They had explored it, climbing miles up cliff paths, taking the perilous trams, walking above the sea-front on the Regency terraces and crescents. Everything seemed very clear and sharp, all the colours were blue and grey and it was cold. Gaily was happier than he had ever been in his life.

'So we won't have oysters, then,' he said, and edged nearer to the seafood stall.

'It smells,' she said.

'Yes. You can have whelks and winkles and freshly-made crab sandwiches. Or shrimps or mussels. Ma likes mussels, they're her favourite food, only she won't eat them in the town, she says they've travelled too far.'

'She's right.'

'Well, do you want something? We ought to eat seafood while we're here.'

'But we already have.'

Only last night the hotel had served crab salad as an hors d'oeuvre. It was a plain hotel, and most comfortable.

'That was at a meal,' Gaily insisted. 'I meant out of a paper cone. Whelks or something. We ought to.'

'Why?'

'Because we're here. You eat pasties when you go to Cornwall, don't you, and that chalky sort of rock when you're in Edinburgh. Well, you ought to eat these things in Scarborough.'

'I don't,' she said. 'I've never eaten a pasty in Cornwall. And I've never been to Edinburgh.'

'Well, you should.'

But he could see the ridiculousness of the notion, although he did not want to give it up, and he grinned at himself. 'All right,' he said, 'you don't like the smell of fish.'

'We were going to see the Sitwell house,' she said. 'Wood End.'

'Of course we are. I hadn't forgotten.'

They walked amicably, happily, beside the cold North Sea.

'The Vikings came across there,' Gaily said.

'Yes.'

'It's a good place this. There's so many different things. Everybody can find the corner they like.'

'Yes.'

They began to climb one of the long, steep, wooded paths up from the shore.

'You will marry me?' Gaily said suddenly, 'won't you? When things are – are clear? That will be all right?'

They paused for a moment, to recover breath.

'I would like that,' she said. 'Yes. I would like that very much.'

Gaily nodded and turned to look back at the steel-grey sea that moved below them, and at the lifebuoy marking a wartime wreck, winking and winking far out beyond the bay.

'I must go now, mother. There is a lot to do. I am still tired from the journey. But I will arrange everything and you will not have to worry. No, not at all.'

Alida Thorne got up and kissed her mother briskly on the forehead, so that Eleanor felt the fur hat tickle her cheek.

'It is a very nice hat, Alida,' she managed to say, having spoken scarcely at all during the past five minutes or so.

'Yes. Rather expensive, but smart. Oh, everyone will be wearing them in London this autumn, you would be astonished.'

'I would.'

'Good night, Mrs Clemency.'

Alida Thorne bowed, and the door clicked shut behind her.

After a time, Mrs Clemency said, 'Yes. It was a very nice hat.' Eleanor Thorne did not reply. She lay in her comfortable bed and looked at the white and blue pattern of her bedspread and could not speak because she could not make clear her own thoughts. They startled her.

'She is a handsome girl,' said Mrs Clemency, and her left hand rustled the top sheet gently with its shaking. 'I wonder that she has never married.'

'Alida never married,' Eleanor said.

'Yes, dear. That is what I have said.'

'Oh.'

'But I do not believe, you know, that an unhappy marriage is preferable to a contented single life. There are a great many people, I think, men and women, who are perfectly satisfied living independently. Of course, that has not always been the general view. *We* were all encouraged to marry, we were branded as failures in our day, if we did not. There was the terrible burden of being the daughter left at home, the maiden aunt. But things are different now. Oh, indeed!'

'Are they?'

Mrs Clemency glanced sharply at her friend, who lay as she had never lain, listless and a little vague.

'Do you not feel well?' she asked. 'Would you like me to ring for someone? You seem so tired.'

'If she had married,' Eleanor Thorne said to the bedcover, 'things would have been different. It would not have been so . . .'

'Yes?'

'But I always knew that she would not, from her childhood. Somehow, I knew it.'

'Perhaps you should try and go to sleep and think about everything tomorrow.' Mrs Clemency had no experience whatsoever of illness, apart from her own, and did not know whether her friend might indeed be ill, or only tired after her daughter's unexpected visit, and the exciting news. Certainly, she was not herself.

'As a child,' Eleanor said, 'she had the most beautiful auburn hair. Very thick and shining, and the truest auburn. Everyone envied it.'

'She must have inherited that,' said Mrs Clemency, anxious to fall in with the whims of conversation.

'Oh, no. Not from me.'

'From her father then. Your husband – had he auburn hair?'

'I do not know,' said Eleanor Thorne, 'I do not remember.'

Mrs Clemency was silent. She should ring the bell and some-one would come to give her companion a warm drink or even a tablet, to look at her and decide and settle her down for the night. But perhaps she would be annoyed and was in perfectly good health, and only a little over-tired. In which case she would simply fall asleep very soon. Mrs Clemency was drowsy herself, her illness made her so, and the disturbance of someone coming in and talking was perhaps not necessary. Not if she just kept very quiet. She did so. The room creaked and settled down into stillness. Mrs Clemency closed her eyes.

After ten minutes, Eleanor Thorne moved her head suddenly, sat up against the two pillows and burst into tears. 'Oh, do not, *do* not make me go,' she said, looking at Mrs Clemency, 'please tell them, ring for Miss Cress. Do not make me go away from here to stay with Alida, do not let them send me home.'

'She died,' said Ma Gaily, 'the following day. Died in her sleep.'

A small sigh came collectively from the listening ward. They appreciated the classical ending to such a story.

'Well!' Mrs Golightly said, 'maybe it was for the best.'

Ma nodded and her nod seemed to be accepted by the rest of the ward as permission to murmur in comment upon the story, or exchange similar ones of their own, between the beds.

At her desk, Sister Theodore did not hide her amusement. She would be sorry, they would all be sorry, to see Mrs Gaily go. She made a difference to the ward, thriving as she did upon the presence of others, she cheered them up and gave them confidence to face their bedridden, pain-filled days.

On the floor below, Kathleen Lavender wanted to show her gratitude to the nurse and hoped that she was doing so by smil-ing but she did not know, that was the trouble, she could not feel her face to know its expression. She hoped that it was true that a smile was revealed best of all in the eyes, for it was only her eyes that she could be sure about. The nurse left the room.

Isabel Lavender, watching from her bedroom window, saw

Alida Thorne, in the new raspberry-pink coat and fur hat, saw her go to Dorothea's house first thing in the morning, and then to the shops and the rectory and finally, in the evening, saw her walk smartly round the green and in the direction of The Gantry. When it grew dark, she switched on her light. People could see that she was in the house and needed nothing, and would therefore be deterred from visiting. So far, at least, this had been the case, apart from the first tedious days, when they had all trooped up the path and hammered on the door, and refused to take silence for an answer, knocking and knocking.

Downstairs, the house remained silent, the doors locked upon rooms that were no longer entered. In the kitchen, tins had been opened, eggs broken, milk bottles drained, but nothing more. She had carried the wireless up to her room and listened to it from time to time, to discussions about famine in India and New Wave films and to isolated episodes of serials and snatches of mid-afternoon plays, to American forces baseball results and police messages about blood donors. Always to voices, never to music. It was Kathleen who had used the radio for musical entertainment, she would not do so.

Returning to her seat by the window with a plate of tinned stewed steak, Isabel Lavender watched Alida Thorne return from The Gantry and go, not to her own house but again to that of Mrs Shottery.

The women of Haverstock, Isabel thought, visiting and chattering, leading frivolous lives, and Dorothea the very worst of them. Dorothea had called four times, no less, during the first two days of Kathleen's absence, prowled round the house from front to back, peering in at windows. But now she went out, every afternoon, to catch the one-twenty-three bus into town, and never returned before early evening. Isabel Lavender would have liked to think that she had a job because she needed the money, but she could not do so, knowing how much money Dorothea had. No, it could not be a job. But by sitting here, she would find out, one day or another.

Alida had gone inside, and Dorothea Shottery's door had been closed. Isabel Lavender began to eat her stewed steak with a dessert spoon.

Chapter Nineteen

'I DON'T want to have to leave,' Florence Ames said suddenly, as they stood under the vaulted Victorian roof of the station waiting for their train. 'I've never been so happy on a holiday, never.'

Gaily nodded, but did not reply. He had asked her to marry him because he could wait no longer to set his mind at rest. It was to be all right. But he had not meant or wanted to ask her yet, it had been much too soon. Things had to be, as he put it, 'clear'. There were decisions to be made, about Ma and their respective houses, a whole way of life was to end and a new one to begin, and he needed to plan for that carefully. He feared that Florence Ames might expect a wedding at once, within a few weeks, and he could not explain that it might not be so. He had only to trust to her knowing the way of his thoughts, and accepting the unspoken state of things.

And there was Ma to be told, the most difficult part of all. Most of the days, and even sometimes during the nights, while they had been in Scarborough, Gaily had pictured himself in the little scenes, telling Ma. In the hospital with the background of the other patients, with doctors and nurses and all the paraphernalia of illness, to act as a kind of support, that seemed to be the best place. But perhaps there would not be the opportunity, she would not be in there for much longer. And whenever his mind began to picture the scenes at home, he turned away from them at once. Nor could he begin to imagine what words he might use.

'I wish they still had steam trains,' Florence Ames said. 'I know about the cost and the smell and dirt, you've told me, but just for stations like this – the others don't look right here.'

'No.'

'But you have to be progressive I suppose – that's what you always say.'

'It's late,' Gaily said, 'and there isn't anything progressive about that. You'll never be able to overcome lateness on the trains. It's human error after all, all the way along the line.' And he laughed with her at the pun which he had not intended.

'We'll get home,' she said, 'we'll be back soon enough.'

'Yes.'

But the lateness of the train annoyed him, he felt in some way responsible. He began to walk about the platform, stamping a little.

Miss Cress had been prepared for Alida Thorne to disbelieve her and to protest. Certainly she would want to march upstairs, disturbing the peace of the house, and confront her mother with the situation, and there would be distress and explanations and possibly tears. Pride would not allow itself to be hurt like this without demanding compensation of some kind.

But Alida Thorne did not protest. She sat comfortably in the Matron's armchair, a new suede handbag on her knee, and nodded.

'Then of course she must not come home,' she said in a sympathetic voice. 'I would not dream of taking her against her will.'

No, Miss Cress thought, certainly you would not, that I can believe.

'She is very old, and the old like clinging to what is familiar. Besides, she has so many sentimental ties with this house in her past, it is only natural that she should wish to remain in it during the last years. Old people need to be secure and to feel secure.'

Miss Cress accepted this teaching with an inclination of her head.

'Besides, perhaps she does not remember her home, and has no notion of where you might be wanting to send her. Yes, that is very likely. She is wandering in her mind. Of course.'

The Matron suppressed her desire to argue, and to deny the

charges so regularly and falsely made by Alida Thorne. The mother's extreme distress had shocked and dismayed her. That should never be allowed to happen again, she should remain here exactly as long as she chose – and that, Miss Cress knew, would be for good.

'I will not see her now,' Alida Thorne said, rising to her feet, 'it would only be an added worry.'

'For her,' Miss Cress asked, capping her fountain pen, 'or for you?'

Alida Thorne looked annoyed. 'Matron,' she said, in the quietest of tones, 'I am a mature woman, I am able to face and accept the realities of life. My mother has always been somewhat sheltered and now she is old. It is of her that I am thinking, only of her.'

'Please,' said Mrs Clemency yet again. 'Please do not worry yourself any more. Miss Cress is a good and truthful woman, a woman of her word. She would not make you go anywhere or do anything against your will. She has said so. Do not continue to be so upset.'

'No,' said Eleanor Thorne, moving her hand restlessly over the sheet. 'No. I am to stay here, that is settled. You have heard them say so?'

'I have. You know that I have.'

'Yes.'

Mrs Clemency had been shocked at her friend's tears and unhappiness, had lain in her own bed and sat in the downstairs rooms and been pushed about the grounds in a wheelchair, and wondered constantly about the background that had caused such a terrible situation. She herself had no family, not so much as a cousin, and to have a daughter, an only child, of whom one was afraid and with whom one hated to stay, was beyond her comprehension.

Eleanor Thorne seemed to have aged suddenly, to be a different woman, ill and anxious. They did not talk together in the way they had talked at the beginning. She now spoke to herself, distractedly, about the past, and forgot who or where she was for hours at a time. And always, in between, was that sad and desperate cry, 'Do not make me go. Do not say that I must go and stay with Alida.' Mrs Clemency had wanted to weep.

Rounding the bend that led up to the green, Gaily decided that he would retire here – *they* would retire here. He planned to buy a cottage with one of the long attics which he would convert into a workroom, in which to make his models, and they would be bigger, more intricate and ambitious, because he would no longer be cramped with them in a single bedroom. He had long wanted to start on King's College, Cambridge, but that needed space – space and time and quietness.

Whenever he thought of it, his imagination took him as far as a picture of himself in his workroom and of Florence Ames in the garden wearing a hat and leather gardening gloves, but he could never place Ma correctly. In the kitchen, he supposed, but by then she would be too old to cook for them, even were she willing, and he could not see her bedridden and idle. Besides, it would be years yet – thirteen years. He forgot that. It seemed only round the corner sometimes. And he knew that he could not place Ma in the Haverstock cottage, because he assumed that she would be dead.

A movement, above eye-level, made him glance up at a woman in one of the house windows. He could not place her. But that was what it might be like, and had he thought about it? Women peeping behind curtains, knowing not only the business you wanted them to know, but other, private matters, and discussing you among themselves. Haverstock was like that. Gaily considered it, as he walked up the path of Dorothea Shottery's cottage. He did not think that, by then, he would very much mind.

It had been Isabel Lavender who saw him and who watched him all the way around the green. The man from the railway, the man from Faith's funeral, who had somehow insinuated himself into their village, and gone so far as to help at the church garden fête. That man was now visiting *Dorothea*. She understood now, about her outings on the one-twenty-three bus into town.

Alida Thorne saw him, too, as she dusted the tops of all her bottles and jars and pots at the dressing-table in the bay window, and she leaned over to see where he called. She had thought that Mrs Florence Ames was his lady friend. If so, it was unchivalrous of him to be visiting Dorothea at eleven o'clock on a Wednesday morning. Alida smiled at her own tranquil reflection in the mirror. It did not alarm her, nothing could alarm her now, because she felt a little detached from it all. And, in five minutes, she would begin to manicure her nails, an activity which she found unfailingly therapeutic.

All the way around the green, Hubert Gaily was observed and recognized and his presence speculated upon. Only Dorothea had not been looking out of her window, but was hanging out some washing on her line at the back of the house when she heard him knocking, so that she greeted him with astonishment and delight.

Isabel Lavender wondered how many people had seen the man from the railway going into Dorothea's house, and in broad daylight. She hoped it was many but feared that it was not. And people should know, they should learn what kind of a woman Dorothea – so well-thought of, so sweet and willing, so eager to support the Parochial Church Council and the Haverstock Council of Residents – truly was. Isabel herself had long suspected the sad mask of widowhood, and the air of present content, but in her sister Faith's day had not dared to speak her thoughts, for Dorothea had been Faith's special friend.

But now, people should have their eyes opened to the real situation. Isabel Lavender knew, after all, how much she herself had been talked about and pointed at and slandered by Dorothea. Patiently and for years, she had disregarded it all. But seeing the man had helped her, she could make up her mind with a clear conscience.

It would mean going out, of course, people must be met and

spoken to, some kind of a public life must once again be led, and it did not accord with her inclinations. Yet it was her duty, and something, something must be done to put an end to the rumours about herself, Dorothea should no longer be allowed to gossip. Isabel Lavender sat down again in the chair beside the window and began to think.

In the white hospital room, Kathleen Lavender closed her eyes for fully ten seconds, and then opened them again and looked at her finger. It was the third finger of her right hand, and three times in the past fifteen minutes she had seen it move. And she had seen it move *because she herself had moved it*.

Nobody came in to see her, it was late morning and the quiet time, and she was able to check and check again the single movement of her single finger. She decided to lift it up, and did so, and to lower it, and did so. And then she moved it to the left, so that it touched against her forefinger. But when she willed it to move back to the right, nothing happened, the message was blocked, and the finger remained still. She closed her eyes again. Well, she thought, I will not be impatient. I will rest a little and forget all about it, and then I will try again. There is all the time in the world.

When the red-haired young nurse came in to feed her lunch, Kathleen Lavender smiled with her eyes, and kept her finger still.

Dorothea had listened most carefully as Hubert Gaily sat at her kitchen table, with the teapot and a plate of scones before him, talking. She had been about to bake when he arrived. It seemed a good idea to continue with it, while he sat opposite, for then she had something to occupy her hands and eyes, so that she need not look at him. Nothing seemed to her more disconcerting than the effort of relating one's problems, or of telling a very personal story, with the listener silent, and staring from across the room. So, she had rubbed fat into flour and kneaded dough and piped icing and greased tins, and now two flans and a tray of small buns were in the oven. At this point, the end of her work, there seemed to be an end to Gaily's story.

214

During a short silence, Dorothea carried her mixing bowl and tools over to the sink.

'Well . . .' he said.

'Would you care for more tea?'

He helped himself, and poured another cup for her. 'It seemed best to talk to you,' he said, 'because you know us. You know her better than I do.'

'Oh, no, I have only known her *longer*. That can't be true!'

Dorothea sat, and took up her cup of tea. 'There is,' she said, 'no doubt whatsoever in my mind. I have often thought about this. I have hoped about it, though one cannot interfere. I detest intrusion of that kind.'

'Match-making.'

'Yes, if you like. Oh, but you must be married! There is nothing else for it, you are so right together. You share so many interests, you have one another's welfare at heart, you are of an age – everything that goes to make a good marriage. There is nothing to prevent it.'

Hubert Gaily moved his forefinger in a pattern along the grain of the table.

'But it is your mother. That is the only problem and that is what holds you back. And that is *all*?'

Gaily nodded. 'Ma . . .' he said, but did not go on.

'I think that she likes Florence Ames. I think she would enjoy her company and affection and support.'

'She's always had me.'

'And why would she not still have you? If you lived in the same house or if you did not.'

'It's selfish,' he said, 'and wrong, but I wouldn't want us to do that. I'd want to be – just to live together. Not to move to the other side of the country of course, no, but I want us to have *our* house. It's a selfish thing.'

'No, it is the inevitable desire for independence, for going away.'

Gaily grinned. 'I've left it late,' he said, 'it's what most people do at twenty, not at fifty-three – leaving the nest!'

'Does that matter?' Dorothea asked. Gaily frowned.

'This is what *you* have done and are doing, it is because it is you that it is different. What has it to do with other people?'

He looked at her in surprise. 'Perhaps,' Dorothea suggested, 'she would be *glad* to have the house to herself?'

'It's too easy, to think that.'

Dorothea stood up and took their cups to the sink. 'Well,' she said decidedly. 'I have given you my opinion, I have told you what I think, and it is what you yourself know is right. It is what you really want.'

'Maybe.'

'But I cannot do your talking for you.'

'No.'

'But I will have your mother here, to stay with me, as she was to come before her accident. I would enjoy her company and it would be good for her. *Then* you would have a chance to make your new start.'

'It's very good of you. It's very kind,' Gaily said, 'but it's only . . .'

'What?'

'I've got to tell her,' he said, and got up, in his agitation, to wander round the kitchen and look out of the window, at leaves on the back lawn. 'She doesn't know anything about it, she'll come out of hospital and I've got to *tell* her.'

'I would not be too sure that she doesn't know anything.'

So that he would have a distraction, Dorothea handed him a cloth with which to dry the dishes.

'Do you think she would have to be told?' she asked Gaily.

He wiped the beating-fork very carefully, in and out of all the wire slats.

'You're perhaps right,' he said.

Dorothea turned to him, in a swift movement, her hands poised over the washing bowl. 'You must not allow it to make any difference,' she said. 'Do not change your mind. Oh, no, for you cannot think how much I want you to be married, you and my friend Florence Ames.'

Gaily smiled at her. 'It's not,' he said, 'so straightforward, so easy, is it? Not like you make it seem?'

'Oh, yes. Yes, it *is*.'

It was for this advice, after all, he told himself, this support, that he had come. Had he taken his day off, travelled all the way here because he wanted her to advise him against the match, deter him from all thought of marriage?

But he needed to argue it out, and needed her to see, not to make it all seem so easy. There was the question of Ma and of the houses. She had asked him, to his astonishment, if he were not using this as an excuse, hiding behind it. He had rejected the suggestion at once, but knowing that he would have to think about it later. He folded the tea towel now, and hung it on its rail. 'I'll get the twelve bus,' he said, 'if I hurry.'

'You – on the bus?'

Gaily smiled, unashamed. 'The buses,' he said, 'are more regular.'

'Then you will stay and have some lunch with me and then why can we not catch the one-twenty-three bus together? I am going to the hospital as usual.'

At one-fifteen, therefore, they left Dorothea Shottery's house and walked slowly, in the thin rain, around the green to the bus stop. From her window, Isabel Lavender watched them and from other windows others watched and commented and interpreted. Dorothea guessed as much, and did not particularly care.

Chapter Twenty

'Now come,' said Alida Thorne, rubbing her hands together briskly and surveying the room. 'It is only twenty people, not a very great number. And all of them may not come.'

'Oh, but they must come, or we shall have so much left, milk and cakes and biscuits . . .'

'You will be surprised,' Alida told her, 'how much will be cleared away. When it is a question of home-made cakes and coffee, few stand back.'

Dorothea accepted her word. Alida had continued to behave so decisively, had taken the arrangements for the charity coffee morning so thoroughly in hand, that she could do nothing else. There is some reason, she said to herself, something behind this alteration. Alida appears to be a new woman, but *is* it only an appearance? But Dorothea was glad, for her sake.

Her sitting-room looked most inviting, with small tables set everywhere, beside clumps of chairs, and on the long sideboard coffee jugs and spoons and strainers, plates of small iced cakes, large fruit slabs, biscuits and cookies and Turkish delight. Because it was a sharp morning, Dorothea had lit a fire, though against Alida's advice. It added so much, she had said, to the welcome of the room, it provided a focus.

'Then we are all ready,' Alida Thorne said, and smoothed her hands down over the beige and brown jersey suit.

Dorothea went to the window. Nobody was yet in sight, the green was deserted.

'And perhaps nobody will come,' she thought, but did not dare to say it aloud. She was not yet accustomed to being afraid of Alida Thorne's sharp tongue. It was simply that she no longer knew her, was unsure of her ground.

'You are aware,' Alida said now, from behind her, 'of course, that it is not considered polite to arrive precisely on time. The clock has only now struck a quarter to eleven.'

Dorothea nodded, and moved rather guiltily from the window. And then, as she caught the glimpse of a figure behind the hedge, turned back.

'But I cannot believe it!' she said, and forgot not to stare between the curtains, in her amazement, 'for here is Isabel Lavender!'

The older doctor, with receding, gingerish hair, leaned over the bed.

'Splendid,' he said. 'Now, I think just once again, to make sure.'

Kathleen Lavender tried to express agreement, on her face.

'Your right hand, is it not, Miss Lavender?'

It was a frustration almost beyond bearing, not to be able to shake her head or frown a correction or speak. All that she could do was to raise, one by one, each finger of her left hand, yet again, up and pause and down. And then lift her left hand up, from the wrist, pause, and let it drop. The *left* hand. The older doctor nodded and smiled. Everybody had smiled, encouragement and praise and satisfaction shone out of their faces.

'Good,' he said, 'splendid. Now your right hand.'

But she could feel nothing there, nothing at all.

'Well, it will come, it will come.'

The younger doctor stepped forward and touched her hand experimentally. Her left hand.

'Do you feel that?'

Kathleen twitched her forefinger. But in her right hand, still nothing, even though they poked it quite hard, with a sharp pin. Nothing. She wanted them to look at her feet now, for she had been sure of movement there, on the left side, and a tingling sensation, like warmth returning to a chilled limb. She tried to point with the useful fingers, but they seemed not to understand, and only smiled some more encouragement. And then the younger doctor was writing busily on his chart.

Then, and it was quite suddenly, the numbness disappeared, and she could feel the muscles of her left leg, moving at her control. She raised the foot, and lowered it, at first imperceptibly, and then harder, so that the bedclothes stirred and the older doctor caught sight of the movement.

'Well!' he said, beaming. 'Well, now!' His plump face was shiny and pink and Kathleen Lavender felt like a child, being applauded for learning to walk.

'I wish to talk to you,' said Isabel Lavender to the Reverend Mr Bottingley, plucking at his sleeve.

The Reverend George Jocelyn Bottingley, his mouth full of almond cake, was caught between Miss Lavender and the sideboard.

'I do not wish the whole room to hear, I am speaking to people individually. Perhaps we might stand in that corner.'

Mrs Marchebanks, whose account of her sister's operation Isabel Lavender had interrupted without apology, turned on her heel. Refilling a cup at the other side of the room, Dorothea did not observe the incident. But she thought about Isabel Lavender, had worried about the cause of her coming since that first peal of the bell. Her manner had been very strange, aloof but purposeful. Gradually, Dorothea watched her as she moved about the room, speaking to one guest after another, taking them on one side and talking directly, earnestly. Her face was still like that of a puppet, without any softening of expression. When she had spoken, she moved away at once, to claim someone else, while the other guests looked embarrassed and shifted their cups from hand to hand. Above all, they avoided her eye, Dorothea's eye, pretended that they did not see her, did not wish for more coffee, were deep in conversation with a neighbour. Those who had been more effusive upon their coming in were now at pains to avoid her.

Alida Thorne had not yet been spoken to but she was in the centre of a chattering circle beside the china cabinet. Dorothea stood alone, therefore, at the edge of her own sitting-room, balancing the two pots in her hand and distressed because she did not know what to do. Isabel was still murmuring to the vicar and Dorothea could not see his face to try and read its expression. Beside her, on a low table near the door, stood the dish, into which everyone would put their voluntary contributions as they left. Alida had decided on that. 'We do not set any price,' she had said, 'and we will get more this way. People are always afraid of being under-generous when others may see. Our charities will benefit.'

As yet, the dish was empty. Dorothea set down the coffee pots suddenly. I will go, she thought, I will go and ask, I will not stand here worrying and building it up in my imagination, I will speak to her directly. And she began to edge through the group of people, towards the corner and Isabel Lavender.

They had brought another doctor into the room, a well-spoken man, severe of face.

'Again,' he said to Kathleen Lavender, as she lifted the fingers, the hand, and arm and leg, of her left side. 'Again – yes. Good.'

'Excellent,' the first doctor told her. 'You are getting better, Miss Lavender – you are doing splendidly.'

And he beamed and they all trooped out, while the green-eyed nurse tucked her sheets back into place, and smiled.

'Before we know where we are,' she said, 'you'll be going home!'

'Well,' said Sister Theodore, holding open the swing doors on the corridor above, 'I shall miss you in my ward.'

Ma Gaily nodded.

'You've entertained us all.'

She had been wheeled round the room, saying her good-byes, receiving them like a queen, and outside the lift her son waited, to accompany her in the ambulance.

'I can't say I hope to be back,' Ma said. 'You wouldn't want that.'

Sister Theodore shook her head. 'And you do as you're told,' she said, turning away, 'or you will be.'

'I know. The physiotherapy,' Ma said, in a tone of scorn.

'Yes, the physiotherapy.'

The lift-doors bumped together, closing her in with the wheel-chair and the silent attendant.

'Right,' said Ma. 'Home James.'

'Isabel . . .' Dorothea said, and turned at an angle so that she could not edge away. 'Do excuse me, Rector, but I would like a quiet word with Miss Lavender. Isabel . . .'

Isabel Lavender began to cough, at first unconvincingly, so that Dorothea judged it an attempt at distraction, but then the cough came in quick, harsh rasps, with unsteady breaths be-tween, and Isabel Lavender's skin paled and then flushed a dark brick-red. Her breathing worsened, a chair was brought and pushed away again, and then a drink, and the windows were opened, people cleared a space around her by drawing back, and then glanced at one another in alarm, over the cups, as she began to clutch at her breast in pain.

'A A A A-aaaahhh,' said Kathleen Lavender on a breath and heard her own voice uttering the soft sound, 'Ah-ah-ah-ah-AAAAAAHHHHHH.'

The white room was empty again. She formed her lips care-fully into a round shape and made the sound come out again, but as an O. 'Oh. OOOOOOOOOhh. OOOOOOOO.'

She tried to say a word, but her mouth would not open to make the shape of each sound quickly enough, and the word only emerged as a curious, strangled cry.

'Oh.'

They were right, she was doing splendidly, she would be home in no time. But she did not like to think of home, of the shut-tered silent house, and Isabel upstairs behind her locked door, black-clothed and censorious. Here, in the white room, she felt freer than she had felt at home, for months, in spite of the paralysis and the recent pain. With the gradual return of movement and now speech, all things became possible, it was like discovering a new world, and the old world held no interest for her. So she did not think of home, but moved her head, as she now could, although slowly, to look out of the window at a patch of chalky-blue sky.

Dorothea hesitated on her own landing, at the head of the stairs. Below, from the sitting-room, the voices of those who were left came up in short bursts, that were somehow subdued, too, between the silences.

They had carried Isabel Lavender up to Dorothea's guest bedroom, and Doctor Sparrow had been sent for. He was there now, with the Reverend Mr Bottingley and Mrs Marchebanks, and downstairs Alida Thorne talked to those who had remained. Dorothea felt dispensable.

Not that they did not know, all of them, though nobody had spoken the words aloud, relying on the absence of certainty until a medical judgement had been passed. At the head of the staircase, Dorothea felt as though she belonged to nowhere at all. The cat Hastings appeared and rubbed around her ankles, and so she sat down on the topmost stair, took him on her lap and fondled him. His purring sounded loudly along the carpeted corridor.

Isabel Lavender was dead, of that there was no doubt. She had died amongst them, in their horrified, disbelieving view, with her handbag and coffee-cup spilled from her grasp, and the hatpin loosened so that her black felt lay askew on her head, and the grey hair wisped over her face beneath.

Everybody had known, those who stared and those who inquired and lifted and telephoned, as well as those who had gone quickly away, not caring to look upon death.

But they said, she is ill, she has fainted, they fetched a doctor and gave advice about blankets and brandy, they did not say she is dead, here in the middle of a charity coffee morning.

Dorothea shook her head. They did not *know*. Doctor Sparrow had said nothing, only gone upstairs two at a time, as usual. They must wait. And think of Kathleen and what amazing things could now be done. The bedroom door opened, throwing light on to Dorothea's seated figure.

'Mrs Shottery . . .'

'I know,' she said at once. 'Yes, I know.'

The Reverend George Jocelyn Bottingley blew his nose.

Dorothea wanted to ask what Isabel Lavender had been saying so urgently, to him and to everyone else, what had made her come here, when she had not left her home for weeks. And now she was dead of a coronary thrombosis and Dorothea could not ask her questions, must only wait and hope to be told.

'There is the question of her sister,' the Rector was saying. Dorothea rose and could think of no way to apologize for having been discovered on the stairs.

'Kathleen,' she said. 'Yes. I do not know if she can be told, we must consult the hospital authorities.'

In the sitting-room, Alida Thorne began to collect scattered plates, though hoping to keep her movements respectful. She did not wish to think of Isabel Lavender, she had turned away from the sight in the corner. But as she gathered biscuits on to a single plate, she thought that the death could not touch her, she was proof, now, against that kind of shock. It was an occasion for decent sorrow and mourning, but it had no personal significance.

To her annoyance, Miss Blade from the post office began to help her with the crockery and to talk at the same time.

'I knew at once,' she said confidently, and popped a ginger finger into her small mouth. 'I know a seizure when I see one. I could tell straight away.'

'Thank you, I can manage.' Alida took the plates from the other woman's hand. 'Perhaps you should go home now,' she said, but politely, showing concern. 'You cannot be of any further assistance, and perhaps the house should now be empty?'

Miss Blade began to reply, and her voice was suddenly loud, the only one raised in the room, as the Reverend Bottingley opened the door. Alida did not look at his face. She knew, as they had all known.

•

'You've got everything you want?' Gaily asked, pausing at the door.

'Thank you very much.'

'Manage the tray all right, can you?'

'What do you take me for?'

'Right.'

'You seem to have got things running smoothly,' Ma said, glancing over her raised fork, 'the pair of you.'

'If there's anything . . .'

'Oh no, *I'm* not complaining!'

'I'll get my own tea, then.'

'I daresay she's keeping it hot for you.'

Ma smiled sweetly back at his angry glance. The door banged shut and then opened again to let the cat in behind him.

Gaily began to eat his meal, not saying anything to Florence Ames for some time. He had not said anything to Ma yet, either, had gone in and out of her room anxiously, fidgeting with this and that, ever since she had come home. But he was unable to speak his mind. Ma watched him covertly, and made no remark, only accepted Florence Ames' care and company, as to be expected. Her leg was healing, but slowly, she would be in bed for some time, and during that time Gaily felt he did not have to decide anything, his situation was held in suspense. He was glad of that.

'It's very good of you,' he said now, cutting into another home-made fishcake. 'Doing all this.'

'You've no need to say that – you will go on and on saying it when I have told you, it's the least anybody could do.'

'No. Not anybody.'

'The least *I* could do, then.'

'I don't see that.'

'Don't you?'

Yes, he did, she considered herself one of the family, bound as much as a relative to take care of Ma. In a way, he was glad of it, the idea had been accepted and became part of their lives. In other ways and in spite of Dorothea Shottery's decided views, it alarmed him, for nothing might work out the way he hoped, and he would have to disappoint her. He wished now that he had not spoken to her of marriage that afternoon on the cliffs at Scarborough.

All that evening, sitting in the chair opposite to her, and later, walking her back to the bus, he thought about telling Ma, trying out various sentences in his head. He didn't want to be asking, but on the other hand didn't want to hurt her, either, with a curt piece of news.

In Ma's room, the cat curled up on her eiderdown.

'You've come now, have you?' Ma said. 'Sent you up out of the way, has she?'

The cat twitched its left ear. Ma turned on the radio, and listened, without being at all impressed, to one half of a religious broadcast about the unity of the churches, until she heard the front door shut and Gaily came in again. He would make their cocoa, then, and come upstairs to bed. Ma stirred her good leg in the bed, frustrated by this enforced idleness, keeping her up here, away from whatever might be going on.

He had better make up his mind, that was all, it was time he did that. The cat coiled itself more comfortably into sleep.

Dorothea Shottery stood outside the door of the white room. Through the glass portholes, she could see her friend, with a better colour in her cheeks and her head turned towards the window. She had improved beyond expectation, they said, everyone was pleased with her, she could move the whole of her left side, and twist her head and speak, though as yet only in a slurred and hesitant way. The charts indicated her condition and her progress.

But Dorothea did not want to go inside. She could give her news, they had decided, Isabel's death would have to be known, and now there was so much improvement ... Dorothea still hesitated. Her friend was ill, after all, and very weak, so might not the news set her back again, was it not better to keep it from her? It was not as though she would be expecting Isabel to visit ... No, they had said she might be told.

Dorothea walked uncertainly a little way down the green

corridor, and then went, with sudden, quick steps, back towards the door of Kathleen Lavender's room.

'It is really very good of you, Miss Thorne, very good and generous.'

'I wish to give service,' Alida said, clasping her hands together over her crocodile bag. 'It occurred to me that I was not pulling my weight.'

'Oh, but you have had your responsibilities at home. Your mother . . .'

Alida nodded. 'But my mother is very well cared for now, in The Gantry, and likely to remain there, Mr Bottingley, and I have recouped my strength with a much-needed holiday. I am ready to be useful once again, that is why I have come to you.'

'The Parochial Church Council elections take place shortly – perhaps you already know?'

'That was why I came at once, today.'

'It is rather a tedious commitment, Miss Thorne, there is nothing glamorous – not that you – no, but serving regularly, week by week, on a committee, helping to do very run-of-the-mill work . . .'

'I would not like you to think I was putting myself forward for anything of greater importance.'

'Miss Blade has spoken to me once or twice about her wish to resign . . . she feels . . .' The Rector raised his hand indecisively, not knowing precisely what Miss Blade felt.

'Then perhaps there might be a chance of my giving you some help, perhaps other people might see their way to electing me. Unless there is someone else in mind, I would not wish to push forward . . . I do not think of bidding for power, Rector.'

The Rector smiled to himself at her seeing the middle-aged church council as a seat of anything like power.

'Oh,' he said, 'but everyone would be delighted, you would be most warmly welcomed.'

'It is the very least I can do, with such time as I have on my hands. And what talents I do possess should not, after all, be buried.'

'Oh, indeed. No. Certainly.'

'And if there is anything else, Rector, if I can be of any further use . . .'

'You are very good, Miss Thorne, I will certainly remember your offer. Oh, indeed.'

Alida Thorne rose. 'I believe that by now,' she said, glancing at the clock, 'Miss Kathleen Lavender will have been *told*.'

The Reverend Mr Bottingley looked embarrassed. 'Mrs Shottery has gone to the hospital,' he said.

'Yes. Mrs Shottery.'

They exchanged a glance. Alida waited for something more to be said, feeling that it was not her place to say it. The Reverend George Jocelyn Bottingley held open the door of his study, saying nothing. Alida adjusted the fur stole about her neck, and bowed, to conceal a slight disappointment. Isabel had talked of Dorothea to the Rector, but nothing was to be said.

'Good morning to you, Miss Thorne, and thank you again. Thank you indeed.'

Alida Thorne walked down the path of the Rectory, feeling calm. When she arrived she had not felt calm, she had been made anxious by the first broken night since her return from London, and by her fearful dreams of Isabel's death.

'You must always find plenty to do, take your mind off yourself as much as possible and turn it to something absorbing and useful, some outside preoccupation,' Doctor Finch had told her. Well, there could be nothing more worthwhile than working for the church and, moreover, she felt that the church would be glad of her. Things needed to be done, improvements could well be made and she had rediscovered her school-mistress's flair of organization. They would be glad of that, too.

When she passed by the Lavenders' empty house, Alida was able to look up, quite untroubled, at the blank windows. Yes, she had done the right thing, and she had been rewarded.

'You do understand, dear?' Dorothea said, yet again. For Kathleen Lavender had shown no distress or shock, hardly even any interest.

'She was taken care of, we did all that we could,' Dorothea twisted her fingers together, uncertain whether to go on or speak no more about the death. Kathleen Lavender lay quite still, looking ahead of her, and the pupils of her eyes were very bright.

'Is-Is-Isabel,' she said suddenly, although the sounds came out softly, sh-sh-sh, as though she were drunk.

'Yes?' said Dorothea.

Kathleen shook her head, and then raised and lowered her left arm.

'Do not worry. She was only ill such a short time, she cannot have suffered much. Do not upset yourself thinking of it.'

Kathleen Lavender said, 'No,' slowly, and then again. 'No. No.' She wished that her mouth would obey her, in forming her thoughts into the correct word-shapes, so that she could set poor Dorothea's mind at rest – pale, distressed Dorothea, whose hands would not be still. So, Isabel was dead, and she was now the last of the sisters. They had been a family of heart cases, mother and grandfather, and the small brother who had died, and Faith. And now, Isabel was dead. But she herself would not die, not yet, though at the beginning she had expected it. Isabel had not been to see her, had not thought of her or cared about her at all. But Isabel had been out of her mind, that was clearer than ever now.

I am not a vindictive woman, Kathleen thought, but I am glad that my sister is dead, for all my life I have suffered under her. She dared not look into her friend Dorothea's kindly face, for fear that the relief and sense of freedom, the complete lack of caring, should be revealed on her own. She could not care that Isabel was dead because she could look forward to her own future.

Dorothea put her hand out and touched that of Kathleen, thinking that she was suffering silent grief.

Ma Gaily examined the skin of the apple carefully, turning it over and over in the palm of her hand.

'It's bruised,' she said at last, 'look for yourself.'

229

Gaily stood in the centre of the room, fiddling with a cleaner inside the bowl of his pipe.

'You let them give you from underneath the stall, you ought to know by now – ask for those you can see, those at the front. Pick your own.'

'I didn't buy them.'

'Oh. Well, she ought to know better, seeing she's got more sense than you have. I'm surprised.'

Ma began to peel the bruised apple with a small knife, not looking at him.

'Look . . .' Gaily began angrily.

'And you thought I didn't know?'

'What?'

'I've got eyes, haven't I? What else was I supposed to think? You coming in here and making a scene out of it.'

Gaily shut his eyes for a second. Though it was all exactly as Mrs Shottery had guessed. He need not have worried, then, and waited for just the right moment through all these days.

'You've been long enough about it. I should think she gave you up for lost. It's a wonder she didn't have to ask you herself.' Ma laid down the single coil of red apple peel. '*Did* she?'

'No, she did not.'

'I suppose that's something.'

'It's all right, is it? I take it you've no objection.'

Ma's eyes grew round and wide. 'Me? What is it to me? I don't . . .'

'You know very well.'

'*I'm* nothing to do with it, you've always gone your own way. I'm not concerned in who you wed.'

'There's no need to be like that, is there? You make everything difficult.'

Ma bit into the apple and did not reply.

'There it is then,' he said.

'So I see.'

'I'm not in any hurry. It isn't a question of that.'

'If I was her, I'd set a bomb off behind you.'

'What?'

'What have you got to wait for?'

Gaily shook his head, puzzled.

'Except finding a house – unless you think you're moving in there. Is that what you've planned?'

'Where?'

'Into her house. That'd be just like you, to do a thing like that, save yourself something.'

'I hadn't thought of anything like that. I hadn't . . .'

Ma laid down the apple again, and looked into his face, making him shift his eyes away. 'You needn't think you can stop here,' she said, 'you two together. If that's what you're working up to. I don't believe in it. Besides, I could do with the place to myself, couldn't I?'

Gaily sucked at the unlit pipe experimentally, not trusting himself to speak, and because she said nothing more, only munched on her apple, in the end he went back downstairs.

Chapter Twenty-One

SCARCELY two rows of pews were full. Alida Thorne glanced a little from side to side, counting heads. But Isabel Lavender had not been loved, and her last weeks of peculiar behaviour had made an impression upon Haverstock.

And now she lay coffined at the feet of the Reverend George Jocelyn Bottingley and, looking at the angles of the wood, Alida tried to picture her shape inside. She had never looked upon the dead, and only called to mind the figures upon commemorative tombs. Would Isabel Lavender look like that?

It is only a short time, Dorothea Shottery thought, in the pew behind, looking at the printed words upon her hymn-book page, only a few months since we were standing here for Faith Lavender. And now here is her sister and where is the difference? Oh, the difference was that Faith had been loved and mourned, but Isabel Lavender she would never miss. Dorothea sang more loudly, feeling bound to pay scrupulous respects, because she could feel no true grief. Isabel had never been an easy woman.

And within a week, Kathleen, the last surviving sister, was to return to Haverstock, and be cared for and comforted back to health by Dorothea.

Outside, it rained upon the leaf-sodden earth, and into the open grave, and at the back of the church Hubert Gaily stood again, and listened to the sound of it, upon the roof. Like Dorothea, he had a sense of the occasion past, but his new life had somehow been marked by a funeral. Beside him, Florence Ames turned a leaf of her prayer-book. It upset her, because she had scarcely known Isabel Lavender, to see so few people here.

The Reverend Mr Bottingley lowered his hands and turned to the altar, and a puff of wind blowing in from an open window or along the stone floor lifted some white petals of a wreath upon Isabel Lavender's coffin.

Propped up against full pillows in the white hospital room, Kathleen Lavender turned the pages of a magazine with her left hand, and read on, unperturbed, about the wives of Arctic trawlermen. She had thought a little, that morning, about her sister's funeral, which must now be over, but without much grief, or even interest. Isabel seemed to have nothing to do with her any longer, and they had always hated one another as children and as girls. Isabel and all the misery she had caused were past. Truth is best, Kathleen Lavender said to herself, and I have found that dutiful feeling is not possible.

Because she had been afraid of Isabel during her lifetime, the experience of vengefulness was a novelty and it satisfied her. She went on reading about the lonely wives of Arctic fishermen.

'Well, we have had a good summer, dear,' said Mrs Clemency, looking out of the window at the sunset. 'A good summer.'

It was for something to say, into the silent, late-afternoon room.

'Oh,' said Eleanor Thorne, and then, 'Yes, I suppose that we have.'

She was no longer sure about anything, this summer or summers past, the change of the days or the activities of the outside world. She could no longer trust her own judgement or even, the worst of all, her own memory. Each day passed, that was all.

Mrs Clemency, who had watched her friend slip into this twilight a little lower by the hour, talked still, to try and cheer or interest or rouse her, or else to soothe her own distress. For perhaps she would grow to be like this, all interest gone, waiting for death. Mrs Clemency did feel herself to be older and sometimes her thoughts wandered and she dozed, frightening herself.

'Yes,' she said now, 'the weather has been good, you know, on the whole. Remember the garden fête. We had an excellent day for the garden fête.'

Eleanor Thorne did not reply.

'Did we not?' asked Mrs Clemency loudly.

'We did,' the other's voice came reluctantly. 'Yes, we did.'

At the garden fête, Mrs Thorne had been excited and full of curiosity, had enjoyed herself and talked about it for some days afterwards. So little time ago, and now this, the sudden concession to age, frailty and incoherence. Mrs Clemency shook with frustration that she could not *do* something to rouse her friend, for she need not, surely, die, for want of any better thing to do. It had been the daughter's fault, something to do with the fear of being sent away with the daughter.

Eleanor Thorne turned her head to the window. 'Is it night?'

'Evening, dear, there is such a wonderful sunset, though it is almost done, now. I do wish you faced this way, to see the sunset.'

'I do not care,' said Eleanor Thorne. She knew, dimly, that she should still care for something. But she was too tired, her eyes and her mind were tired, she only wanted to be left to sleep here all the days.

Sadly, Mrs Clemency lifted up her book again. There was nothing she could do, nothing at all. It was too long ago.

On the morning of 1 October, Kathleen Lavender left the hospital and was driven in an ambulance to the house of Dorothea Shottery. On the way around the green, she passed by her own shuttered and empty house, but behind the darkened windows she did not see and did not care. It was a dead house, in which, for two-thirds of her life, she had lived.

On the doorstep, Dorothea and the cat Hastings waited for the pleasure of her company. We shall look after her, Dorothea thought, everything will be well. She thought gladly that there was not, after all, to be a sad ending to the summer.

'Thank you,' said Alida Thorne that same evening, 'thank you so much.' And nodded to each one of them around the table in the bleak church hall. She wore her best jewel-green mohair and the fur hat, a smart, confident woman. They had elected her on to the Parochial Church Council in place of Miss Blade. Dorothea Shottery had voted with hesitation, thinking that the duties might either be too trivial or too tiring for Alida, yet admitting that she no longer knew anything about her.

The Reverend Mr Bottingley blew his nose. 'You will keep us up to the mark, Miss Thorne. I am sure of that, yes indeed.'

Alida nodded. She intended to do so. She did not intend to spend time in looking back.

'I shall not take my duties lightly,' she said, 'I only desire to be of use.'

Dorothea shifted in her chair, with embarrassment. But nothing could be said, nothing at all.

'It's got a fur collar,' Ma said. 'Very nice and warm.'

'I thought you didn't care for fur. You've always said so.'

Ma picked up a magazine. 'There's a pattern here,' she said, 'for a cable-stitch waistcoat. You could do with a new waistcoat.'

'You used to say fur next to your skin made you shudder.'

Ma shifted her leg, only bandaged now, on the stool before her.

'What made you change your mind all of a sudden then?' Gaily asked in a voice she knew better than to ignore.

'This is different. Quite a different sort of thing altogether.'

'Oh, it is?'

'If I didn't make the effort you'd have something to say.'

Gaily finished sharpening a pencil into the coal-bucket.

'You won't be allowed to do things like that, either,' Ma told him. 'Chippings all over her clean floor.'

He sat down to mark his piece of balsa wood. 'It'll give you less to clear up,' he said. 'I don't see why you should complain.'

'I'm not complaining. Be glad to see the back of you.'

'Oh, yes?'

Ma lifted up the magazine to her face.

It wasn't long, Gaily thought, a week, not so long, and he had no idea, really, what she felt. Not that they were going far away, scarcely worth the bus ride.

'Glad I'm not living in it,' Ma had said of the house. 'Walls like paper.' Though in the presence of Florence Ames she had voiced no criticism, found no fault.

Gaily would have liked to ask her what she thought, how much she really minded and did not mind the wedding and his removal and being left alone. But he couldn't say. He was unsure, now, how he felt himself, all the change it involved. Only when he took himself over the future and looked this way and that, he was satisfied, things would be right. And when he saw his life as it had been and imagined its continuing, he knew, too.

'Nobody's going to put up with your carpentry in the living rooms, either,' Ma said, taking off her glasses.

'No,' said Gaily, marking off another line. 'Very likely not.'

'Well.'

'Well.'

He looked up and caught her eye. Ma nodded in acknowledgement of his smile. He bent over his work again, satisfied.

On the wedding day of Hubert Gaily and Florence Ames, in the early hours of the morning, Eleanor Thorne slipped from sleep into death, and Mrs Clemency waited for a little time before ringing the bell, wanting to stay quietly with her friend.

A mile away from The Gantry, Alida Thorne slept in her scented room among the cushions and lotions and creams and Kathleen Lavender slept without dreaming of the empty house.

Downstairs, the cat Hastings slid out of the kitchen window into the garden and the first, thin sunlight of a winter's daybreak.

Afterword

People often ask novelists which they think is their best book. I never know what to answer about my own, but I have no hesitation in naming *Gentleman and Ladies* as my *favourite*. It is a novel of which I am extremely fond, both for its own sake and for the particular place it occupies in my work.

I do not remember when I first started writing fiction – I had always done so, from early childhood. By the time I was fifteen, I wanted to write a novel, I suppose because I thought that that was what proper writers did, and so, with all the confidence of extreme youth, I simply settled down and wrote one. It was about a middle-aged theatrical couple going through a period of marital crisis, a subject about which I knew nothing at all, characters that were completely unknown to me. But because I was still at school when I wrote it, and it was accepted by the first publisher I sent it to, it got quite a lot of publicity, of the 'Sixth Former Writes Sex-Novel' variety. It was published during my first year at university, and my second novel a couple of years after that. They were both pretty bad, but I had to begin somewhere. I was experimenting, writing the sort of books I saw other adults writing – a bit like a child trying on mother's clothes. At the time, it was the best I could do.

But for five years after that I wrote nothing, partly because I was struggling to earn a living as a free-lance reviewer and too much reading of other people's books wasn't conducive to writing my own, but mainly because I had not yet found my own voice, a style, a way of writing which was entirely and completely my own and which would lead somewhere. I didn't have anyone or anything to write *about* either, I was waiting for a book to come to me – which is all a novelist ever really can do. None did. But below the surface, in my sub-conscious – or wherever the place is in which an imaginative writer's work is begun, and grows – something must have been stirring.

Circumstances gave me the impetus I needed to write again. The newspaper for which I worked got a new editor, and I got the sack. I had no income, no savings, no qualifications, and I could not get any more work as a reviewer.

I went to my bank manager and asked for an overdraft for six months, to write a novel. In a gesture of great faith, he gave it to me. His requirement was that I must repay the loan from the advance given to me by a publisher (I don't know what was supposed to happen if no one had wanted it!) and give him a signed copy of the book.

With enough to pay the rent, and basic bills, I settled down to write *Gentleman and Ladies*. It took only three of the allotted six months, and was accepted straight away by a new publisher, Hamish Hamilton.

I had begun again, and this time it was a true start, I felt quietly confident that at last I had found myself as a writer. *Gentleman and Ladies* opened a sort of floodgate; in the following six years, I wrote five more novels, two books of short stories, and a good many radio plays – virtually all the serious fiction writing I have done.

So, the novel is special to me, the first 'real' one I wrote, the first of which I was not – and am still not – ashamed, no longer apprentice work. Re-reading it now, I am proud of it, though it certainly isn't flawless; but its faults do not embarrass me, and I do not think they spoil the whole.

I think the seeds of it were sown when I was a child living in what was then a rather genteel watering-place, the Yorkshire spa town of Scarborough, just after the war. In it lived a good many older, retired people, many of them struggling on fixed incomes, in poverty which they had not been brought up to, keeping up standards they could not afford. There were unmarried daughters tied to ageing parents, widows, spinster sisters living together, all within a few blocks of our house; I saw them on my walks – at the shops, in restaurants – and we visited them. Many of them were ill and died in my godmother's nursing home where I spent so many hours. The sort of people who inhabit *Gentleman and Ladies* were familiar to me, I remembered them, and those memories were all stored away.

Then, in 1965, I went for a week's holiday with my mother to a quiet country-house hotel in the Cotswolds, and there they all were again, the same old people I had known all those years before. For a week I watched them, listened, speculated. The novel began to brew.

None of the characters in *Gentleman and Ladies* is 'real' – that is not the way I work, they are all wholly invented, but they are distant relatives of those hotel guests and country-town residents, as well as of the people from my past.

In some ways I suppose it is a sad book, about sad, restricted lives, shrinking horizons – or else, perhaps even sadder, horizons which have never expanded at all, about people clinging to the old order. It is sad that Alida feels so bitter about her mother, resentful that her own life has been spoiled because an old woman, as she sees it, has gone on living too long; sad that Isabel Lavender, because of her own cruelty and mental instability, makes life so miserable for her sister Kathleen. But the overall tone is not sad. One of the reasons I remain so fond of it is that I think it is quite funny, in a very gentle way, the only remotely funny book I have written – and as I grow older, I appreciate humour in fiction more and more. I like the human jokes – that old Eleanor Thorne is so happy in the home to which she has been consigned, that Hubert Gaily's mother takes so completely to Florence Ames; I like the incongruity of the Gailys, in the ladylike Haverstock community. And I am very fond of the cats!

But most of all, I like the fact that so many of the characters are *good* people, good in a simple, quite ordinary way, essentially good, and that no one is really bad. Although Alida and Isabel do bad things, they can be readily understood and therefore forgiven, so there is no serious moral blame to be apportioned.

It's a sunny book, I think, with a happy ending – or rather, a series of happy endings, in spite of the fact that the final paragraphs are about a death. It if has some caricatures rather than characters, if it seems slightly dated now, if it is about a way of life that no longer exists (or does it?) I hope none of that matters enough to spoil the whole.

It may seem rather boastful of a writer to speak about their own work in the way that I have. But the truth is that when a book was written more than 20 years ago, it begins to seem like one by quite another person, which can be praised or condemned by the author quite impartially.

Anyway, it isn't so much admiration as affection I feel for *Gentleman and Ladies*, a novel which I hope will continue to give some quiet pleasure, as well as food for thought.